A CHRISTMAS GIFT

Books by David Saperstein

Cocoon
Metamorphosis: The Cocoon Story Continues
Fatal Reunion
Red Devil
Dark Again

Books by David Saperstein and George Samerjan

A Christmas Passage
A Christmas Visitor

Books by James J. Rush

Durner's Spring
Naked in the Streets
Time Frames
Cousin Harry

A CHRISTMAS GIFT

DAVID SAPERSTEIN *and* JAMES J. RUSH

KENSINGTON BOOKS
http://www.kensingtonbooks.com

KENSINGTON BOOKS are published by

Kensington Publishing Corp.
119 West 40th Street
New York, NY 10018

All Kensington titles, imprints, and distributed lines are available at special quantity discounts for bulk purchases for sales
promotion, premiums, fund-raising, educational, or institu-
tional use.

Special book excerpts or customized printings can also be cre-
ated to fit specific needs. For details, write or phone the office
of the Kensington Special Sales Manager: Attn. Special Sales
Department. Kensington Publishing Corp., 119 West 40th Street,
New York, NY 10018. Phone: 1-800-221-2647.

Kensington and the K logo Reg. U.S. Pat. & TM Off.

ISBN-13: 978-0-7582-4711-7
ISBN-10: 0-7582-4711-7

First Kensington Books Trade Paperback Printing: October
2009
First Kensington Books Mass-Market Paperback Printing:
October 2009
10 9 8 7 6 5 4 3 2 1

Printed in the United States of America

Acknowledgments

Sara Camilli, our agent, who encouraged us this time to write the novel before the screenplay.

Audrey LaFehr, our editor, who once again has shown her good taste and wisdom.

Ivan Saperstein, Esquire, who takes intellectual property ownership very seriously, and always has our backs.

The late Joseph F. McDonough, the quintessential "Ad Man" who introduced us in another time, in another place, in another galaxy.

CHAPTER 1

ROUND ROCK CREEK BRIDGE

Florence Chalmers leaned forward and peered through the school bus's windshield. The wipers could barely keep up with the vision-blurring sheets of rain. The sky was getting darker. She squinted and gripped the steering wheel tightly.

"A mix of sun and clouds . . . a mix of sun and clouds . . ." she muttered. "If anyone else was as wrong as often as the weather bureau, they'd be fired in a New York minute!"

"What did you say, Miss Chalmers?" Jimmy Yates asked from his seat directly behind her.

"Nothing, Jimmy," she answered. "Just thinking out loud." A flash of lightning that lit up the dark sky was immediately followed by a loud clap of thunder. It rumbled through the bus with a deep growl, silencing the children. "That's just great," Florence said softly. She leaned forward again and wiped the window with her handkerchief.

Katie Williams, seated next to the window, with her best friend, Melissa, beside her, was three rows behind Florence. Melissa had her mathematics text open on her lap.

"That was a big one," Melissa said, looking out the window past Katie. She turned back to her math book and let out a big sigh. "I still don't understand this stuff about dividing fractions."

"It's really not that hard, Melissa," Katie said. She reached over and pointed to the example in the math book. "All you have to do is invert and—" Another bright flash of lightning and an almost simultaneous clap of thunder interrupted her. Katie spun her head toward the window, as though she had been summoned, and then she closed her eyes.

"Are you okay?" Melissa asked. Katie raised her hand to quiet her friend. She then clenched her jaw in concentration.

"What's wrong?" Melissa put her hand on Katie's.

"Wait!" Katie said as she shook her head. Then her eyes popped open. "Let me out!"

"What?"

"Let me out," she repeated, standing up.

"Why, Katie?"

"Melissa!" Katie insisted. "Do as I say! Now!" Surprised and confused at her friend's insistence, Melissa got out of her seat.

"Okay, okay," she said, annoyed as she stood up. Katie slid out of her seat and pushed past Melissa. Her eyes were focused on Florence, whose grip on the steering wheel had whitened her knuckles. Katie held on to the edges of the seats for balance as she hurried to the front of the bus.

"Miss Chalmers! Miss Chalmers!" she shouted.

Florence glanced back quickly to see who was calling her name. "Katie Williams! What are you doing? Get back to your seat!"

The bus suddenly hydroplaned to the right. Florence turned her attention back to the road. She steered the bus sharply to the left. The move caused Katie to stagger for a moment before she gained her balance. She then stepped forward and stood next to Florence.

"Did you hear what I said, young lady? Get back into your seat!"

"But you've got to stop the bus."

"Is somebody hurt? Sick?"

"No. No, Miss Chalmers. It's the bridge!"

"The bridge?" Florence asked as she peered ahead. The bridge over Round Rock Creek was a few hundred yards down the road. "What are you talking about, child?"

"The bridge. It's going to wash away!"

Florence was confused. She strained to see the bridge ahead, but it was hidden by the heavy rain and darkness. "The bridge? You can't see the bridge."

"I can. I can. Please stop," Katie cried. "Pleeeze!"

"Stop this hysteria now, Katie Williams. You're distracting me and scaring the other children."

But Katie did not listen. She stared out the front window. Her eyes widened.

"Look!" she screamed. "The bridge! Look!"

Florence Chalmers, whose head had been swiveling back and forth between Katie and the road ahead, now looked once again through the windshield. Her eyes widened with fear as she saw the bridge through the rain, now no more than fifty yards away. It was slowly beginning to break apart from the pressure of the raging creek. And then suddenly, like a rubber band stretched to its limit, the bridge tore away from its moorings and slid away downstream.

"Oh my dear God!" Florence exclaimed. She jammed her foot on the brake pedal and grabbed Katie by the arm to keep her from falling forward. The bus skidded on the slippery rain-soaked road. The sudden deceleration caused some of the children to fall out of their seats. Melissa, who was still standing next to her seat, went sprawling onto the floor. Jimmy Yates lurched forward into the plastic partition behind the driver's seat, face-first, bloodying his nose. Florence Chalmers pumped the brake pedal furiously, but the bus continued to slip and slide toward the roaring river ahead. She was nearly standing on the pedal now. "Hold on, children!" she screamed, tightening her grip on Katie and steering with her free hand. The bus spun around and slipped sideways for a second or two.

Then with one mighty pump of the brake pedal, Florence turned into the skid and brought the bus to a stop in a small culvert on the side of the road, not more than ten yards from the raging creek.

For a moment, there was complete silence except for the furious sound of the rushing water, the hammering of the rain on the bus roof, and the groaning of the bridge as the last vestige of it broke free. Then, a few children began moaning in pain from their injuries. A few of the girls and one young boy began to cry.

Florence Chalmers, shaking from the ordeal, got up out of her seat. She realized that she still had Katie's arm in her grip and let it go. "Are you all right, Katie?"

"Yes, Miss Chalmers. You're a great driver."

Florence Chalmers was close to tears. She pulled Katie to her breast and hugged her. "God bless you, Katie," she said, kissing her on the forehead. She then hurried down the aisle to check on the other children while at the same time dialing 911 on her cell phone.

CHAPTER 2

A THANKFUL TOWN

Everything in Hamilton still glistened and dripped from the rain, although it had passed two hours ago. As the skies had cleared, the temperature dropped rapidly. The wet roads were getting slick from the cold front that had rushed in behind the storm. Fallen branches were scattered everywhere and several trees were down. Everyone in town was focused on the near disaster of the school bus and the raging Round Rock Creek.

The visitor and emergency parking lots of Clayton Memorial Hospital were crowded with the cars of anxious parents. Two of the three sheriff's patrol cars and the town's two new pale green fire trucks that had responded to the emergency were still at the hospital. Two volunteer ambulances were parked at the emergency entrance. Clayton Memorial, named for Barry Clayton, a decorated young soldier from Hamilton who had died in Vietnam, was a small, forty-bed facility, typical of a growing, fairly prosperous midwestern town. Because of its size, the sheriff and hospital security people had limited the visitors inside to parents and a few reporters.

Katie was in the emergency waiting room with Melissa. They were holding hands, fascinated by the activity and attention around them. Katie's parents, Carol and Tom Williams, chatted with Melissa's mother, Barbara. Nearby, Florence Chalmers was going over her story again with Sheriff Mark Keller. Several other parents stood or sat with their children, some of whom wore bandages. One boy had his arm in a sling. Jimmy Yates's nose was bandaged. The skin around both his eyes and nose was a swollen, angry reddish blue. A few parents were starting to leave, saying their good-byes and praising God that disaster had been avoided. Several glanced at Katie, and then smiled and nodded at Carol and Tom. One mother stopped and quietly hugged Katie.

"God bless you, child," she whispered. Katie blushed and looked down.

Melissa tightened her grip on Katie's hand. "You're like a real hero, Katie."

"I didn't really do anything . . . It was just—"

"No, Katie," her friend said firmly. "You are a hero and that's cool." At that moment, Sheriff Keller turned to Katie's parents.

"That's quite a young lady you've got there, Mr. and Mrs. Williams," he announced in a loud voice. The sheriff was an elected official and never missed a chance to promote his public presence.

"She surely is," Florence Chalmers chimed in. "I will never, in all my born days, understand how she knew what was going to happen to that bridge! I mean, the rain hadn't been falling that long and we couldn't see the bridge. And how could Round Rock Creek rise so fast?"

"That storm dumped five inches of rain in one hour up in the Middleton watershed where the river originates," Keller said.

Florence Chalmers shook her head. "But how could this child know that?"

"Maybe ESP," the sheriff suggested, with a wink toward Tom Williams. Tom gave a slight dismissive wave with his hand. "How about a woman's intuition? Or a girl's anyway?"

Keller suggested lightly. But there was no doubt he was interested in an answer. Carol Williams was about to respond when a voice called out from nearby.

"Carol! Tom! And, Katie! Katie!" Anne Yates, Jimmy's mother, shouted excitedly as she joined them, almost dragging Jimmy by the hand behind her. His bandaged nose gave the appearance that he was wearing an oversized surgical mask. "I just want to thank you, and especially dear Katie here, for saving everyone today."

"Thank you, Anne," Carol said. "We're sorry about Jimmy's nose. Is he going to be all right?"

"Oh, he's just fine. Nothing's broken. Kids' bones are soft," Anne said as she rubbed the top of Jimmy's head. "But he's going to have a couple of beautiful shiners."

"Well, that should be the worst of it," Carol said.

"Amen," Anne answered. "He's alive. They're all alive and safe, thank the Lord, and that's all that matters." She looked at Katie. "Thank you again, sweetheart. And we'll all make sure Jimmy doesn't sit behind the driver anymore," she added with a rueful smile. "Well, we have to be going," Anne Yates added. "Jim Senior is on his way home now and as you can imagine, he's upset." She took Jimmy's hand again and left as abruptly as she had arrived.

"I think we'd better be going too," Tom told Carol.

"If you don't mind, Mr. Williams, before you go I'd just like to ask, uh . . ." Keller looked at Katie. "You know, we sometimes use people like Katie who . . . well, might sort of see things? Call it ESP, intuition, or, well, just a gift. A special, wonderful gift. I could tell you about several cases where—"

"It was just something she felt, Sheriff," Carol Williams interrupted. "Nothing more."

"I suppose. But you never know about these things. Anyway, I was thinking you just might want to check that out with young Katie here. They do these things over at the State University Psychology Department. See if she's got, you know, the gift."

"We just might do that, Sheriff," Tom said quickly, as he took Katie's hand. "Ready, Carol?" he asked. She nodded.

"Well, whatever it was, or is, young lady, you have the thanks of this entire community," Keller said.

Florence Chalmers leaned over and gave Katie a hug. "Especially this very, very grateful bus driver."

CHAPTER 3

A LITTLE WHITE LIE

Later that afternoon, Carol and Tom Williams sat at the kitchen table sipping coffee as they watched Katie attack two peanut butter and jelly sandwiches, washing them down with two glasses of milk. They were emotionally exhausted from the morning's events. Katie was the opposite—emotionally charged and excited. At her insistence, she had, for the third time, just finished describing everything that had happened up until their arrival at the hospital.

"That's all there was to it," Katie concluded. "No one was really hurt badly. Since I was up front, I helped Miss Chalmers get the other kids out of the bus. Then Deputy Sheriff Michaels was there in a few minutes and then the sheriff and then the fire trucks and ambulances . . ." She took a big gulp of milk and a bite out of the last half of her second sandwich. Tom, though obviously happy his daughter was safe and sound, had a look of concern on his face. He cleared his throat.

"Look, Katie," he began, "each time you tell the story, you go quickly by how you seemed to see that the bridge was going to wash away."

"Uh-uh," Katie said, taking another drink of milk to wash

down what was in her mouth. She held up her hand, chewing and swallowing, indicating she would answer in a moment. Finally she spoke. "I didn't *seem* to see it, Daddy," Katie said matter-of-factly. "I *did* see it."

"But how could you see it? Miss Chalmers said you were sitting in back when the bus was a quarter mile or so from the bridge. I mean . . . Look . . ." He took a deep breath and exhaled loudly. "Is this like that fire thing in the movies last year?"

"Yes, Daddy," Katie answered quietly.

Tom looked at Carol and then back at his daughter, who stiffened as though she knew what was coming. "What are we going to tell people this time? I mean, so they won't think you're some kind of . . . of a . . ." He exhaled again loudly and raised his hands in frustration. "With the fire, we decided you smelled smoke."

"You decided," Katie answered softly. "I didn't smell smoke, Daddy. I saw the fire."

"Let's not go there again," Carol suggested as she saw Tom's lips tighten and his jaw clench. "It was just a little electrical fire in the bathroom and no one was hurt. And everyone got to see the movie again free."

"Well, this time I just won't bother telling anyone anything," Katie said quietly. She then finished the last of her sandwich and milk.

"You're going to have to say *something*. Everyone is going to ask me what happened. What do I say?" Tom's voice was strained with frustration.

"Do we really have to go into this now, Tom?" Carol asked, noticing that Katie was on the verge of tears.

"Yes, Carol. I think we do. Beth said there were already nine calls about this at the office."

"How about we say that Katie saw a documentary on The Weather Channel yesterday about flash floods?" Carol suggested. "And there was this bridge that got washed away and, well, it was on her mind when it began to rain so hard?"

"But that's not true. I didn't," Katie said.

"Yes, dear. We know that. But it's an explanation that will stop all the questions."

"But I don't want to lie again like I did about the smoke at the Mall Quad."

Carol reached over and patted Katie's arm. "It's not really a bad lie, sweetheart. Sometimes, when people don't understand these kinds of things, we have to, well, sort of give them a reason they can accept. It's called a little white lie."

Katie frowned as she grappled with Carol's suggestion. "I guess," she finally said, reluctantly.

Tom stood up and looked at his watch. "I've got a closing at three. Katie, what Mom says is a good idea. That's what I'm gonna tell people if they ask. But when I get home later, I want to discuss this 'seeing things' business."

Frustrated, Katie felt her eyes filling with tears and, shaking her head, she jumped up and ran from the room. Tom started to go after her.

"Tom!" Carol said sharply. "Let her be. She's exhausted and confused. I'll talk to her."

Tom stopped at the kitchen door. His shoulders sagged. "I'm really worried. What's going on with her? I mean, when the sheriff starts to talk about ESP and intuition and gifts . . . well, I've read about people like that and a lot of them wind up having terrible lives."

"Not our Katie. Trust me. It's just preadolescence, hormones, and an overactive imagination."

Satisfied, Tom looked at his watch again. "A female thing, huh? If you say so. We'll talk later. Please, tell her I love her and that what I am is, well, that I'm just concerned. Okay?"

"She knows that, dear. But I will. I surely will."

Tom came back to the table and kissed Carol gently on the lips. "I love you too, babe."

Carol stroked his cheek. "Yeah. Me too. Now go close that house sale and bring home the bacon."

Tom smiled and left through the door that led to the garage.

Carol rose and walked out of the kitchen, down the hallway, and up the stairs. She noted that Katie's bedroom door was closed. She listened at the door but heard nothing. At least Katie wasn't crying. Carol then went to her bedroom dresser, opened the top drawer, and took out an envelope from underneath her jewelry case.

CHAPTER 4

MIRANDA

Katie's door was closed. Carol knocked.

"Katie?"

"Come in, Mom," Katie's soft, sad-sounding voice responded. Carol opened the door and saw her daughter sitting on the edge of her bed. Her head was hanging down. Carol sat down beside her as Katie spoke in tearful tones.

"I just wish Daddy would try to understand that this . . . this . . . it just happens. I don't know why. I can't help it."

Carol put her arm around Katie's shoulder and pulled her close. "I know, dear."

There was a long pause as Katie drew a deep breath. "Do you? Do you really?"

"Yes. Now listen carefully. There's something important that I want to tell you." Carol's tone of voice got Katie's attention. She straightened up and looked directly at her mother as Carol continued. "You see . . . well, this is something I was going to tell you when you got a little older, or when this business of seeing things . . . well, I thought it might just be a passing coincidence. Something that might just go away. But now I see it hasn't and probably won't."

Katie's eyes focused and brightened questioningly. "What won't go away, Mom?"

Carol lifted up the envelope that Katie had not noticed before. She handed it to Katie. "Look at this."

Katie took the envelope and opened it. She carefully took out a faded photograph of a young, pretty, dark-haired, dark-eyed woman looking into the camera with a kind of smile Katie had never seen before. Katie looked at the picture carefully for several seconds. At first she was curious, but then an expression of surprise came over her young, pretty face. She looked up at Carol.

"Who is this?" she asked.

"That's your great-grandmother," Carol said softly. "Her name was Miranda. She died before I was born."

"Your grandma? But didn't you tell me her name was Mary?"

"She changed it to Mary after she ran away with my grandfather."

"She ran away with him? Wow!" Katie was intrigued.

Carol smiled as she remembered her own feelings when her mother told her the same story. "Yes, she told my mother, your grandma, that they were madly in love. They were very young and his parents didn't approve of Miranda's family."

Katie looked back at the photograph very carefully. "She looks very young."

"Do you see anything else?" Carol asked her daughter.

Katie looked at the photo of Miranda again. "She looks something like you." Then, looking one more time, she said, "But I think she looks a little more like me, only maybe older . . . do you think?"

"Yes, sweetie. You resemble her very much. And not only that. According to things my mother told me, you seem to be a lot like her too."

"Like her? How am I like her?"

"Great-grandma Miranda's parents were from eastern Europe. They were, uh, sort of what you would call circus people. I guess they were, well, if the truth be told, they were Gypsies. And Miranda's job was to tell fortunes."

"You mean like with a crystal ball and everything?"

"I guess. Maybe. I don't really know. But my mother told me that Miranda really didn't need tricks or gimmicks. She could . . . she could really see things. Things that were about to happen. Things she had no way of knowing about. Do you understand what I'm saying?"

Katie looked away toward the window. The sun was out now and a strong wind was blowing, rattling the bare branches of the sycamore in their front yard.

"You mean seeing things like I do sometimes?"

"Yes."

Katie frowned and then relaxed. She turned back to Carol. "Did it ever happen to Grandma or you?"

"No."

"Never?"

"My mother never had any experience like it. She watched for it to happen with me, but it never did. There were stories that generations before Miranda had this, uh, gift. But after two generations, my mother believed that the 'gift' was unique to Miranda and not a hereditary thing."

"But that isn't true, is it?"

"After today, I would say you're right." She touched Katie's chest. "It's here, in you."

A chill ran down Katie's spine and her heart beat faster. She shivered slightly.

Carol saw the reaction and pulled Katie to her breast. "I believe it is a gift from God. But I'm afraid Daddy doesn't believe in such things. When I first told him about Grandma Miranda, he dismissed it as a fable from the old country—a superstitious fairy tale."

"But it's not, Mommy. What I see is not a fairy tale."

"No, it's not. You have Miranda's gift." She released Katie, who once again gazed at the old photograph and for the first time saw in that young, pretty face, with its dark eyes and knowing smile, a beckoning.

CHAPTER 5

CHASING A CAPER

The next morning was bright, cloudless, and cold, with a blustery wind from the northwest—what is known in weather circles as a Canadian clipper. It left no doubt that yesterday's unusual warm weather was an exception. Winter had now settled into the Midwest, and that seemed proper as Christmas was fast approaching.

Marty Richards and Al Steel pulled into the crowded Ridgeway Mall and looked for a parking spot on the western edge of the complex. After driving up and down three aisles, they found a Honda Element backing out in front of a hardware store. It was a stroke of luck because not too far away, past a McDonald's, a dry cleaner, a bakery, and a drugstore was what they were looking for—Kaplan's Jewelry.

Al Steel, heavyset, six-foot-three, with gray eyes and a broad, flat face, turned off the engine and turned to his smaller crony.

"So that's it, huh, Marty?" he asked, pointing.

Marty Richards, five-foot-nine and thin, with close-set brown eyes, squinted into the sun's glare and nodded. "Bingo. Let's do it."

Both men, in their late thirties, wore leather jackets. Al's was black while Marty's was a replica of a brown, World War Two bomber jacket, with a fur collar and a faded old Army Air Force patch on one sleeve. He wore a navy blue woolen navy watch cap. Al sported a Cleveland Indians baseball cap. Both wore jeans and dark scuffed work boots. As they got out of their black Chevy Blazer, Al took off his cap and smoothed his thick black hair. He then put the cap back. He left his jacket open. Marty, in contrast, zipped his jacket up to his chin and pulled his watch cap down over his ears.

"Shoulda wore gloves," Marty muttered as they headed for Kaplan's.

"Whaddaya gonna do when winter really gets here?" Al joked.

Marty didn't respond other than to throw a contemptuous glance in his partner's direction. He then picked up the pace and hurried along. In less than a minute, they arrived at Kaplan's Jewelry Store. The window display was sparse and tasteful. Several stones that looked like diamonds, rubies, emeralds, and sapphires were scattered about in delicate mounds of fake snow. Colorful ribbons were woven among them. The display was lit with white-hot, xenon pin lights. The effect was sparkling and festive for the Christmas season.

"Jeez," Al said. "Check out all that ice."

"It ain't real."

"How do you know?"

"You really think they'd put real stones in a plain glass window like that?" Marty answered.

Al frowned. He knew that when Marty used that tone of voice with him, it was a put-down.

"You ready?" Marty asked.

"Yeah. Sure. I'm ready," Al said sullenly. The door was locked. Marty found the admitting bell button and pushed it. A buzzer sounded in response and Marty opened the door. He went into the store. Al took a deep breath and followed.

The layout of Kaplan's was similar to that of many jewelry stores of its size—display cases on either side of the store filled with nice, but not too expensive watches, bracelets, rings, pins, and pendants. There was one more case across the rear of the store that had higher-priced items and the cash register. Behind it was a glass-enclosed area where Ed Kaplan, a studious man in his fifties, sat peering through a loupe as he worked repairing a gold and jeweled lady's wristwatch. Joan Kaplan, a tall and well-groomed forty-eight, Ed's wife of twenty-five years, was behind the rear counter waiting on a woman customer. Susan Cole, a bright, pretty woman about thirty, was behind the right-side display case waiting on a young couple.

After she buzzed in Marty and Al, Joan pressed a button under the counter to alert her husband that there were new customers in the store. Since she and Susan were occupied, Ed would have to wait on them.

The winter sun, low in the sky, shone through the front window behind Marty and Al. Joan Kaplan could not see their faces clearly, but she felt a pang of anxiety in her stomach as they entered. Ed Kaplan removed his jeweler's loupe, got up from his workbench, and put on his jacket. He then left his glass cubicle, opened the locked gate at the end of the rear counter, and walked, smiling, to Marty and Al.

"Good morning, gentlemen. How may I help you?"

Marty cleared his throat. "I'm lookin' for a bracelet for the little lady. Somethin' special. It's gonna be ten years next week."

Ed smiled and nodded. "Ten years. Well, congratulations! We've got a very nice bracelet selection. You can look in here," he said, gesturing to the counter on the left side that had a display of bracelets. "But let me get you our catalogue. There's a lot more. I'll be right back." With that, he hurried to the back of the store and through the gate, past his work area, and through a door in the back of the store.

The two men then stepped casually over to the display side case where there was an array of bracelets and watches. Marty bent over, pretending to study the bracelets.

"Soon as he gets back, we go," he whispered to Al.

"No sweat," Al said, nodding. He looked over at the watches. "Ya know, I always wanted one-a dem Movados. But, jeez, they're expensive."

"Not to worry, pally," Marty said in a hushed tone. "After this, you'll be able to get one for both wrists. Your ankles too." Al grinned.

A moment later, Ed Kaplan came out of the back room holding the bracelet catalogue, a loose leaf with several manufacturers' bracelets in it. Joan excused herself from the customer she was waiting on and met her husband at the gate.

"What do they want?" she whispered.

"A bracelet. The short one is married ten years."

"He's not wearing a ring," Joan said suspiciously.

"Most men don't. Maybe I can sell him one."

"Don't joke. I don't like their looks."

"They're customers, my darling. Not everybody looks like you want everybody to look. It's Christmas. Business is a little slow. If you haven't noticed the news, people are using the word 'recession' now. Look harder at those two and you'll see a sale. And that customer you're waiting on is one too. Okay?"

"Just do me a favor and keep an eye on them."

"I will. Love you," he whispered.

She blushed slightly and smiled. "You're impossible, Edward Kaplan. But I love you anyway." She left him and went back to her customer.

Ed put on his best sales face and, smiling broadly, returned to Marty and Al, this time walking down the aisle behind the display case. Marty noticed him approaching and straightened up. Al followed suit. Ed laid the catalogue on top of the display case in front of the two men.

"You know," he said, "gifts for tenth anniversaries used

to be tin. But now it's diamonds." As the last word came out of Ed's mouth, Al let out a gagging cough and began to sway. As if to keep himself from falling, he leaned the upper part of his body over the top of the counter, grasping the edges.

Marty's eyes widened in alarm. "What's wrong, pally?"

"Oh, man, I don't know," Al moaned. He put his hand to his mouth and let out a huge burp.

Marty leaned over and put his hand on Al's shoulder. "Jeez. What is it? You okay?"

"I don't know, man. I feel weird," Al muttered. He let out another moan. "I feel sick. Like real sick. Maybe it was them oysters."

Ed stood frozen at this sudden turn of events. Susan stopped talking to her customers, who had turned and were now looking at Al and Marty. In the rear, Joan felt another wave of anxiety come over her as she too stopped talking to her customer and looked toward her husband.

"You got a bathroom?" Marty asked Ed. Ed glanced quickly back and forth between the two men.

"Uh, well, yes. But it's for employees. I, uh—"

Al let out another, even louder, burp.

"Look. The thing is, I think my buddy here's about to hurl," Marty announced, "and if you don't want it all over your store here . . ."

Ed raised his hands. "No, no. Of course not." Then, beckoning, he said, "This way. In the back."

Marty put his hand under Al's arm and helped him straighten up.

"Edward? Is everything all right?" Joan called out, a worried tone in her voice. Ed started toward the back with Marty and Al following on the other side of the display cases.

"Nothing serious, dear," he answered. "One of the gentlemen isn't feeling well." Ed stopped at the gate and opened it for Marty and Al. "They need the bathroom." Joan balled her fists, her knuckles turning white with worry.

"Should I call someone? A doctor, maybe? Or an ambulance?" she asked Ed, not looking at the two men who made her inexplicably uneasy.

"No. No. He just needs the bathroom." Ed then led Al and Marty past his work cubicle toward the back door. As they passed, both Marty and Al shot a quick glance into it and spotted a large safe sitting behind Ed's raised stool. "In here," Ed said, opening the rear metal door that led into the store's rear storage area. Al held his stomach and moaned as the two men followed Ed. The metal door had a tight spring that automatically closed it behind them.

"Easy, pally," Marty said, trying to soothe Al.

Ed pointed to a nearby door. "The bathroom's right there."

"Thanks, man," Marty said, leading Al to it. "Here's the john," he told his supposedly sick friend as he opened the door. Both men quickly went inside, closing the door behind them. Marty immediately turned on both faucets over the basin. Al put his mouth under one, filled it, stepped over to the toilet, and expelled the water into the bowl, making a loud splashing sound. At the same time he bellowed, grunted, and let out a loud guttural sound, followed by a moan.

"Keep your head in the toilet," Marty said loudly.

Outside, Ed stood listening, his brow furrowed. "You all right in there?" he called out.

"Yeah, he's gettin' it out," Marty called back. Inside, Al went back to the basin, filled his mouth with water again, then stepped back over to the toilet and repeated the action. While Al was doing this, Marty examined the room carefully. He noticed there was a drop ceiling. The basin had a mirror over it. The toilet was in the far corner of the small, clean bathroom. An oversized, ornate medicine cabinet took up nearly half of the rear wall. A few feet to the right was a small, barred window with alarm wires, some of which ran from the window up and behind the drop ceiling so they were between the ceiling and the roof. Other wires ran along the back wall. Marty noticed that the wires on the wall did not go behind the medicine cabinet but around it. To be sure he went over to the cabinet, opened the door, looked inside, and noted with satisfaction that they didn't.

"How're you doin'?" Marty shouted to Al. Al responded with more moans. "Just keep your head down in there and take deep breaths." Marty then silently pointed out to Al that the wires along the back wall did not go behind the medicine cabinet but around it. With that, he closed the cabinet door and gave Al a thumbs-up sign.

"Everything okay in there?" Ed called from outside.

"He's lookin' a little better, sir!" Marty shouted back. "Just a few minutes, I think, and we'll be out." He then signaled for Al to get more water and throw up again. While that was happening, Marty reached into his bomber jacket pocket and took out a tape measure. He quickly measured the distance from the edge of the window to the middle of the cabinet. Then, he measured the length and width of the cabinet. He carefully wrote down all the measurements on a small pad.

"You sure that's it, pally?" Marty asked loudly.

"I got no more to give," Al answered as he flushed the toilet. "I'm gonna sue that lousy restaurant."

Marty stepped over to him, a conspiratorial smile on his face. "Ready?" he asked in a low voice. Al nodded and grinned. Marty took him by the arm and opened the bathroom door, stepping out into the back room where an anxious Ed Kaplan waited.

"Better?" Ed asked.

"Much," Al said. "Still a little queasy, but better."

"Maybe you should see a doctor," Ed suggested.

"Nah, I don't need no doctor," Al answered. "I'll be okay now."

"You're sure," Ed said, more a statement than a question. "I heard there's this salmonella thing going around."

"Nah. This was just some bad oysters." Al leaned slightly on Marty, who was still supporting his arm.

"Listen, uh, is it Mr. Kaplan?" Marty asked.

"Yes. Ed Kaplan."

"Well, thank you, Ed Kaplan. Thanks for lettin' us use the john and all," Marty continued as he guided Al back to the sprung metal door that led to the store. "That was real good of you to do that." He stopped just as Ed was reaching for the doorknob. "Tell you what, Mr. Kaplan. I'll get this bum home and come back to check out that catalogue. Okay?"

"We're open till seven," Ed said. He pulled the door open and let the two men pass ahead of him back into the store.

"I'll be back way before seven," Marty said. "See you then."

There now were no customers in the store. As Marty, still supporting Al, headed for the front, Joan and Susan made eye contact. Susan gave a slight shrug and rolled her eyes as if to confirm these two were "characters." Joan shifted her eyes back to the retreating Marty and Al. That uneasy sensation in the pit of her stomach returned.

"How'd ya know about the medicine cabinet and the wiring?" Al asked as they walked back to the Blazer.

"I didn't exactly," Marty answered. "But I knew that store used to be a salon and it had a bathroom back there. So I figured if there was a hole anywhere in security, it'd be there. That's where they always are."

"Kinda small to be a bar, huh?"

It took a moment for Al's question to register with Marty. "Salon! Salon! Not *saloon*."

"Oh. Oh. I get it. Like haircuts for dames."

Marty did not respond. They reached the car and Al beeped open the door locks.

"This could be real sweet," Marty said, getting in on the passenger side. "You see that old safe?"

Al got in behind the wheel and smiled. "Yeah. Like a sittin' duck."

"More like a sitting duck's egg," Marty said as Al started the engine. "Just waitin' to be cracked open. Now all we gotta do is find a guy good at crackin' 'em."

CHAPTER 6

THE GOVERNOR'S GIFT

Billy Etheridge and Paco Rodriguez trimmed the official Harrison Falls State Penitentiary's Christmas tree under the watchful eyes of Sergeant Ray Metz, a twenty-year career guard of the state penal system. Billy and Paco, both serving fifteen to twenty-five years for armed robbery, had finished stringing the last of the colored lights and were opening the boxes of tinsel when Charlie Williams walked by. He was escorted by a new guard, a tall black man who was, like many of the inmates, an obvious bodybuilder.

"Lookin' good, guys," Charlie called out. "Very festive."

" 'Tis the season to be jolly," Billy said.

"I hear that."

"How ya doin', amigo?" Paco asked.

Charlie Williams, just short of thirty-one, was at least ten years younger than Paco and Billy. He walked the walk of a longtime convict, but in fact, had only served nine years of his fifteen-to-twenty-five-year armed robbery sentence.

"I'm not doing anybody today," Charlie answered, grinning. "Not yet anyway." Although he had a comfortable air about him, underneath, and not too deep, there was a bitterness that always manifested itself in edgy sarcasm. "Any word on what Santa's bringin' you guys?"

"Yeah," Billy said quickly. "A set of wings for all of us to fly the coop."

Charlie laughed and began to sing. "Yeah, wings like an angel, which is what I am. . . ."

The rookie guard escorting him grasped Charlie's arm and shoved him along. "Put a sock in it, Williams. The warden's waiting."

"Okay." Charlie put his hands up in a gesture of surrender. "Okay, Chief." He glanced back at Paco and Billy. "Merry Christmas, guys."

"You too, Charlie," Paco called back to him.

"And good luck," Billy added.

Moments later, Charlie stood in front of a small gray metal chair in the warden's conference room. Warden Jeremiah Sloane was a portly, gray-haired man in his fifties. He wore a dark, slightly wrinkled suit, a white shirt, and a plain gray tie. He was flanked by Hal Cherry, a thin-faced, bearded man in his forties whose worn brown tweed sports jacket, tan turtleneck sweater, and tortoiseshell glasses gave him a professorial appearance. On Sloane's other side sat Nancy Lockwood, also in her forties. She wore frameless glasses. Her hair was pulled back in a tight bun. Her dress was a greenish Anne Klein knockoff with a wide yellow collar that seemed out of place in the spartan surroundings. The three sat behind an imitation-wood metal table in front of a small window. The blinds were drawn tight. They were the Parole Board. Lying in front of them were files pertaining to Charlie Williams's court and prison records. The somber grayness of the room's walls was accentuated by the cold, bright, overhead fluorescent lighting.

"Good morning, Warden, and Merry Christmas," Charlie began cheerfully.

"Hold on, Williams," the guard said, tightening his grip on Charlie's arm again.

"That's okay, Corell. Good morning, Charlie. Have a seat."

Charlie slipped his arm away from the guard, winked at him so that the board didn't see, and sat in the chair.

"Nice tie, Warden," Charlie said.

"Wha? Oh, thanks. The, uh—"

"And that sure is a lovely scent you're wearing, ma'am."

"Thank you, Mr. Williams," she responded pleasantly. As Charlie turned to Mr. Cherry, searching for a compliment to pay, the warden raised his hand.

"That's enough of that, Charlie."

"Sorry, Warden Sloane. Just trying to be friendly."

The warden nodded. "Yes. Well, thank you. Now here's the deal. With your sentence, you wouldn't be coming up for parole for another three years. But Ms. Lockwood, Mr. Cherry, and I are here to bring some holiday cheer your way."

Charlie fought to keep his face calm and uncommitted. He blinked once and locked his gaze on Warden Sloane. Beneath his stone-faced facade, his heart skipped ten beats.

"You've kept your nose clean these past nine years," Sloane continued. "The governor took a hard look at our budget and overcrowding here and, well, we've been authorized to give early paroles to a population we feel are low-risk recidivists."

The words were sinking in, but the final confirmation had yet to come. Could it be? Charlie took a deep breath. He could not exhale.

"Bottom line, Charlie, is, I've recommended you for immediate parole, and," he said with a smile, "the board here agrees."

Slowly, Charlie Williams let out his breath, and with it he felt as though he was cleansing himself of a nine-year nightmare. Then, unable to contain his cool, he broke out into a large, joyful grin. "Jeez . . . that's . . . wow! Thank you, Warden, sir, uh, ma'am. Thank you all. Thanksgiving twice this year!"

An event like this was one of the better parts of the warden's job. He liked Charlie, but he knew what nine years in prison could do to a young man, especially one who never wavered in his insistence of innocence. He recalled his first interview with Charlie Williams when the young convict explained that he had no idea one of his cohorts was packing a gun. So robbery became armed robbery and the state sentencing guidelines were firm.

"Just don't let us see you back here, Charlie."

"Oh no," Charlie said, shaking his head. "No, sir. And you can take that to the bank." He immediately realized the irony of his statement and grinned sheepishly. "Uh, I guess that's kind of not exactly what I should . . . I mean, a bank and all . . . I, uh—"

"Charlie," the warden interrupted. "I want to remind you that you have two felony convictions. One more and you'll never come before a parole board again. You understand?"

"Yes, sir," Charlie answered. "Totally. Three strikes and I'm out."

"No, Charlie," the warden said. "Three strikes and you're in. Forever! Now just go with Mr. Corell and process out!"

"Right. Right." Charlie got up and started for the door with the rookie guard leading the way. Then he stopped and turned back to the board. "Merry Christmas to you all." They all responded with "Merry Christmas" and a smile. Other than dour Corell, who had no feelings for convicts, everyone else in the room felt something good and positive in the air.

CHAPTER 7

THE MYSTERIOUS PHOTO

Katie and Melissa were sprawled out on the floor of Katie's bedroom doing their homework in the late afternoon. It was a bright and colorful room. The winter sun streamed in through her filmy, pale yellow curtains. Bright yellow and orange pillows were scattered across the white bedspread. Bubblegum pop posters, taped on the light blue wall, added to the room's colorful ambiance. A computer with a flat screen sat on a white desk. Across the room, a high-def TV/DVD and a CD player sat at eye level on the shelves of a matching white bookcase. The floor was covered with pale green carpeting. Pop music blared from the CD player's surround-sound speakers that were suspended from the ceiling in each corner of the room. The music didn't affect their concentration. Katie finished a calculation as Melissa shook her head in disbelief.

"It's hopeless. I still don't see how you solved that, Katie," she said with a frown.

"Well, I figured out a lot of it in my head," Katie answered.

"But we have to show all our work on paper."

"I will. After you leave, I'll write it down."

Melissa frowned again. "But I still don't understand how . . .

wait! I know. It's like on the bus. You close your eyes and it just appears."

Katie was not happy with Melissa's apparent sarcasm.

"Noooo," she said. "It's not like that at all."

"Then you're a witch and you must be burned at the stake!" With that, Melissa jumped up and grabbed a pillow from the bed. She playfully bopped Katie on the head. "You must be subdued and disposed of, Witch!" she shrieked, laughing and swinging the pillow again. Katie dodged the pillow, rolled away, got up from the floor, and grabbed another one.

"Oh, really? We'll see about that." She stepped toward Melissa. "I'll get you, my pretty. I'll get you . . ." Katie cried out, imitating the Wicked Witch from *The Wizard of Oz.* ". . . and your little dog too." She swung her pillow, but missed as Melissa ducked and then jumped up and bopped Katie on the head once more. She then ran from the room laughing. Katie chased after her and caught up with Melissa in the hallway. The two girls started pummeling each other, laughing and running. Melissa yelled, "Witch, witch," and Katie responded with loud, witchlike cackling.

The pillow fight continued downstairs into the family room, where Melissa suddenly stopped, turned, and threw her pillow at Katie. Katie ducked and the pillow sailed into the wall behind her. Katie then threw her pillow at Melissa, but it went wide and hit a glass-framed photo sitting on an end table. The picture flew off the table and smashed down onto the hardwood floor. As its wooden frame came apart, the glass shattered.

"Oh no!" Katie cried. "That's my dad's army picture." She moved quickly to see the damage.

"Be careful. Don't cut yourself," Melissa warned. Katie carefully avoided the glass shards as she knelt and picked up the photo and backing. As she did, another photo slipped out from behind the one of her father in uniform. She examined it closely. It was also of her father, but he was younger than in the army photo and he had his arm around a teenaged boy. Katie cocked her head and frowned.

"What is it?" Melissa asked.

"This picture. I wonder who this is with Daddy."

"Let me see," Melissa said. She moved over to Katie, who stood up and showed her the photo.

"This person," Katie said, handing the picture to her best friend. "The one with my father. He kind of looks a little like him, doesn't he?"

Melissa studied the photo. "Yeah. Kind of. . . ." She handed the photo back to Katie, who studied it again. "Maybe he's your uncle or cousin."

"No. I don't have uncles. Just one aunt. My mom's sister, Iris."

"Well, I think he looks like a relative," Melissa insisted.

Katie stared at the boy in the picture. Melissa was right. He looked a lot like her younger father next to him.

"This is a week of old pictures," she said softly.

"What?" Melissa asked.

"My mom showed me an old picture of my great-grandmother. Her name was Miranda. She was a Gypsy."

"A Gypsy? Wow! Does that mean you're a Gypsy too?"

"Maybe. Part Gypsy, I guess."

"Did she live in a wagon and play the violin?"

Katie looked quizzically at her friend and frowned. "What are you talking about?"

"I saw an old movie once. In black-and-white on Nickelodeon. It was about this Gypsy girl and she played the violin for money. Her family lived in this funny wagon and cooked over a fire."

"No. That wouldn't have been my great-grandma. She was a fortune-teller and she fell in love and—" Katie was about to tell Melissa about Miranda running away with her great-grandpa and telling fortunes, but she was interrupted abruptly by the sound of the front door opening.

"Katie! I'm home, dear," Carol's voice sang out. Melissa's eyes widened.

"It's your mom!" she said in a loud whisper. Katie put the photo into her pocket and both girls knelt and began to clean up the broken frame and glass.

CHAPTER 8

A ROOM AT BENJIE'S

The Trailways bus carrying Charlie Williams pulled into its outside platform at the Hamilton bus terminal. Charlie rose from his seat, stepped into the aisle, and pulled a battered old valise off the overhead rack. Then, after waiting a few moments for other passengers in front of him to gather their belongings, he followed them off the bus.

It was a typically blustery early winter day, the sky filled with low, scudding clouds with only an occasional patch of blue showing through. The terminal had been refurbished and expanded since Charlie had been there last. He now found himself unsure of his surroundings. Then he spotted a familiar landmark, a monument to the men and women of World War Two. Now confident of his bearings, he started off in the direction of Main Street. *Nine years is a long time,* he thought as he walked, noticing several new buildings, stores, and widened streets.

It was just after five P.M. when Charlie Williams got to the heart of town. There was much more traffic than he remembered. Both sides of Main Street were crowded with people, many of them carrying packages. Because he had no gloves,

Charlie kept one hand in his jacket pocket, switching the valise to the warm hand when the other one got too cold. As he walked along, he strained to see if he recognized any faces. But there were none. Most of the store windows had Christmas decorations—lights, glitter, and greetings. There were cheery holly wreaths with broad red ribbons on several of the doors. Quite a few stores also had HAPPY HANUKKAH signs and menorahs with two of the eight candles lit, plus the center master candle. It all felt vaguely familiar to Charlie, and yet somehow he felt like an outsider, a stranger in the town he grew up in. His nine years in prison seemed more like a lifetime. The world had moved on while he had remained frozen in place.

A half hour later, Charlie reached his destination, an old Victorian house that had seen better days even before he had once roomed there. He mounted the wide, worn, wooden steps leading up to the porch. The old sign jutting out from the wall next to the door had aged, but not changed—ROOMS BY THE WEEK OR MONTH. When Charlie rang the bell, he smiled as he heard the familiar chimes of Beethoven's Fifth. It was a comforting sound from the past. He pushed the button one more time.

"I'm comin' . . . I'm comin'," a familiar voice growled. The front door opened and a man with a two-day growth of beard and a sour expression confronted Charlie. He wore an open, thick gray sweater over a black T-shirt and paint-splattered jeans. The T-shirt had a gold Harley-Davidson logo across its front. The man squinted at Charlie and then down to his valise.

"Yeah?" he said flatly. "Whatever you're sellin', we ain't buyin'."

"How ya doin', Benjie?" Charlie said with a broad grin.

Benjie's squint deepened into a suspicious frown. "Do I know you . . . ? Whoa! Charlie? Jeez. Charlie Williams? 'Zat you?"

Charlie put down the valise and spread his arms wide in a "Ta-da" gesture.

"In the flesh, Benjie."

Benjie gave a short laugh. "Wha'ja do, kid? Bust out?"

"Nope. A Christmas present from the guv." Charlie suddenly became aware of his cold hands. He stuffed them into his pockets and hunched his shoulders. "So do I sleep out here, or do ya have a room for me?"

"Oh, Jeez. Sorry. Sure. Come in, Charlie. Sure, I got a room for you. Always." Benjie moved to one side as Charlie stepped into the foyer. Benjie closed the door behind him. "It's really good to see you again, kid."

"Good to be back," Charlie said. He noticed that the foyer still had the same musty smell.

"C'mon in here." Benjie led Charlie past the foyer to his apartment/office. Next to the door was a wall-mounted pay phone with a pencil and small yellow pad beside it, both attached by a piece of string.

"So you're out. That's great. Got any plans?" Benjie asked as he walked over to an old, scarred wooden desk. An open can of Budweiser sat on it. Several circular stains from previous cans dotted the desk. Papers and mail in a state of disarray covered most of the rest of the desk.

"Yeah," Charlie snorted. "Find me a new life."

"A new life, huh? So then, what brings you back to this old burg?"

Charlie shrugged. "Last address. Jurisdiction that arrested me. So my parole officer is here. Once I get straightened out, I'm gonna make like Roadrunner. Neep, neep, and I'm gone."

"I hear that," Benjie said. "Home sweet home ain't sweet no more."

"Yeah," Charlie answered sardonically. "You got that right. Anyway, let me sign in and get settled." Benjie nodded and opened a ledger.

"Sign here," he said, indicating a line on the registration page. "The parole officer will want to see it to confirm your address. I got your old room open."

A half hour and a Budweiser later, Charlie Williams finished putting his belongings into a double dresser that looked like it predated the old boardinghouse. Furnishings in the room were minimal. Besides the dresser, with a discolored mirror over it, there was a double bed, a floor lamp to one side of an old overstuffed wing chair. An eating area contained a small wooden table with a hot plate on it. The table had a drawer under it that housed a few pieces of flatware. A shallow cabinet, screwed into the wall over the table, held some cracked pottery. A small TV sat on a metal stand opposite the wing chair. The only natural light came from two rear windows that faced an overgrown backyard. A door on the right led to a small bathroom, which Charlie remembered was shared with the room next to his. He didn't know if the room was occupied. Inside the bathroom, a small glazed window faced a neighboring boardinghouse. A small refrigerator next to the bathroom door hummed noisily.

Charlie turned his attention to the TV set. An attractive, but heavily made up, African-American woman was interviewing a group of women who were seated on a long couch. Charlie went over to the set, picked up the remote, and clicked it. The screen filled with another woman. This one, who was Caucasian and dressed in judicial robes, sat behind a raised desk lecturing a young man and woman who stood before her. Several people, an audience, were seated in rows behind. It all seemed a little weird to Charlie. He had watched TV in prison, but had seen nothing like this. He clicked from channel to channel looking for something to interest him. He passed cartoons, cooking shows, talking heads, stock market reports. Finding nothing that interested him, he turned off the set, stood quietly for a moment musing, and then swept up his jacket from the bed and left the room.

Downstairs, he knocked on Benjie's apartment door that was next to the office on the other side of the pay phone.

"Bring it in," Benjie called out. Charlie entered. Benjie sat on a couch, a Bud in hand, watching the woman judge on a large TV screen that was flat and hanging on the wall. "What's up, Charlie?" he asked.

Charlie stared at the TV. "That's a big TV set. What kind is it?"

"High-def. High definition. Forty-seven inches. I guess they didn't have it in the joint. It's my one indulgence." Charlie noticed that Benjie, who usually spoke like an uneducated longshoreman, at times revealed that he possessed a large vocabulary. "It's super sharp and has great sound. Surround sound," he said, pointing to five speakers around the room. "I love to watch the ball games and movies on it. They got football on Monday, Thursday, and Sunday night now."

"No kidding?" Charlie said. Of course he knew that. Sports were a big distraction in prison. "That's a great picture."

"Puts ya right in the seats. So whaddya need?" Benjie asked, slipping back into his "whaddya" mode.

"You still got those weights down in the cellar?"

"Yeah. You want to use 'em? Be my guest."

"Thanks. I'm gonna go out now. Do I need a key?"

Benjie reached into his pocket and flipped a key to Charlie. "Sorry. I meant to give it to you before. So, where ya off to?"

"I don't know. Just itchy, I guess. Have a look around. See what's changed in nine years. Maybe I'll grab a bite. Maybe do some shopping . . . like that."

All the while that Charlie spoke, Benjie's eyes never left the woman judge and the courtroom drama on the high-definition TV. "Ya got anything lined up? The parole officer's gonna want to know."

"No. Tomorrow I'll call him. See if he knows of anything."

Benjie looked up at Charlie for only the second time since

he had entered the room. "Sounds like a plan. You gonna see any family?"

"No way," Charlie said firmly.

"I hear that. So I'll catch you later." Benjie went back to the TV, where the judge was scolding the defendant. Charlie shrugged and left.

CHAPTER 9

UNCLE WHO?

Tom, Carol, and Katie Williams were seated at their kitchen table having apple pie and vanilla ice cream after a chicken dinner. The photo that Katie had discovered of young Tom with his arm around a younger boy was in the middle of the table. Katie now knew that it was a picture of her father and his kid brother, Charlie. Tom spoke slowly, directly to Katie. Carol had a rueful expression on her face as she listened and watched her daughter's reaction. Katie was rapt.

"With our parents gone, our aunt Belle tried her best to raise us," Tom said. "But what with her working to make ends meet and everything, well, she had her hands full. Charlie and I were what you might call 'active' kids. And being five years older, I didn't have that much to do with him outside the house." He looked away and down at the floor for a moment. "Practically nothing, now that I think of it. When you're nearly eighteen and your brother's only twelve or thirteen . . . that's a big difference. I felt like I had my own life, Charlie had his, and they were very different. You understand, Katie?"

Katie nodded. "Sure. You were probably going out and things like that."

"Yes." Tom smiled at Carol. "Going out on dates that didn't mean much until I met your mother. Anyway, then when Charlie got into his teens, he began hanging out with the wrong crowd. I was in the army and when I was home on leave I guess I didn't really notice. Maybe I figured it was just a stage and he'd work things out himself. Only he didn't." Tom smacked his lips in thought. "I guess I let him down."

"You did the best you could," Carol said. She turned to Katie. "By then, Daddy and I were dating. He told me Charlie was a little wild."

"I should have paid more attention."

"But why did he go to jail?" Katie asked.

"Well, the first time—" Tom began.

"The *first* time?" Katie interrupted. "You mean he went to jail more than once?"

"When your mother and I got engaged, Charlie was what?" Tom asked, looking at Carol before answering himself. "Seventeen?"

"That's right. Seventeen. It was a year before you were discharged."

"So he was hanging out with some bad apples. One of them was a real thug. Charlie had dropped out of school. I didn't know it. Aunt Belle was sick then and couldn't control him."

"She died a few months later," Carol interjected.

"Oh," Katie said.

"She was a real nice woman, Katie. You would have liked her."

"Anyway," Tom went on, "I was discharged and found out that Charlie and this thug had gotten into a big fight. Charlie beat him up good. A few months later, this same guy was caught holding up a Burger King in Hillsdale. It turned out the one driving the car, this guy's cousin, got scared during the holdup and took off without him. That's why he got caught. When the cops brought him in, instead of giving them the

name of his cousin, he said it was Charlie driving the car."
Katie picked up the photo of Tom and Charlie and studied it.

"No, Daddy. It wasn't Charlie," she stated flatly. She said
it in a knowing way, but it went unnoticed by Tom. But not
Carol.

"He was framed," Tom continued. "But Charlie had no
alibi. And he had a juvenile arrest record for some minor
stuff."

"What did he do?" Katie asked, now very interested.

"Well, when he first got involved with that crowd, he got
caught doing some shoplifting. And there was a stolen car,
but they never proved he took it."

"So they thought he was a criminal?" Katie asked.

"We . . . Mom and I . . . tried to convince the family court
judge that we'd look after him . . . that he was innocent, but
we couldn't. And Charlie didn't help his case. He was angry
and sullen in court. The judge sent him to juvenile hall until
he was twenty-one."

"But you did go to visit him." Carol again noticed the
knowing way in which Katie said this.

"Daddy and I both went to see him, Katie. As often as
possible."

"And when he got out," Tom said, "I gave him a job in the
hardware store I had before I went into real estate. But it just
didn't work out." He shook his head, remembering, and let
out a long sigh. He looked away and down to the floor again.

Carol saw that Tom was getting upset reliving those days.
"We did everything we could, Katie," she said. "But the business wasn't doing too good at the time. Daddy was working
sixteen, sometimes eighteen hours a day. I was pregnant with
you and . . ." Carol's voice trailed off.

"And because he was framed by this guy," Tom went on,
"he was angry and bitter. Having lost all that time in juvenile
detention for something he didn't do, well, as it turned out,
he, uh . . . you see, Katie, he kept in touch with some of the
guys he was in there with."

"In juvenile hall?"

"Yes. And then one of them came up with what he thought was a foolproof plan to rob a bank."

"Oh no!" Katie said, as though it was something she could prevent.

"Sadly, yes. My brother went along with them. It was far from foolproof. Disaster is a better way to describe it. We can only be thankful no one got hurt."

"What happened?" Katie asked.

"One of them, the one who had that brilliant plan? Well, it turns out he had brought a gun with him and didn't tell the others. And that's armed robbery. A class-A felony."

"What's that?" Katie asked.

"A major crime with a mandatory sentence," Tom told her.

"It seems like my uncle Charlie is always paying for the mistakes of others," Katie said. It was the first time she had called Charlie "Uncle."

"The first time, yes, but he did go to rob that bank," Carol told her daughter.

"But not with a gun. That's a big crime like Daddy just said."

"Yes," Carol agreed, "you're right. In that sense, maybe it was unjust."

"We borrowed money," Tom went on, "and even took out a second mortgage to hire the best lawyer we could. But the jury said it was armed robbery, and the prosecutor made sure that they got a tough judge. She sentenced them all to fifteen to twenty-five years."

Katie slowly rubbed her fingers over the photo image of young Charlie. "But this time, you didn't visit him," she said flatly.

"We tried to, honey," Tom said, not questioning how she knew. "But when your mother and I got to the prison we found he had us taken off his visitors' list. We called and wrote but he never came to the phone or answered our letters. We finally rationalized that he was too embarrassed or too ashamed, and so I guess we just sort of gave up."

Katie gazed at the photo. "Well, you did try, Daddy."

"Yes," Tom answered softly. "But maybe not hard enough." His face then suddenly brightened. "Hey, you know what? I'm glad you found that picture. I'm going to call that lawyer again. I'm going to see if there's not some way we can persuade Charlie to let us see him again. Find out at least how he's getting along and when he's getting out."

"But he *is* out, Daddy," Katie said brightly.

"What?"

"I said he *is* out. I could see him. Before. When I picked up this picture." She held the photo up.

"Katie, sweetheart," Carol said gingerly, with a sense of foreboding. "He had a very long sentence. He couldn't possibly—"

"No, Mommy," Katie interrupted. "I saw him. He was in a small dark room, all alone."

Tom smiled and took Katie's hand. "That's exactly what a prison cell is, dear," he told her softly. "Small, dark, and lonely."

"No, Daddy. I could see him in a room with a bed and a lamp and a window, and a TV, and a . . ." She stopped and looked at her father and mother. They were staring at her with worried expressions. "You don't believe me," she said, disappointed.

Tom smiled indulgently and then let out a long sigh. "It's not that, sweetheart. I mean, with the bus thing and all . . . well, there's some explanation, maybe. But what you're saying about Charlie . . . I mean, it just doesn't make any sense. He's in prison and will be for, well, I don't know how many more years . . . eight or nine at least."

Katie jumped up, her eyes brimming with tears. "Why don't you believe me when I tell you I can see things? You didn't believe me about the fire, but there was a fire. You didn't believe that I could see the bridge washing away, but it did. And now you don't believe me when I'm telling you that my uncle Charlie, my *only* uncle in the whole wide world, is *not* in prison!" She stood motionless for a moment, then turned and ran from the room crying. Tom was on his feet and moving away after her when Carol stood up and grabbed his arm.

"Tom!" she said firmly, stopping him. "Stop. We have to talk. Now!"

CHAPTER 10

SANTA'S HELPER

The next morning, after hanging up the phone in the downstairs hallway, Charlie went up to his room, put on a jacket and hat, came back downstairs, waved good-bye to Benjie—who called out, "Good luck"—and left.

Outside, Charlie walked to the corner bus stop and waited. It was a cold, gusty day and had the feel of snow in the air. The warmth of his morning coffee was just beginning to wear off when the bus arrived.

Ten minutes later, Charlie stepped off the bus into an even older part of town than where Benjie's rooming house was located. Referring to a note in his hand, he walked a half block to the Church of Saint Francis where a cornerstone declaimed A.D. 1912. Charlie stood in front of the church for a few moments trying to figure out where the entrance to the basement could be. Finally, he decided to simply walk around the church starting with the alley on his left. A few seconds later, he said to himself, "Good choice," as he reached the end of the alley and saw a flight of stairs leading down to a wooden door whose dark green paint was peeling in a few spots.

Charlie descended the stairs and knocked on the door. No

answer. He waited and knocked again. Still no answer. He tried the doorknob. It turned and Charlie pushed the door open.

A rush of warm air greeted him from a dark hallway.

"Hello?" Charlie called out.

"We are down here," came the reply from a man who had a slight Hispanic accent.

Charlie entered, closed the door behind him, and walked down the hallway to a large room on his right. The room was harshly illuminated by two banks of fluorescent lights suspended from the ceiling.

"I'm Charlie Williams," Charlie said, stepping into the room and extending his hand to the man standing inside.

"Lefty Lopez," the other man answered, stepping over to Charlie and shaking his hand.

Lefty, a man in his late forties and about five-foot-ten, had graying black hair and was built like a slightly out-of-shape football linebacker. Charlie could see he had been handsome as a young man but that his face had taken its share of punishment through the years. In particular, his nose had obviously been broken and, from its looks, more than once. He was wearing old jeans, sneakers, and a sweatshirt with SAINT FRANCIS printed across the front.

"Ron Taylor call you?" Charlie asked.

" 'Bout an hour ago."

"Everything cool?"

Lefty raised his left hand. "Cool. Ronnie's a good guy. 'Specially for a parole officer."

"Yeah, he seemed like that."

"You'll see when you meet him. Coupla years ago I messed up and he coulda fried my butt, but he didn't. So I owe him big."

Lefty half turned and made a sweeping gesture with his hand. "Right now, this is the only gig we got goin'. Maybe after Christmas there'll be somethin' else."

"I'm not complaining."

Lefty nodded and started away, saying, "Let me introduce you to Leon."

He led Charlie into a small room off to the side. The only illumination there was a naked bulb on a wire hanging from a beam. An African-American man was in the center of the room pulling pieces of a Nativity scene out of a large box. He was slightly taller than Lefty and very dark skinned with close-cropped, curly black hair. He was wearing a Santa Claus outfit with black plastic leggings around his shins and black sneakers. His face too had the look of one that had weathered a lot of physical action through the years.

"Hey, Leon," Lefty said. "Say hello to Charlie Williams."

Leon looked up with a sideways glance. "Yassa, Mr. Boss Man." Then, to Charlie: "What's happenin' there, Mr. Charlie?"

"Hey," Lefty said. "Can it. He just graduated."

Leon laid down a piece of scenery on the floor and stepped over to Charlie. "Jus' funnin', homeboy." He then reached out his hand and he and Charlie shook. "Well, bro," he continued, "welcome to the land of the free but unwanted."

"Thanks," Charlie said with a smile.

"How you doin', Lee?" Lefty asked.

"Short a sheep and two chickens."

"Well, they're plastic so we know no one ate 'em."

"Man, rats'll eat anything," Leon said.

"Well, there are no rats down here, thank God," Lefty said. Then, turning to Charlie: "C'mon, I'll set you up with your ho-ho-ho outfit while Lee keeps looking."

In the larger room, Lefty went over to a clothes rack where two Santa outfits hung. He took the larger one down. "Here. This should fit you okay. The other one'd be too small."

Charlie took the outfit from Lefty and fingered the material. "Doesn't feel like it'd be too warm."

"It's not. That's why you wear your clothes under it. That way it'll give ya extra girth too."

Charlie took the outfit over to a bench, where he took the jacket off the hanger and slipped it on.

"Hmm, not bad," he said.

"Yeah, it'll be fine," Lefty said.

Charlie sat on the bench and pulled on his Santa pants, stood up, tied the drawstring, and flopped the jacket over them. He then sat down and wrapped the black plastic leggings around his shins.

"Good thing I'm wearing black running shoes," he said.

"Yeah, that helps," Lefty answered. "Okay. You put on the hat and we're outta here." He turned and called out, "Hey, Lee! We're ready to roll."

Leon appeared in the doorway, smiling. "I guess the rats didn't get the sheep or chickens."

"You found 'em?" Lefty asked.

"They were taped to the back of the stable."

"Okay, let's go," Lefty said. He walked over to two cardboard chimneys, picked one up, and handed it to Charlie. Leon picked up the other one and they walked out of the room and into the hallway. Lefty followed, turning off the lights on his way.

Moments later, the three men emerged through the basement door and walked to the parking lot behind the church where a few cars and an old van was parked. Lefty led them to the van and climbed into the driver's seat. Leon went around to the rear and opened the back doors so he and Charlie could put their chimneys inside.

"Okay," Leon said, closing the doors. "Let's go."

He walked around to the passenger's side and climbed into the seat next to Lefty. Charlie followed and got into the seat behind him, and as soon as he closed the door, Lefty started out of the parking lot and into the street.

Some twenty minutes later, Lefty pulled up in front of a bank inside a mall.

"See you at five," he said to Leon, who had already opened his door.

"See you guys," Leon said with a wave as he got out and went to the back of the van to get his chimney.

Lefty then drove across the mall to a spot in front of a jewelry store, which was next to a toy store.

"We found these are the two best spots," he said to Charlie. "The bank back there and the jewelry and toy store here."

"Okay," Charlie said, opening his door and starting out. He then stopped. "Uh, what do I do with the chimney when I have to go to the head? And speaking of that, is there one around here I can use?"

Lefty pointed to a McDonald's down at the end of a line of stores.

"There's a McDonald's there you can use," he said. "And if for some reason you have to leave your chimney, you can park it in the jewelry store. Kaplan's. That's where I always put it. The owner? Ed Kaplan? He's a good guy that way."

"Okay," Charlie said, getting out of the van. "See you at five, then."

"Ring that bell!" Lefty yelled after him.

CHAPTER 11

AN OLD ENEMY

As Charlie was setting up his chimney on the sidewalk in front of Kaplan's, Marty Richards and Al Steel were directly behind it. They were on the narrow dirt path that ran behind the row of stores that Kaplan's was part of. On the other side of the path was a deeply wooded area. At that moment, Marty was measuring the distance from the barred window that led into Kaplan's bathroom to the spot where he knew the medicine cabinet was on the other side of the wall. As he did, he carefully marked off what he knew would be an outline of the cabinet with a series of dots from a black marker.

"This'll be our doorway in," he said to Al, who was a few feet away, leaning against one of the trees.

"The safe won't fit through there," Al said, motioning at the wall. "And if we can't take it out, how we gonna crack it?"

"I'm workin' on that."

"Well, I was thinkin' like maybe we could blow it up. I gotta cousin, Tiny, could get us some dynamite. From a construction job he's on."

"Tiny?"

"Yeah."

Marty finished marking the wall. " 'Cause he's got a tiny brain? Like you?"

"Huh?"

"Do me a favor, Al. Don't think anymore, okay?" Marty put the pen and tape measure back into his pockets. "Let's go. We're done here."

As Marty turned and started toward the end of the stores, he didn't see Al grimace in anger and rub the fist of his right hand into the palm of his left.

Suddenly, Marty stopped and turned, as if realizing his remarks to Al had been maybe a little too abrasive.

"Easy, Al. Chill. Like I said, I'm workin' on it. There's a safecracker I heard about in Cleveland. And I got Jimmy Falco checkin' him out."

To his surprise, Charlie found he was enjoying playing Santa. It seemed he was in a good spot as Lefty had said. Maybe, he thought, it was because after spending money in the toy or jewelry store, people felt a little guilty if they didn't contribute to the welfare of those less well off.

"Merry Christmas," he said to passersby over and over, occasionally adding, "Thank you. Santa thanks you and Saint Francis thanks you."

He had just finished saying just that when his body froze in reaction to the sight of Marty Richards and someone he didn't know coming around the corner from the area behind the stores. Charlie almost couldn't believe his eyes. Here was Marty Richards, the punk who had framed him as a teenager for something he didn't do, which had sent him to juvenile hall, walking directly toward him.

As Marty and Al continued on their approach, Charlie's first instinct was to turn his back to them. He wanted no part of Richards. But almost immediately, he realized that Richards wouldn't recognize him behind his Santa's beard.

And so as Marty and Al came abreast of Charlie, he felt an almost impish impulse take over him.

"Something for the homeless, gentlemen? Families and children?" he said to them.

Marty threw a look at Charlie and kept moving. But Al stopped, fished into one of his pants pockets, took out a wad of bills in a money clip and removed a couple of dollars.

Marty stopped. "Whaddaya doin'?" His question sounded more like a demand. Al ignored him and dropped the bills into Charlie's chimney.

"Thank you and Merry Christmas," Charlie said.

"Yeah, you too," Al said, putting the money clip back into his pants and starting after Marty, who was standing a few feet away.

Then, as they walked away, Charlie overheard Marty say, "What's the matter with you? Don't you know that's a racket?"

Marty and Al continued down the sidewalk for several more feet before stepping off and walking to a late-model black Chevrolet Blazer. Charlie watched them get in and then as they drove away he repeated their license plate number over and over to himself until they were out of sight.

CHAPTER 12

DO I KNOW YOU?

The people and donations kept coming and he was pleased. But Charlie was also beginning to feel pangs of hunger. He looked down the row of stores in his part of the mall and ze-roed in on the McDonald's. But his thoughts of eating disap-peared when he spied a young woman walking quickly toward him. She was coatless and obviously cold in the win-ter air as she carried her McDonald's takeout bag close to her body.

Could it be? Charlie wondered. Then, as the young woman came to within a few feet, he found himself blurting out, "Susan?" The woman stopped and looked at him.

"Yes?" Charlie's mind raced to say something.

"Uh, you're looking real good," he said, smiling through his white Santa beard.

"Why, thank you, Santa." Susan continued on a few more steps, then stopped as she recognized something in this Santa's voice.

"Do I know you?" she asked.

"You already forgot your first boyfriend from grammar school?"

Susan's mouth opened and her eyes widened. "Charlie? Charlie Williams?"

"Ho, ho, ho, that's me."

"Oh my God! What are you doing here? I thought you were in . . . I mean . . ."

"It's okay," Charlie said. "I was. But that's all behind me now. I'm out. And for good."

For a moment, they stood staring at each other, their minds reeling back through the years.

"You were my first boyfriend. That's true," Susan said, smiling warmly.

"And you were my sweet patootie," Charlie said, smiling back.

Susan let out a whoop of laughter. "Oh, Charlie," she said, laughing. "I forgot you used to call me that. And I always used to laugh because it was such an old-fashioned expression." Her eyes drifted off to one side. "Wow. That was a long time ago."

"Too long," Charlie said so softly Susan barely heard him. As he did, Charlie looked down at Susan's left hand, which was holding the bag. No wedding ring, he noticed.

"I heard you got married," he said.

"Yes. I did. It didn't work out."

"Sorry," he said, as he felt his heart skip a beat.

"Thanks. It's okay. The parting was amicable."

"Any kids?"

"No. I guess it was all part of growing up."

Charlie nodded his agreement. "Yeah. Only it takes some of us, like me, longer to do that." A strong gust of wind suddenly caused Susan to shiver.

"Hey," Charlie said. "You'd better get inside. You're not like Santa, you know. Living at the North Pole, I'm used to cold weather." Susan smiled. It seemed radiant to Charlie.

"Nice to see you still have your sense of humor, Charlie. Well, I have to get back inside anyway." She shifted her package and extended her hand. "I'm really glad you're, uh, out, and, well, you know . . . it's nice to see you."

He took her hand in his. As cold as the air was, her hand was warm and soft. "Yeah. Nice. Where do you work?"

"Kaplan's. Right over there," she said, half turning and pointing. "Oh, and listen, we have a coffee machine inside and, uh, facilities if you need to. I know Mr. Kaplan wouldn't mind your using them."

"Thanks," Charlie said. Susan gave another shiver. "You'd better get inside before you catch cold."

"Mmmm," Susan said, smiling. "Good idea." Their eyes held for another second before Susan turned and ran to Kaplan's, where she was buzzed in.

Jeez, she looks great, Charlie thought, watching the door close behind her. And he felt an old familiar ache inside his chest, something he hadn't felt for longer than he could remember. At the same time, a voice inside his head said, *Be careful. Don't get involved. Remember the new life. You're not staying around here.*

A half mile away, Katie and Melissa sat in their art classroom. Along with several other children they worked on a seasonal display for their school lobby. It was a snowy winter scene depicting their town with little figures of people and replicas of the town stores and, in the background, the town mall.

At the moment, Melissa and a boy named Jules were working on a Santa, his sleigh, and his reindeer. Katie was working with two other girls, pasting cotton snow on the display. As she worked, Katie happened to glance over at Melissa's Santa. The bright red suit that Melissa was handling caught her attention. As she focused on it, her eyes glazed over and her mind produced an image of a man in a Santa suit. Then, shaking her head as if she were rousing herself from a trance, she left the two girls and went to her desk. There, she opened her notebook and took out the picture of her father and Charlie that she and Melissa had discovered. Katie's brow knitted in deep concentration as she gazed at her uncle's face for several seconds. Then, raising her eyes, she startled her other classmates by exclaiming, "He's a *Santa!* He's a *Santa!*"

CHAPTER 13

YES, MY DARLING DAUGHTER

Looking through her living room window, Carol watched Tom's Jeep pull into the driveway. She put her magazine down on the couch, rose, and moved rapidly toward the front door.

Outside, as Tom swung his tall, lanky frame out of the Jeep, he was surprised to see his wife step outside into the cold air, without wearing a coat, and close the door behind her.

"Whoa," he called out. "What are you doing out without a coat on?"

Carol stood on the front stoop and put her hands around the upper parts of her arms for warmth. "I wanted to see you before Katie did."

"Something wrong?"

"No. I just wanted to remind you of our little talk the other night." Carol paused before going on. "Katie says she saw Charlie again. This time in the mall. In her mind's eye," she added quickly.

"And?"

"And just listen to her and what she has to say. Please don't disparage her. You know how sensitive she is. Okay?" Carol turned and opened the door.

"Okay. But what did she say?"

"I'll let her tell you. Now remember. Please."

Tom followed her into the house.

"Okay. Okay," he said amiably.

"Daddy?" Katie called out from her bedroom.

"Yes, sweetheart," Tom called back. Immediately he heard Katie running down the hallway from her room. She bounced down the stairs, ran to Tom, jumped up into his arms, and kissed him.

"You'll never guess what happened today in school."

"In school? No, what?" Tom asked, putting her down.

"In my art class. We were making the lobby display for Christmas and Hanukkah and Kwanzaa."

"Sounds like you've got everyone covered. So what happened that's so exciting?" Tom asked with a smile as he took off his coat.

"Wellll," Katie began dramatically, "Melissa and a boy named Jules were making a Santa and . . . well, you see, I had this sudden kind of, you know, thought . . ."

Tom felt a tingle go down his spine. "A thought. Like on the bus?" The moment he said that, he was sorry he had. Carol rolled her eyes in disapproval, thinking Katie would clam up, but she didn't.

"Exactly!" she said. "I went to my desk and took out that picture of you and Uncle Charlie . . . you know the one."

"Yes," Tom replied softly.

"Right. And as I looked at Uncle Charlie, I suddenly saw him dressed up as Santa Claus in our mall!"

Tom raised his eyebrows. "You saw Charlie as a Santa at the mall?"

"Yes, Daddy. Now, I know you probably don't believe me—"

"Hey," Tom interrupted. "I never said that."

"I know. I know. But I can tell what you're thinking," Katie said in a singsong manner, wagging her finger at him as she did. "Anyway, I would have gone to the mall today when

I got home from school but I had the piano lesson, and besides, Melissa couldn't make it. So we're both going to walk over there tomorrow after school. I know you think it's silly and all that, but even Melissa said—"

Tom held his hands up in front of him and laughed. "Whoa. Slow down there, young lady. I said no such thing. I think it's a good idea. A very good idea. Sure, you go check on whether Uncle Charlie's there or not." Tom looked from Katie to Carol with raised eyebrows as if to say, Did I do right? Carol smiled and nodded.

"Really, Daddy? You don't mind?"

"Not at all. I put in a call to Uncle Charlie's lawyer today. He's out of town and won't be back until next week."

"You did?" Carol said, pleased but surprised.

"Sure. I said I would, didn't I? And, while I'm waiting to hear back from him, I think you should go check on what you think, uh, on what you saw today. Okay?" Katie hugged Tom.

"Oh, thank you, Daddy," Katie said. "I've got to call Melissa." She then bounded up the stairs.

"Dinner will be ready in about fifteen minutes," Carol told Tom. "How about a glass of wine?"

"After today? Sounds like a good idea."

Carol and Tom moved toward the kitchen.

"Something go wrong today?" Carol asked.

"Not exactly," Tom answered. "I just can't seem to close on that Jenkins parcel over in Sunnyside. We were supposed to meet this afternoon to iron out the details, but the buyer's lawyer canceled. She said there was an 'emergency' she had to deal with. We're on for four tomorrow. But the whole thing'll take a couple of hours and we were supposed to go for the tree and wreath tomorrow night." Tom opened a cabinet and took out a bottle of red wine. "Join me?" he asked. Carol nodded and Tom took out two glasses from another cabinet.

"Well, instead of your coming all the way home," Carol

suggested, "Katie and I can meet you at the nursery. Say, six, six thirty. Call when your meeting's over. That way we can be back home for dinner around seven thirty. Okay?"

"Perfect." He poured the wine and brought Carol's glass to her. He clinked his glass against hers, and executing a terrible imitation of Humphrey Bogart, said, "Here's lookin' at you, schweetheart."

Carol laughed. "That was awful. You have no future as an impersonator." Tom nodded his agreement. She took a sip from her glass. "But you're a great father. The way you encouraged Katie made her very happy. I must say I was somewhat surprised. I thought at best you'd just say, Okay."

"Well, I figured the best way to put this whole thing with Charlie to bed is to let her go see for herself that she's just imagining these things. By tomorrow night, she'll understand that."

But Carol knew that the legacy of her grandma Miranda was alive and well within her daughter. *Yes, my dear,* she thought to herself. *And so will you.*

CHAPTER 14

A COLD DISH

That same evening, shortly after 5:20, Lefty pulled up in front of Benjie's Rooming House with Charlie and Leon aboard. As soon as the van stopped, Charlie hopped out.

"Take it easy, guys. See you tomorrow." He then turned and hurried up the worn steps. When he stepped inside his new home, going from the heated van into the near-freezing air sent an involuntary shiver through his body. Charlie noticed the door to Benjie's room was open. Looking in, he saw Benjie sitting on his couch watching television with a cup of coffee in his hand.

"Hey, Benj," he called in.

"Charlie boy," Benjie answered. "How ya doin'? How's the Santa business?"

"Good. Made a nice haul today."

"Glad to hear. That church does good things. Like a cup of coffee? Warm yourself up? Just made one for myself."

Charlie hesitated a moment. "Uh, okay," he said, and stepped into the room. Benjie got up, walked to his stove, and turned it on. He then stepped over to the cupboard, took out a cup, and spooned some instant coffee into it.

"Milk?"

"Black, thanks." Benjie turned toward Charlie, his eyes studying him carefully.

"So, ya made a nice haul today, huh?" he asked idly.

"Yeah." Moments later, the kettle started whistling. Benjie turned off the gas and poured the steaming water into the cup. He stirred it once and then brought the coffee to Charlie.

"Siddown," he said, motioning to an old overstuffed chair. Charlie took the cup and sat. "So, what's on your mind?" Benjie asked.

Charlie raised his eyebrows. "What do you mean?"

Benjie shrugged. "Somethin's on your mind. I can see it. Spotted it the minute you looked in. Don't forget I was once a guest of the state myself. I know the look." Instead of answering, Charlie took a cautious sip of his hot coffee. Benjie sat down on the couch and looked at him. Charlie paused a moment, then cleared his throat.

"Could you find the address of someone if I gave you the license plate number?"

"I don't know. What's the number?" Charlie reached into his jacket, pulled out a piece of paper, and handed it to Benjie.

Benjie looked at it. "Who is it?"

"Guy named Marty Richards." Benjie made an almost inaudible groan.

"Charlie, Charlie, what's the matter with you? Don't you know the old saying, 'Any man who goes after revenge only keeps his own wounds open'?"

"It's not that—" Charlie started to say.

Benjie raised his hand and interrupted. "Hey . . . don't try to kid a kidder, huh? You just can't forget that Richards lied you into juvie hall for three and a half years and got away with it!" Charlie turned back to his cup and took another sip. Benjie's eyes remained on him. "So where'd ya see him?"

Charlie looked back up. "The mall. With another guy. I didn't know him."

"Big guy? Beefy?"

"Yeah."

"That'd be Al Steel. Metal head, they call him. Not the sharpest knife in the drawer. Yeah, I heard he'd hooked up with Richards. Did Richards make you?"

Charlie shook his head, his mouth forming the barest hint of a smile. "No. I'm Santa Claus, remember?"

Benjie took a gulp of coffee. "Look, Charlie. You're out. You're a free man. Why d'ya wanta go stirrin' up trouble?"

"I don't want any trouble. Just curious, is all."

Benjie snorted. "Yeah. And pigs can fly. Look, I can understand seein' him gets you steamed about that whole thing, but, Charlie, you're a big boy now. That part of your life is over. Finished. Finito! Let it go, man."

"Look, Benjie, if you don't want to do it, then—"

Benjie held up his hand. "Whoa. I didn't say that. I'll do what I can. But I can't promise anything. And I gotta tell you, it's against my better judgment." Benjie rose and started toward the stove. "Ya want any more?"

"No, thanks," Charlie answered. Then, as Benjie reached the stove, he added, "Hey, Benj?"

"Yeah?"

"You know that other old saying?"

"What one's that?"

"Revenge is a dish best eaten cold."

Benjie sighed and dropped his head. "And that, Charlie my boy, is also a dish that can lead you straight back to the lousy dishes they serve in the joint."

CHAPTER 15

UNCLE WHO?

Instead of going home when they got off the bus, Katie and Melissa headed straight for the mall. Katie couldn't wait to prove her uncle Charlie was indeed there, working as Santa.

Along the way, two boys a few years older than they were, wearing baseball caps turned sideways on their heads like rappers, whistled, and waved at them from across the street. The two girls, flattered that they were the center of attention from what they considered "much older boys," giggled.

"They must have been fourteen!" Melissa said.

"Maybe even fifteen!" Katie said as she smiled and rolled her eyes in agreement.

A few minutes later, they entered the mall. Almost immediately, Katie grabbed Melissa by the arm.

"Look!" she said excitedly. "There's a Santa right there! Right in front of the bank!"

The girls hurried over to the Santa, who was standing with his back to them and ringing his bell. Katie went up behind him and tapped him on the back.

"Hi, Santa," she said expectantly. Leon turned around.

"Well, hi there yourself, young lady," he said. "And a Merry Christmas to you." Katie's eyes widened and her mouth dropped open in disappointment. She turned to Melissa, who was giggling. "Somethin' wrong, honey?" Leon asked.

"Uh, no," Katie answered, feeling her face turn red. "I just thought you were someone else."

"Guess you didn't know ole Santa's a brother, huh?"

Katie looked at him uncomprehendingly.

"My brother?" she asked.

Leon let out a short laugh. "Yeah. Kinda like that. Look, sweetie, if it's the more 'traditional' Santa you're lookin' for, maybe you should go to the other side of the mall." He pointed. "Over there. See that sign, Kaplan's Jewelry Store?"

Katie turned and looked. "Yes."

"Well, that's where the other Santa works."

"Thank you. I didn't mean to . . . I mean, I just thought that . . . well, that is . . . well, thank you again." With that, Katie grabbed Melissa by the arm again. The two girls smiled at Leon and started across the mall through the parked cars. In a few minutes, they stepped up onto the sidewalk in front of Kaplan's. This time, they could see the Santa was a white man.

Katie walked up to Charlie, who was thanking a shopper for dropping money into his chimney. And as she did with Leon, Katie tapped Charlie on the back.

"Well, hello there," he said, turning to her with a smile.

"Hello there yourself," Katie answered, almost unable to contain her excitement.

"And have you been a good girl this year?" Charlie said, widening his eyes and raising his eyebrows. "I mean, *all* year?"

"Yes, I have, Uncle Charlie," she blurted out. The smile disappeared from Charlie's face. Instinctively, he looked around to see who else might have heard.

"Uncle Charlie?" he asked. "Who's Uncle Charlie?"

Katie's face broke into a big smile. "You are! *You're* my uncle Charlie. And I'm your niece, Katie!"

Charlie looked at her. *Yes, of course,* he thought. There

was no denying that face. In it he saw his brother's wife, Carol. Same eyes, same smile. A dead ringer. And, like Carol, she was an exceptional beauty. But, *how?* he wondered. How did she *know?* How did she *find* him? In any case, he decided to deny his way out of it.

"I'm awfully sorry, uh, Katie, is it?" Katie nodded energetically. "Look, Katie, I'm real sorry but much as I'd love to be your uncle, especially to such a pretty young lady, I'm afraid you've made a mistake. I have no nieces."

Katie smiled indulgently. Melissa, who was embarrassed, tugged slightly on Katie's coat sleeve.

"You made a mistake," she told her friend. Katie ignored Melissa and pulled her sleeve free.

"Yes, you do," Katie said firmly. "You're my uncle Charlie and I can prove it." With that, she swung her backpack off and reached into one of the pockets.

As she did, a man and woman who had come out of Kaplan's passed Charlie's chimney and dropped a bill into it. Relieved at the distraction from Katie, Charlie turned to them.

"Thank you, folks! Thank you! And a Merry Christmas!"

"Merry Christmas to you too, Santa. Keep up the good work," the man said as the couple walked away.

Charlie, his back now turned to Katie, began ringing his bell and calling out, "Something for the homeless families and children? Merry Christmas . . ."

A young woman came out of the toy store with a couple of Christmas-wrapped packages and walked toward Charlie. She juggled the packages while trying to open her pocketbook, but couldn't manage it. "Here, let me help you," Charlie said, going over to her. The young woman handed the packages to Charlie, opened her pocketbook, took out a couple of dollars, and handed them to Charlie.

"Thank you. Thank you," Charlie said, handing the packages back to the woman. "I'll put them in my chimney. Merry Christmas to you."

"Merry Christmas to you," the woman responded.

Katie, who now had the photo of Charlie and her father in hand, waited patiently for Charlie to come back to his chimney.

"Here, Uncle Charlie, look!" she said, holding the photo up for Charlie to see.

I've got to end this once and for all, Charlie thought. He dropped the money the woman had given him into the chimney.

"Look, young lady. You're very nice and very persistent, but you've made a mistake," he said. "I've got work to do."

"It's not a mistake," Katie said, now raising the photo up to Charlie's face. "My daddy is your brother, *Tom*. Please just look!"

Charlie looked and indeed did remember the day the picture was taken.

"I don't know who either of those people are," he said firmly. "Now, I'm busy here trying to raise money for a very worthwhile cause. So why don't you and your friend here run along?"

"I know where you *were* and what *happened*. And I know you're all alone and—"

"And?" Charlie interrupted. "And Merry Christmas." With that, Charlie picked up his chimney and walked away with it to a spot in front of the toy store.

Katie stood, hurt. She could feel her eyes filling with tears. Melissa put her arm around Katie's shoulder.

"Maybe he really isn't your uncle, Katie."

"No," Katie insisted. "He *is* my uncle Charlie. He's got the exact same blue eyes as my father."

"Well, then he doesn't want to admit it. So, what are you going to do?" Melissa asked.

"I'll see what my mother says," Katie answered. "C'mon, let's go."

Charlie was relieved to see Katie and Melissa walk away. *Now what?* he wondered. But this thought was interrupted by the sight of Susan coming out of Kaplan's. She walked to him.

"How come you moved over here?" she asked.

"Thought I'd try a different neighborhood," Charlie answered lightly. Susan smiled.

"Well, I'm off to McDonald's," she said. "Joan, Ed's wife, is having a chocolate chip cookie fit. And to tell you the truth, so am I."

"Hey, Susan," Charlie said, "I was wondering, uh, do you go out for lunch?"

"I usually bring something in with me. Why?"

"Well, like I said, I was wondering, uh, if maybe you'd like to join me tomorrow at Micky D's."

"Why, I'd love to, Charlie," Susan said. "I take my lunch break at one. Is that okay?"

"Perfect," Charlie answered.

"Then it's a date. Now I've got to run. We're busy and need that chocolate fix."

Charlie raised his hand to her with a smile. "Then by all means, run."

As Susan left, Charlie found himself wondering why he had so impulsively asked her to lunch.

Remember, he told himself again, *you're not staying here. Don't get involved.* And then he remembered Katie, his beautiful niece, and sensed that no matter how hard he was trying, his past life in his hometown was catching up with him.

CHAPTER 16

WHO CAN CRACK A SAFE?

Giacomo ("Jimmy") Falco pulled up in front of a bar in a 2003 Nissan he had picked up for only nine hundred dollars at an auction. As he turned off the engine, it coughed and shuddered, reminding him it was not as good a deal as he had thought. He cursed his bad luck.

A small man, compactly built, Jimmy moved with short, quick steps toward the bar. The bar's name, the official name on its business license, was The Flamingo. But since the outside neon sign with its name and flamboyant pink flamingo had been blown away in a tornado, its patrons had come to call it "The Bud" because of the red neon Budweiser sign that hung in the center of the front window—a window that looked as if it hadn't been washed in years.

Jimmy Falco walked up to the heavy, solid wooden door that had three locks on it, and entered. The Flamingo was basically a long narrow store with a bar on the left side and four small tables with two chairs apiece lined up against the opposite wall. The walls on either side were exposed brick whose plaster had been removed several years before Paul Gaglione, the new owner, took over.

The only illumination came from a few rose-tinted fluorescents behind the bar and four banks of white fluorescents that hung from the ceiling in a line from the front door to the restrooms in the rear. These overhead lights gave off a harsh glare, broken only by the flickering of some of the aging tubes.

Paul Gaglione was placing a bottle of beer in front of one of the three men sitting at the bar as Jimmy walked in.

"What's up, Jimmy?" he asked with a nod as Falco passed by.

"This 'n that, Pauly," Jimmy said, nodding in return.

In the rear of the bar were eight larger tables with chairs around them. All were empty except for the farthest one in back where Marty Richards sat, a beer in front of him. Jimmy walked up to the table and extended his hand.

"Whaddaya say, Marty? How's it goin'?"

Marty shook Jimmy's hand. "You tell me. And why are we meetin' here in this dump in the first place?"

"This is where I do mosta my business," Jimmy said.

"In here?"

"The place kinda grows on ya. And Pauly's got a mouth like a clam."

"Ya coulda told me what I wanted to know over the phone."

"I don't like doin' business over the phone. Ya never know who's listenin'. Besides—" Jimmy stopped in midsentence as Marty held up his hand for silence as Pauly approached with a glass of red wine for Falco.

"Thanks, Pauly," Jimmy said. Paul nodded, then looked at Marty and pointed at his near-empty glass. Marty lifted his hand and shook his head. Paul turned and walked away. Jimmy sipped his wine and continued. "Besides, this is the only place I know where you can get homemade red. Pauly's got an uncle who still makes it."

"I'll have to put that in my memoirs," Marty said sarcastically. "Meanwhile, what's with Cleveland?"

Jimmy took another sip of wine and smacked his lips. "Forget Cleveland. That guy, Marseller? He's doin' four to seven in Wisconsin."

Marty exhaled in disgust. "Great. So that's why you wanted to meet me here in this rat hole? To tell me you got nothin'?"

Jimmy leaned across the table, his glittering eyes so dark brown they appeared black. "Hey, Marty. Chill. Wait'll ya hear what I got. Somethin' even better. Someone right here in this burg."

"There's nobody in this burg. I already went through everyone who—"

"This guy just blew in," Jimmy interrupted. "And it's someone *you* know," he said in a singsong manner.

"Who?"

"Charlie. Charlie Williams."

"That homemade wine's makin' you nuts," Marty said. "That jerk got at least three more to go before he's even up for parole."

"Did, Marty. Did."

"Whaddaya talkin'?"

"Did have a few more years to go. Up till a few days ago. Seems the joint became a full house. They was runnin' outta room. And, from what I hear, money too. Budget's tight. Recession. So the governor sprung some of 'em early. Bingo— Charlie Williams is free as a bird."

"So they sprung him." Marty shrugged. "So what? What's that got to do with me? Or my problem?"

Jimmy smiled slyly.

"I guess you don't know that Charlie Williams shared a cell with Winkie Cohen for a spell."

"Winkie Cohen?" Marty could barely believe his ears. "The Master?"

Jimmy sipped his wine again and nodded. "Prob'ly the best safecracker ever lived. Like you said, the Master. A lotta the old-timers called him 'the Genius.' Even 'Houdini.' But nobody ever like him. Nobody."

"Where's Winkie now? Maybe he—"

"Forget about it. He don't got another shot at the board for, oh, maybe five years."

"And Williams bunked with him?"

"Word is Williams was his best pupil."

Marty sat back in his chair as the news sank in. He smiled. "So Charlie Williams knows how to crack safes. Will wonders never cease?" He let out a short laugh. "And he's right back here, ya say?"

"His parole officer, a guy named Taylor, hooked him up with Lefty Lopez over at Saint Francis. Ya know where that is?" Marty nodded. "And Lefty's got him workin' a Santa gig over in the mall."

"A safecrackin' Santa Claus." Marty chuckled. "Whaddaya know? Where's he floppin'?"

" 'At's all I know."

"Well, I can find out," Marty said. He rose from his chair. "Jimmy, ya did good. Thanks a lot."

"Have another beer."

"Thanks, no. I gotta talk to Al. See ya around." Marty left the table and headed for the door. He passed Paul, who was carrying another glass of wine to Jimmy.

CHAPTER 17

NOT LOOKING BACK

The mall was crowded with Christmas shoppers. The nearest parking spot to Kaplan's that Carol could find was two rows away.

"There he is, Mommy," Katie said, pointing through the front windshield to the man in the Santa suit ringing his bell.

"I see him," Carol said. "Okay. Now you stay here."

"But, Mommy, I want to—"

"No, sweetie," Carol interrupted. "He's seen you. I want to surprise him. He probably won't recognize me until I'm next to him. That way he can't turn and walk away or whatever."

"O-kay," Katie said, disappointed.

Carol opened the door, got out, and beeped the locks shut. She then walked through the rows of cars before stepping up on the sidewalk in front of Kaplan's.

Charlie was thanking an older woman for her contribution as Carol approached him from behind. Then, as the woman left, Carol stepped up and dropped a couple of dollars into Charlie's chimney.

"Thank you and Merry Christmas," Charlie said.

"You're welcome. And a Merry Christmas to you, Charlie."

But even before Carol finished her greeting, Charlie knew who she was. It was the same beautiful face, the same lovely voice he remembered.

"I guess I'm busted," he said with a grin. "How are you, Carol?"

"I . . . we're fine."

Charlie gave a quick chuckle.

"That daughter of yours? Katie? She's quite a package."

Carol nodded, smiling. "Believe me, more than you could imagine. But why didn't you let us know you were, uh, you know . . ."

"Out?" Charlie shrugged his shoulders. "They gave me a quickie parole. I'm a victim of budget cuts," he added sardonically. Carol's eyes widened questioningly.

"So why didn't you *call?*" she asked, almost beseechingly. "I mean, Tom's your *brother.* Your *only* brother. And we're *family.* Your *only* family."

As she spoke, Charlie could feel his chest tightening. He took a deep breath and exhaled slowly. "Well, you know . . . Look, Carol, I'm not going to be around here long, so why be a burden to you or Tom?"

"How would you be a burden to us?"

"I'm an ex-con, Carol. Look, I—"

But Carol was having none of it. "That doesn't matter, Charlie. We're family!"

At that moment, two women, loaded with gifts, walked up.

"Is this for the Community Chest?" one of them asked as she opened her pocketbook.

"No, ma'am," Charlie answered. "It's for the Saint Francis homeless families' fund."

"That's just fine," the woman said, dropping a dollar into the chimney.

"Must be a long day out here in the cold, young man," the

other woman commented as she also dropped a dollar into the chimney.

"Yes. Until five. But it's for a good cause," Charlie said.

"Yes, it is," she said, snapping her pocketbook shut. "Well, Merry Christmas."

"Yes," the first woman said. "And God bless."

Charlie raised a hand and nodded. "Thank you, ladies. And a Merry Christmas to you and yours."

"As I was saying . . ." Carol began as the women left. "We're your family."

Charlie could feel his chest tightening again. "I'm not *out* out. I'm on parole! I'm a two-time loser. An ex–bank robber."

"That's all in the past."

"Maybe. But I can't change what I did. And I can't get back those years in prison. All I can do now is look ahead."

"Rejoining your family isn't looking ahead?" Carol's voice was soft and her tone pleasant but, as Charlie noticed, persistent.

"I'm sorry, Carol, but it's not for me. I want a new life of my own. On my own."

"You can still have your own life without cutting yourself off from your family."

Charlie shook his head. "The only reason I came back here was that my parole begins in this jurisdiction. My parole officer got me this job. Obviously, it's temporary. After Christmas, I'm going to ask to move to Florida."

"Fine," Carol said. "But being with us now, over the holidays, that wouldn't interfere with your plans, would it? I know Tom would love to—"

Charlie held up his hand. "Carol, I'm sorry. No. It's like everything here reminds me of my mistakes. The things I want to forget. Now please just let me be." With that, Charlie turned his back to Carol and began ringing his bell. She stood for a moment in a state of confusion and frustration. Finally, she turned and walked away.

* * *

Inside the jewelry store, Joan Kaplan looked out the front window. Ed walked up next to her.

"What's so interesting, my love?"

"Our Santa Claus," Joan answered. "The one you told Susan it was okay for him to come in here for coffee and to use the john?"

"Yeah? Susan said he's a nice guy."

"Well, I was noticing. About an hour or so ago, young Katie Williams was talking to him. You remember her? Her father used to have the hardware store?"

"Yeah, sure. I think he's in real estate now."

"Right."

Ed gave a slight shrug with his shoulders. "Well, so? Everybody likes to talk to Santa. Especially kids, right?"

"I know, dear," Joan said patiently. "But now Katie's mother, uh . . ." She paused, mentally searching.

"Carol."

"Yes. Carol. She was also talking to Santa. And it looked like, well, I don't know if I'm reading something into it, but it looked like they were having a very sort of personal and heavy conversation."

"Heavy?"

"You know what I mean. *Serious.*"

Ed looked at Joan and shrugged. "You are always looking for the dramatic, sweetheart. Maybe she just was giving Santa her Christmas wish list."

"Don't be so smart-alecky with me, Edward."

"Never, my love. Meanwhile, I've got to get those links added to Mrs. Reiff's tennis bracelet."

"She put on weight again?"

Ed shrugged and walked away. "Who am I to say? That would be smart-alecky."

* * *

Back at the car, Carol beeped the locks open and climbed in next to Katie.

"It was Uncle Charlie, right?" Katie asked.

"It was Uncle Charlie, sweetie."

"What did he say?"

"Well, it seems your uncle Charlie would rather not see us."

"But, *why?*"

Carol rolled her head from side to side. "Oh, for a lot of reasons, honey. But maybe Daddy—" She stopped in mid-sentence. "Now, there's an idea."

"What?"

"Maybe if Daddy were to talk to him, he could convince him to get together with us for the holidays. But talking to him in the mall while Charlie is working isn't good. But where, is the question?" Her eyes narrowed in thought. "Is it possible you know where your uncle Charlie lives?"

"No. I just can see the room, but no address."

"Oh." Carol thought for a moment. "Wait a minute. I heard Charlie say he gets off at five. That's less than half an hour from now. So why don't we see where he goes from here? Maybe we could find out where he lives."

"But, Mommy, aren't we supposed to meet Daddy to get the tree tonight?"

"Not till six or six thirty. And if this takes longer, I can always call Daddy's cell."

"Good," Katie said. There was excitement in her voice. "This is like a secret adventure."

"Yes," Carol said, sliding down a bit in her seat. "I suppose it is. So let's keep our heads down and our eyes open."

As Katie slid down her seat, she couldn't help smiling.

CHAPTER 18

FOLLOW THAT VAN

It had begun to snow lightly when a few minutes after five o'clock, the Saint Francis van, with Lefty driving and Leon sitting next to him, pulled up to the curb in front of Kaplan's. Charlie picked up his chimney, opened the van's rear hatch, and put his chimney inside. Then he brushed off the snow on his Santa suit and climbed into the van behind Leon.

"Hi, guys," Charlie had said. The other two men returned his "Hi" with their own. "Maybe a white Christmas, huh?"

"Could be. How'd it go today?" Lefty asked.

Charlie pulled off his cap and beard. "Better than yesterday."

"Yeah, same here," Leon said. Lefty lifted one hand off the steering wheel and gave them a thumbs-up.

"Good. That's good," he said as he approached the mall exit. "People usually loosen up as the holiday approaches."

Carol and Katie watched the van, peering just above the car's dashboard. The snow partially obscured their view.

"I think they're leaving!" Katie exclaimed with excitement. Carol started her car and windshield wipers, and then swung out into the lane parallel to the van. She drove slowly to be sure it would be ahead of her as they left the mall lot.

What she didn't see was a black Chevrolet Blazer pull out from a nearby spot and fall in behind her.

"**H**ey, Charlie, you startin' a fan club?" Leon said to Charlie, half turned from the front of the van. "Or Santa groupies or somethin' with young girls?"

"What are you talking about?" Charlie asked.

"I mean like two cute girls came up to me lookin' for you this afternoon. Seemed disappointed when they saw I wasn't a white Santa."

"Oh, yeah, that . . ." Charlie waved his hand dismissively. "One of them thought I was someone she knew. It was nothing."

As the van drove slowly through the traffic on its way to drop off Charlie, Marty was puzzled by the car between them and the van.

"Am I imaginin' things," Marty asked, "or is that car in front of us followin' them also?"

"Yeah. I seen that too," Al said. "Sure looks like it, huh?" They both watched with heightened interest as the van made a sharp left and then right. Carol's car followed it, skidding slightly on the wet pavement.

"You see that?" Marty said. "That guy sure is followin' it, all right. And he don't seem to be makin' no bones about it neither."

"Look how close behind it he is," Al added. Just then, a truck came along from the opposite direction, its bright lights silhouetting Carol's head.

"Is it a guy or a woman?" Al asked. "See? Look at the head," he added as now a car passed Carol's car, once again silhouetting her head. "See how it's all puffed out? That's a woman's hairdo."

"Maybe it's a guy wearin' a hood," Marty suggested.

"Maybe. But it sure looks a woman's head to me," Al countered.

"You could be right," Marty conceded. "So what's she doin' followin' our boy? And who is she?"

When the van pulled up in front of Benjie's, Charlie hopped out and looked up at the falling snow.

"Hope this is just a dusting," he said, noting that the snow was beginning to stick on the grass. "See you guys in the A.M." As he started to close the van's door, Carol's car passed them.

"Crazy," Lefty said.

"What's that?" Charlie asked. Before Lefty could answer, Marty and Al's Blazer passed by.

"That car and then that SUV that just passed us," Lefty said. "I coulda sworn they was both followin' us."

Inside the Blazer, Marty was smiling. "Now we know where Williams lives. Benjie's place. I shoulda figured that. It's where he flopped before he went away."

"And it looks like that gal or guy or whatever in front of us wanted to know that too," Al said, as up ahead, Carol made a right at the first corner.

"Follow her," Marty said as they pulled up to the corner stop sign.

"What for?"

Marty made an annoyed sound with his mouth. "To see where she lives, Einstein."

"And what's that gonna tell us?" Al asked, frowning and puzzled.

"I'm thinkin' maybe there's some connection between them

and our boy Charlie Williams, and I wanna know what it is. I gotta hunch it jus' might come in handy."

Because Carol was so intent on following the van, she never noticed she was being followed. She glanced at the dashboard clock.

"Let's call Daddy," she said to Katie. "It's almost six."

"I can do that, Mommy," Katie offered. "Where's your cell?"

"In my bag. Right on top."

Katie found the phone and speed-dialed her father's number.

Not quite fifteen minutes later, Carol drove into the parking lot of the plant nursery.

Marty and Al, who had followed at a discreet distance, pulled up in the street outside the nursery entrance where they had a clear view of Carol's car.

"This don't look like where someone lives, unless they're a tree or somethin'," Al said, amused at his own words.

Marty threw him a sideways look. "You're a real riot, Al. Anybody ever tell you that?"

"I was jus' jokin'."

"Right. I knew that. But did it ever occur to you they might be stoppin' to buy somethin' on the way home? Like maybe some Christmas stuff, bein' as how it'll be Christmas in a few days?"

Al could feel the anger rising within him. He hated the way Marty always talked down to him like he was a moron or somethin'. *When this job is over,* he thought, *I'm gonna flatten his face.*

"They ain't gettin' outta the car," Marty said, interrupting Al's thoughts. "They're jus' sittin' there."

"Ya think they spotted us?" Al asked.

"I don't think so. Maybe they're waitin' for someone. Yeah, that's it. Okay. We wait too. And even if they did spot us, whadda they gonna say? We was followin' them? We'd say we don't know what the hell they're talkin' about."

Just as Marty finished his rationale, Tom's Jeep passed by them and pulled into the nursery parking lot. It then slowed almost to a stop before moving over to Carol's car. As it pulled alongside, Carol and Katie both got out. A moment later, Tom got out of the Jeep.

"Ah, see!" Marty exclaimed. "I was right! Papa Bear, Mama Bear, and Baby Bear. Huh?" He nudged Al's arm. "Huh? What'd I say about them shoppin'? Huh, dummy?"

Al kept his eyes on the Williamses and merely nodded. *Keep it up, Marty,* he thought. *Keep it up. You'll get yours.*

Tom gave Carol a hello peck on the cheek, and then gave one to Katie.

"How are my two girls?" he asked, smiling broadly.

"Fine, Daddy," Katie answered, brimming with excitement. "And guess what?"

Carol held up her hand. "Wait. Before we tell Daddy, sweetie, we have to congratulate him on closing a very important deal today." She turned to Tom and hugged him. "Congratulations!"

"Congratulations, Daddy," Katie said dutifully.

"Thank you, thank you," Tom responded, bowing slightly. As Katie opened her mouth to speak, Tom continued. "I have to tell you, though, for a little while there I thought the whole deal was going to slip away. But then halfway through, I could tell he really wanted the land and was just trying one last attempt to get me to lower the price. I was stubborn and didn't budge. He gave in." He turned to Katie. "Sometimes, being stubborn when you really believe in something pays." Tom nodded and then held his hand palm up to the snow. "Now we'd better get that tree before this gets any worse."

As they began to walk toward where the Christmas trees were displayed, Tom took his daughter's hand. "And now, young lady, why don't you tell me what I can see has you jumping up and down inside?"

"Daddy," Katie blurted out, "we saw Uncle Charlie today! He's playing Santa Claus in the mall! Just like I pictured him in school yesterday."

Tom stopped in his tracks and turned to Carol. She nodded with a small smile on her lips.

Marty leaned over to the driver's side and turned on the ignition.

"Whaddaya doin'?" Al asked.

"I just want to get some heat in here," Marty answered. With the ignition on, Al turned on the wipers to clean off the windshield, letting them flick back and forth a few times before turning them off. The snow had let up quite a bit.

"I'm gettin' hungry," Al said.

"You're always hungry. You should try to lose some weight."

Al ignored this remark. "I could use a drink too."

"And ya drink too much," Marty said.

"And you're Mr. Perfect," Al retorted.

"At least—" Marty began to say, then stopped and pointed through the windshield. "Here they come."

Al saw Tom, Carol, and Katie exiting the nursery with an attendant pushing a wagon that held a full blue spruce and a wreath with a large red bow on it.

Tom put the wreath in the back of the Jeep and then he and the attendant tied the tree onto the roof. While Tom and the attendant were doing this, Carol and Katie got into Carol's car and with waves and a beep of the horn drove out of the parking lot and away.

Al shifted the Blazer into gear.

"No, no," Marty said. "We follow him."

"Why him?"

" 'Cause his mind'll be on keepin' that tree from fallin' off, not on someone followin' behind. Who knows? Maybe the broad did spot us before but just thought it was a coincidence. Now, if she was to see us followin' her again, she'd know it was no coincidence. And even though she couldn't prove nothin', I don't wanna get into no hassle with cops."

With the tree now tied to the roof of the Jeep, Tom pulled out of the parking lot and, to Marty and Al's surprise, drove away in the opposite direction.

"Where the hell's he goin'?" Marty asked.

"I don't know," Al said, turning on his headlights and shifting into gear, "but you're the one who said to follow him, so we'll follow him."

Tom drove slowly down the street checking the house numbers. When he saw the large number 59, he pulled up to the curb and stopped. He sat there for a few minutes gathering his thoughts and trying to decide how he was going to greet his brother, and what he was going to say. As he did, he found himself half wishing his brother would not be home, but out for the evening.

CHAPTER 19

OH, BROTHER

Halfway down the block, Marty and Al sat in the Blazer watching.

"What's goin' on?" Al asked.

"You're askin' me?" Marty said.

"What's he gonna do?" Al persisted. "Just sit there?"

"How the hell should I know?" Marty asked with some heat.

Both men were now irritable, having been cooped up inside the Blazer together for more than two hours, and not having eaten in several more.

"D'ya think he made us? And is waitin' to see if we're gonna get out?" Al asked. Before Marty, annoyed by Al's questions, could answer, they saw Tom get out of the Jeep and walk up the steps to Benjie's house.

"So who is this guy?" Marty wondered aloud. "And what's his connection with Williams?"

"You're askin' me?" Al said, repeating Marty's question of a few moments before while smiling to himself. Marty turned his head slowly and looked at Al, who kept his eyes on Tom, who was now on Benjie's porch.

* * *

Tom rang the doorbell and waited. A few moments later the door opened.

"Yeah?" Benjie asked. Tom took in a deep breath.

"Hi. I'm Tom Williams. Charlie Williams's brother. Do you know if he's in?"

Benjie eyed Tom. "He expectin' you?"

"No."

Benjie hesitated a moment while he considered telling the stranger that Charlie was out. Then he relented. "Well, seein' as how he's your brother, I guess it's okay." He stepped back and opened the door wide. "Normally I don't do this unless someone tells me they're expectin' someone."

Tom stepped inside. "I appreciate it."

Benjie closed the door behind him. "I hope *he* does. Me? I don't like no surprises."

"Well, a lot of people don't, I guess," Tom said, trying to be as agreeable as possible with the crusty old man.

"Just remember," Benjie went on, "it ain't easy bein' dropped back into civilian life after bein' in the joint."

"That's why I'm here," Tom said. "To see if I can help with the transition." They had reached the foot of the stairs. Benjie pointed up the stairs.

"Second door on the left," he told Tom.

"Thanks."

When Tom reached the top of the stairs, he noticed Benjie was still standing below obviously waiting to see what Charlie's reaction would be to the surprise visitor. Tom stepped over to the second door on the left and knocked gently. He could hear music coming from the room. Then he heard his brother's voice.

"Just a sec." Tom heard the clang of iron along with the thump of a heavy weight being put down. A moment later, the door opened. Charlie stood in the doorway wearing only khaki shorts, white socks, and black running shoes. His upper body was glistening with sweat. Tom couldn't help noticing that Charlie's arms and shoulders, which had always been muscular but slim, were now heavily muscled.

"Hello, Charlie." Tom could hear his voice cracking involuntarily.

"Hello, Tom." Charlie's voice was flat and emotionless. They stood for a few seconds staring at each other in silence.

"How'd you find me?" Charlie finally asked. "Nah, never mind," he said quickly. "After Carol and your kid made me I figured you'd be along sooner or later. Come on in," he said, stepping back inside.

Downstairs, Benjie turned and walked away as Tom stepped into Charlie's room.

"You're looking good," Tom said as Charlie went over to a black steel bar with some large weights on it.

"Yeah," Charlie said, lifting up the heavy bar. "This is about the only thing you can do when you're, uh, away. This and read." Charlie carried the weights over to a corner of the room and put them down.

Tom looked around and noticed how neat and orderly everything was. A far cry from the way Charlie used to keep his room when they were kids, he mused. "Carol said you got an early parole."

"Yeah," Charlie snorted. "Ha! More like getting thrown out. You know, there was actually one guy there who didn't want to leave at all. Said he had nowhere to go. Guess he had found a home."

"Maybe he shouldn't have been on such good behavior," Tom offered.

Charlie picked up a sweatshirt and pulled it on. "Good behavior had nothin' much to do with it. It was a budget crunch. I think they're only keeping in murderers, rapists, and child molesters. And politicians," he added with a sardonic laugh.

Tom smiled despite his discomfort. "Look, Charlie . . . I, uh—" he began.

"Sit down, Tom, sit down," Charlie interrupted, motioning to an easy chair off to the side. He then pulled up a small wooden chair and sat, straddling it as Tom sat.

"As I started to say," Tom began again, "I . . . well, I guess I don't know where to begin."

"There's nothing to begin, Tom," Charlie said simply.

Tom made a smacking sound with his lips as he opened his mouth to speak. "Well, I think there is, Charlie. First of all, you're my brother. And because all these years when I guess I could have, I mean, no, should have . . ." Tom's voice trailed off as he could suddenly feel himself starting to choke up.

Charlie held his hands up in front of him. "Hey. Tom. You didn't shut me out. I shut you out. I never blamed you, if that's the weight you're carrying."

"I still should have come to see you," Tom insisted.

"Ahh," Charlie said, gesturing with his hands apart. "*Shoulda, woulda, coulda.* I wouldn'ta seen you. I was a screwup. I didn't care. For *you.* For *me.* For *anyone.*"

"Still," Tom went on, unable to accept Charlie's explanation, "the first time, when you went to juvenile hall, if maybe I had gotten a better lawyer . . ."

Charlie rose from his chair. "If! Maybe! Tom, it's all water under the bridge. Drop it. Please. All I want is a new life. A life I can call my own."

"What about us?" Tom asked. "Your family? Aren't we part of that life?"

Charlie began pacing in the small room. "Tom, look . . . it's not you. Or Carol. This town has bad vibes for me. And worse? Memories. I can't stay here. So I'll be moving on as soon as they let me."

Tom shook his head. "I still don't know why you don't want to even see us."

Charlie got up, stepped away from Tom, and went to his bed, where he sat down. "It's like this . . . that's what prison does to you. As one of the guys I was in with said, 'It's the most dehumanizing place in the world.' The only way I could keep from going crazy was to work out and read. I got me a high school diploma and some college credits too." He shook his head. "Nine years. I shut everything out of my life. You . . . this town . . . everything. Truth be told? I was ashamed of myself. Just plain ashamed. And in some ways, I still am."

"That's no reason to keep shutting us out," Tom persisted.

Charlie looked away, off into the distance. "Sorry, Tom. That's how it is."

Tom's mind raced. He couldn't lose his brother this way. Not after all these years. He decided to change the subject.

"Know how we found you?" he asked.

Charlie turned to face him. "Yeah. Your daughter, Katie. She spotted me."

Tom smiled. "But do you know *how?* Even though you were dressed up as Santa Claus?"

Charlie frowned. He obviously had never considered this.

"Haven't a clue," he said.

"Your *niece,* Katie," Tom said, purposely emphasizing the relationship between Charlie and Katie, "has, well, I guess you could call it a 'gift.' Somehow, she 'sees' things. She knew you were out!" Tom looked around the room. "She described this room in detail!"

Charlie was confused. "What are you talking about? She was never here. Not while I was here anyway."

"That's *just* what I'm talking about. This gift, as Carol calls it, seems to let her see things. I know. It's weird. Carol said it runs in her family. They're Romany. On her mother's side."

"They're Italian?"

"No, no. Not Roman. Romany. Like Gypsies. At least her grandmother was."

"So you mean Katie sees things like a fortune-teller? Or at least like they say they do?"

"I guess." Tom shrugged. "I don't get it myself, but there it is. And like Carol and me, she wants her uncle Charlie to be part of her life."

Charlie smiled ruefully. "Tom. Guilt trips don't work on me. I've laid enough of them on myself to last a lifetime."

"No guilt trips, brother. She and you and Carol and me are family. If there's any guilt here, it's mine."

Charlie held his hands up, palms toward Tom. "Like I said, I was the one who refused to see *you*. *I* was the one who returned your letters *unopened*."

"Charlie," Tom sighed, "you'd still make me feel a lot better if . . . Look, for old times' sake, remembering when we were without parents together, would you come over for dinner some night? I mean, you have to *eat,* right? *Tomorrow!* How about tomorrow night? We'll have a roast. Carol's a fantastic cook. I mean really fantastic. She could be a chef. Really!"

Charlie looked down and off to one side. "I . . . I don't know."

"C'mon, Charlie. Like I just said, you have to eat, right? And if you're going to leave here soon, or as soon as you're able, you could spend at least one evening with us." Tom gave a small chuckle. "I mean, it wouldn't *kill* you."

Charlie gave an involuntary smile as memories of him and Tom flooded his mind.

"No, I guess it wouldn't," he said.

Tom jumped up. He wanted to seal the date before Charlie changed his mind. "Great! That's great! Carol said you get off at five?"

"Yeah."

"Then why don't I pick you up at the mall?"

"You don't want me to go to your house in my Santa Claus outfit, do you?"

"Okay. I'll pick you up here, then. At what? Six?"

"Sounds good."

"All right, then!" Tom could barely restrain himself.

"Uh, one question, Tom. What do you do now? You don't have the hardware store anymore. I mean," he said with a chuckle, "unless you changed your name from Williams to Wong."

Tom smiled. "No, I sold it to Johnny Wong a few years back."

Charlie nodded. "I figured something like that when I saw the new name out front."

"Yeah, I'm in real estate now. And, incidentally, I'm doing a lot of business with Asians. You'd be surprised how many have moved in around here."

"How'd the old establishment in town take it?"

"Oh, there was some grumbling for a while. 'Our way of life is changing' and all that. But it didn't last long. Not that they had any choice. Hey, except for the Native Americans, we're all immigrants, right? Some of us just got here sooner than others. These new people are hardworking family folks. And good neighbors too."

A few seconds of silence followed as both men seemed to realize they had run out of things to say.

"So," Tom said, finally, "I'll see you here at six tomorrow night, then." Charlie raised a hand and nodded. "Okay, then," Tom said, getting up from the chair. "I've got to get that tree tied to the roof of my car home."

Charlie rose from the bed. "A *tree?*"

"Christmas tree."

"Oh, right. Christmas."

Charlie stepped over to Tom and extended his hand. Tom shook it, then let it go and impulsively embraced his brother. For a moment, Charlie stood without moving. Then he reached up, wrapped his arms around his older brother, and hugged him back.

"See you tomorrow, then," Tom said, his voice husky.

"Yeah, bro," Charlie answered in the same choked voice.

"**H**ere he comes," Marty said as Benjie's door opened and Tom came out.

"Mmmph . . . wha?" Al mumbled, coming awake.

"Some lookout you'd make." Marty sneered as Tom ran down the steps and hurried to his Jeep.

Marty and Al watched as Tom tugged the sash cord that held the tree atop his Jeep before getting inside and driving away.

"Okay, let's see where he takes us," Marty said.

Al started the Blazer and shifted into gear. "Prob'ly back to that broad and the kid."

"Unless . . ." Marty said as they followed Tom from a good distance.

"Unless what?"

"Unless that broad and kid ain't his. Maybe it's somethin' he's got goin' on the side."

"With the kid there?" Al said. "Never happen."

"Al, never say never to somethin' before you know what you're sayin' never to."

Thirteen minutes later, as Marty noted on the dashboard clock, Tom pulled into the driveway of his home.

"Keep goin'," Marty said. "Then make a U-ey down the end of the street and come back."

Al did as Marty said and when he drove back and came abreast of the Williamses' house on the other side of the street, Marty told him to pull over to the curb. He reached into the glove compartment and took out binoculars, aiming them at the lit Williamses' picture window. "I can see him with the broad and the kid," Marty said. "Looks like they're havin' a big discussion. She's smilin' and the kid's jumpin' up and down and clappin' her hands. Now he's takin' off his coat and walkin' away somewheres. The broad and the kid are huggin' each other. Now they're walkin' outta the room." Marty lowered the binoculars and put them back into the glove compartment. "Okay," he went on, "let's go. We now know they're connected to Charlie boy. What we have to figure out next is how."

Al merely shrugged as he shifted the Blazer into Drive and they drove off down the snow-dusted street.

CHAPTER 20

MIRANDA'S LOCKET

As Marty and Al drove away, Tom went out to the Jeep and began to untie the Christmas tree to bring into the house. Carol and Katie went to Katie's room.

"There's something I'd like to give you," Carol said as she closed Katie's door behind her.

"It has to do with Great-grandma Miranda, doesn't it, Mommy?"

"Yes," Carol answered, taken aback but not surprised that Katie would have known. Katie was filled with excitement as she watched her mother reach into her jacket pocket and take out a small box. It was made of dark wood and had intricate carvings on the top and sides. To Katie it had the look of something very old, even ancient. Carol took the box over to the bed and sat down. She patted the spot next to her. "Sit with me." Katie sat down close next to her. "I was waiting to give you this sometime in the future," Carol began, "maybe when you turned eighteen and I was sure you had the, uh . . . well, anyway, I think it's time to give it to you now." With that, she handed the box to Katie.

As she reached to take it, Katie had the sensation that the air was charged with some sort of mysterious energy pouring out of the box. She held it and closed her eyes, unable to contain her excitement. Her body shuddered slightly. Then, a smile crossed her face and she felt a wonderful calmness come over her.

"It's from Great-grandma Miranda, isn't it?"

"Yes," Carol said, shaking her head in wonder.

Slowly, Katie lifted the lid of the box and peered in. Inside, she saw a gold locket with a Romany cross engraved on it and a delicate gold chain around it. She reached in, lifted it out, and dangled it before her. She closed her eyes and held it to her breast, her face radiant.

"How beautiful you are, Great-grandma," she said in almost a whisper. With her eyes still closed, Katie slid her right index finger along the rim of the locket till she found a tiny clasp. She pressed it and the locket sprang open. Katie then opened her eyes and saw that inside the locket was a small compartment on either side.

"Where did Great-grandma get this?"

"It was passed down to her from her mother, who got it from her mother. It is very, very old. Who knows how old? Miranda gave it to my mother, who gave it to me."

Katie fingered the locket gently. "It has, like, a . . . like a magical feel to it. Or like it has some really great power."

Carol smiled knowingly. "I'm not surprised you feel that. The story is that it began with the Magi. You know the story of the Magi, don't you?"

"Sure. From Sunday school. Balthazar, Caspar, and Melchior, right?"

"Yes. And do you know what those Three Wise Men brought to the Baby Jesus?"

"Gold, frankincense, and myrrh. Of course gold was valuable, but frankincense and myrrh were also very rare and valuable spices."

Carol nodded, proud of her daughter's knowledge. Katie's eyes widened and she couldn't keep herself from bouncing on the bed excitedly. "Mommy, you're not trying to tell me this locket really, *really* came from the Magi!"

"That's the story that my mother told me and that Miranda told her. It's been handed down through our family for generations. And I was told that this is made from the very gold they brought to the Baby Jesus, and that inside is some residue of the frankincense on one side, and the myrrh on the other."

"No wonder it has a magical feel to it. Here," Katie said, handing the locket back to Carol. "Would you put it around my neck? Please?" With that, Katie bounced her body around on the bed so her back was to Carol.

Carol took the locket, snapped it shut, and then opened the clasp on the chain and slipped it around Katie's neck. When it was fastened, she faced Carol and, closing her eyes, placed her hands over the locket.

"I can see her, Mommy," she said, smiling.

Carol felt a light-headedness coming over her. "You can?"

"Yes. And she is so beautiful. And she is very happy that you gave this to me now."

Carol stared at her daughter, awestruck by the knowledge that through the locket, Katie was not imagining this vision; that she was in an actual communication of sorts with her great-grandmother, or her great-grandmother's spirit.

CHAPTER 21

THERE'S THE HOOK!

Al entered the cheap apartment he and Marty were renting carrying a black plastic bag decorated with gold fleur-de-lis.

Marty was sitting on a sprung couch and reading a newspaper in their small, cramped living room. He looked up and saw the bag in Al's hand. "Whyn't ya lay off the stuff? Least till this job is over."

Al walked past Marty into their tiny kitchen area. His large body almost filled the space.

"Why?" Al asked. "We're just sittin' around here doin' nothin'." He removed a bottle of Scotch from the bag, placed it on a counter, and put the bag into a garbage pail.

"We're gonna leave in a little while and go back to Benjie's place," Marty told him. Al opened the bottle, poured some Scotch into a glass, and carried it into the living room.

"For what?" he asked, sitting on an old, frayed easy chair that creaked under the strain of his weight.

" 'Cause I figure this guy's been in stir for a lotta years and I just can't see him comin' home every night and sittin' around his room. I mean, not every night."

"Maybe he just wants to be alone," Al suggested after he took a sip.

"No way. He'll have to wanna go out somewheres, some-time. At least a coupla nights a week."

"So?"

"Whaddaya mean, 'So'?"

"I mean, so he goes out. So what? Whadda we gonna do? Follow him?"

"Yeah. We follow him. See where he goes. Get some sorta hook into him."

"And that's because . . . ?"

"Because, dummy, when we squeeze him about crackin' our safe, if he says no, we have some leverage on him."

Al, bristling at the word "dummy," took another sip from his glass to keep from saying anything. *When this job is over,* he thought once again, *when this job is over . . .*

Shortly before five thirty that evening, the Saint Francis van drove up in front of Benjie's and Charlie got out. Half a block away, Marty and Al sat in the Blazer watching. The van pulled away and Charlie walked up the steps and disappeared inside the house.

"What if he don't come out?" Al asked a few minutes later.

Marty cocked his wristwatch to one side so it was illuminated by an overhead streetlamp. "We'll give it till six thirty . . . seven."

"Six thirty or seven?" Al asked disbelievingly.

Marty could smell the Scotch on Al's breath. "Hey, Dumbo. We gotta give Charlie boy time to change out of his Santy Claus suit and maybe clean up. And maybe he'll wanta take a pop or two before he leaves."

Al gave a long sigh, letting out a lungful of Scotch-scented breath. Marty leaned over, turned on the ignition, and then lowered the window on his side.

"Hey! Whaddaya doin'? It's cold out there," Al protested.

"It smells like a distillery in here. Next time, you don't drink before we do a stakeout and I won't open the window."

Just wait, buddy, Al thought. *You just wait.*

Just as this thought was going through Al's mind, Tom's Jeep passed them and pulled up in front of Benjie's.

"Hey, isn't that the—" Al started to say.

"The guy we followed," Marty interrupted. "The one with the Christmas tree." Then, as they saw Tom get out of his Jeep and start for Benjie's, Marty snapped his fingers. "Yeah! That's the same guy all right."

"Maybe he's just gonna visit like last night," Al said.

"Sure. Maybe," Marty said with a slight shrug. *Why'd I get involved with this bozo?* he thought. *I shoulda kept tryin' to get Billy Murray. He's a better wheelman than this guy will ever be.*

The two men didn't have to wait long for Tom to reappear, but this time Charlie Williams was with him.

"Ya happy now?" Marty asked. "Let 'em get a little distance before you go." Al waited till Tom drove to the end of the street before starting the engine and following at a safe distance behind.

After they had made a few turns, Marty said, "Ya know what? I think they're goin' back to that guy's house." Al nodded and slowed down slightly to let the distance between the two SUVs widen.

"Hey, don't lose 'em," Marty said. "I might be wrong."

"I won't lose 'em," Al answered, annoyed at what he considered a criticism of his driving expertise. "There ain't many cars on the road and I don't want them makin' us."

"There they go," Marty said as Tom's Jeep made a turn in front of them. "Just like last night. That's where he's goin' all right. Now the question is, why? Why is he takin' our boy Charlie back to his house?"

Several minutes later, they followed Tom's Jeep onto the street where he lived. The night before, the street had been empty of cars, but this night there were several parked there. This allowed Al to pull up closer to Tom's house, in behind two cars, as Tom and Charlie got out of the Jeep and walked toward the house.

Marty watched the two men. Then he remembered. The realization struck him like a clap on the back of his head.

"It's his *brother!*" he almost shouted. *"His brother!"*

"What?" Al asked.

"It's Charlie's *brother.* The walk! The walk! Look at the way they walk! The two of them! The same walk! I shoulda known! I shoulda remembered he had a brother. My brother and me? We had the same walk as our old man. I remember a woman neighbor of ours pointin' it out to me as a kid. And she said walks run in families. Same as blue eyes or brown eyes. That's the connection! They're brothers! Bingo! Oh, baby. We got 'im now!"

"Got him how?" Al asked.

"*How?* Look in the window there, dummy." Marty pointed toward the house where Tom and Charlie could be seen through the living room window being greeted by Carol and Katie.

"See that little girl there? Jumpin' up and down? That's gotta be his niece. So if Williams says he won't do the job, well, all we gotta say is, you wouldn't want anything to happen to that little girl, would you?"

"Somethin' happen?" Al said, concerned.

Marty didn't pay any attention. "Oh yeah, man. Your cute little *niece?* Your brother's *daughter? Your own flesh and blood?*" Marty slumped back into his seat, satisfied. "Oka-ay," he said. "We got our hook. Let's get outta here."

CHAPTER 22

HAPPY BIRTHDAY, UNCLE CHARLIE!

As Tom and Charlie entered the house, unaware they were being spied upon from the outside, Charlie felt his emotions rise. For the first time since childhood, he was in a home. A home! With a family he was part of. He blinked rapidly to keep the tears in his eyes from brimming over.

After kissing Carol somewhat awkwardly on the cheek, he then bent to do the same to Katie. Unable to contain her happiness, she wrapped her arms around his muscular frame and hugged him. He stood stiffly for a moment and then, as she released him, he smiled at Tom, who was grinning back.

The warmth of the room was also filled with tantalizing holiday aromas from long ago—a roast beef in the oven, a cake being baked, intermingled with the piney scent of the Christmas tree near the window. He quickly wiped away a tear before it rolled down his cheek. Blinking didn't help after all.

Tom noticed the emotions welling up in his brother. He put an arm around Charlie's shoulder. "Welcome home."

Charlie couldn't speak. He merely nodded his thanks. Then, to save himself any further embarrassment, he turned toward the tree.

"That's a nice tree," he said hoarsely.

"I picked it out, Uncle Charlie," Katie said proudly.

"Well, you've got a good eye, young lady," Charlie said. "And good taste." Katie clapped her hands together.

"Wait till you see it after it's all decorated and lit up!" she blurted out.

"That sounds great," Charlie told her.

"Will you help us do it?"

"That would be my pleasure, Katie."

At the sound of her name coming from her one and only uncle, Katie was ecstatic. "Mom! Dad! Did you hear that? Uncle Charlie is going to help decorate the tree!"

Carol saw the emotional strain in Charlie's face. She also noticed the tear he'd wiped away before and sensed he was a bit overwhelmed by this family reunion. Carol placed her hand on Katie's shoulder and smiled. "Of course he will. In the meanwhile, why don't you come to the kitchen and give me a hand?"

Katie didn't want to leave, but at the same time she didn't want Uncle Charlie to think she disobeyed her parents.

"Okay, Mommy," Katie said reluctantly. She followed Carol toward the kitchen.

"How about a drink?" Tom asked. "A beer or something?"

"Beer'll be fine," Charlie answered.

Katie had just reached the kitchen door. She whirled around and said, "You like Budweiser. Right, Uncle Charlie?" Charlie turned to her and stared at his niece.

"That's absolutely right," he said, mystified. "Bud's my beer."

"I'll get it for you," Katie offered. "You too, Daddy?" she asked.

"Sure, honey. Thanks."

"Okay," Katie said, and disappeared into the kitchen.

"She knew I drink Bud," Charlie said to Tom. "How'd she know that?"

"Remember what I told you about her sort of, well, seeing things?"

"Yeah, but I thought that was just like, you know, a father talking proud about his daughter and, uh . . ."

"I am proud, but it wasn't just talk."

An hour later, all four of the Williams family were sitting around the dining room table, the only light coming from two scented Christmas candles on the table. They had burned halfway down.

"Have some more, Charlie," Carol said as Charlie downed the last piece of meat from his plate.

"No, no," he said, patting his stomach. "Thanks, Carol, but I've had it. I am full and content."

"You're sure? I mean, you don't have to be shy or polite here. We're family."

"No. Really. I'm full. It was great. That's the first home-cooked meal I've had since before"—he gave a short laugh—"well, since I can't remember when." Charlie could hear his voice giving way with emotion. Carol stood up and started to collect the plates on the table. To cover his emotions, Charlie stood too. "Let me give you a hand."

"I wouldn't hear of it," she told him. "Please. Sit down. Relax." She nodded in the direction of Katie, who was already standing. "Katie and I can handle it." Charlie sat down.

"Go again on the Bud?" Tom asked.

"Thanks, no, Tom."

"Well, I hope you have room for the cake," Katie said as she stacked some plates. "I baked it!"

"You did?" Charlie asked, arching his eyebrows with surprise. Katie put a mischievous smile on her face.

"It's your favorite. Chocolate!" She picked up the plates and went to the kitchen.

Charlie sat, staring after her before turning to Tom. "After all these years you remembered I was a chocoholic, huh?"

"I never told her," Tom said, shrugging. "Like I told you,"

he continued, "somehow she sees and knows things. It's weird, but true. And sort of scary."

"Must be," Charlie said, still not sure just what it was that Katie could do.

Tom leaned back from the table and looked at his brother. "I can't tell you how happy I am, we all are, that you're here with us."

"Not as happy as I am, Tom. I'm glad you pushed me to come. Sorry I sort of gave you a bad time about it at first. I was, you know, sort of disconnected from everything."

"Hey, I understand."

Charlie looked down at the table. "Being here with, well, seeing you and your family—"

"Your family too," Tom interrupted.

"Yeah. Thanks. Being away and all. I sort of forgot. Anyway, all this makes me realize how much I've changed. And lost."

"Charlie. Look at me," Tom said. "Want some advice from your older brother? There's an old saying. 'Today is the first day of the rest of your life.' Put the past behind you. What's done is done. Start living for the future. Okay?"

"Easier said than done, bro," Charlie answered after a moment. He knew his brother meant well and he heard the love and concern in his voice. But there were feelings Charlie was experiencing that he had suppressed. And the idea that he was a free man was finally settling in his mind. "Sometimes the things you remember most are the things you'd like to remember least. Like living in a tiny, concrete, windowless room with bars for a door. See, it's not really living. Just existing. The world? That's something somewhere out there." He gestured with a sweep of his hand.

Before Tom could respond, Katie, followed by Carol, came out of the kitchen carrying a chocolate cake with ten lit candles on it.

"Surprise!" Katie shouted. "Happy birthday, Uncle

Charlie!" Charlie looked from Katie to Carol to Tom, an un-comprehending look on his face.

"Happy birthday?" he said. "It's not my birthday." Katie walked over to the table and put the cake down in front of Charlie.

"It was my idea," she said, her eyes wide and her face beaming. "This is for all the birthdays you missed with your family." Charlie put his hand to his mouth and shook his head slightly, unable to believe how emotional he felt. He couldn't speak. "And you get to make ten wishes," Katie continued.

Charlie felt his eyes tearing up again. He took in a breath to blow out the candles, but stopped. Something deep inside made him turn to Katie and put his arm around her. He gave her a tender hug.

"Thank you, sweetheart." His voice cracked a bit. "This is great. Thank you." He looked at Carol and Tom. "Thank you."

"Oh, you're welcome, Uncle Charlie," Katie said, wrapping her arms around his shoulders and hugging him back.

Then, with his vision blurred by tears, Charlie blew out the candles with one big puff. Katie, Carol, and Tom cheered and clapped their hands.

Katie then led them all, singing a loud, and in-tune, "Happy Birthday to You," to her one and only lost uncle.

CHAPTER 23

HORMONES

The winter morning sunlight shone weakly through the kitchen window where Katie and Carol sat eating breakfast. They could hear Tom whistling upstairs in the bedroom as he came out of the shower and dressed for work.

"Daddy sounds happy," Carol said. Katie didn't respond. Carol saw she was moving her spoon slowly around in her bowl of oatmeal.

"You'd better eat that while it's hot, Katie. It's cold outside."

"I know," Katie said, her eyes cast down on her bowl.

"Is something wrong?" Carol asked, becoming concerned.

"I don't know, Mommy. I just have this awful feeling something bad is going to happen to Uncle Charlie." Acutely aware of her daughter's gift, Carol was alarmed.

"What is it?" she asked.

Katie rocked her head from side to side. "That's it. I don't know."

"Well, is it something we should warn Uncle Charlie about?"

Katie frowned and thought for a moment. "No. Not now anyway."

"Well, what should we do?"

"It's nothing that will happen right away. Maybe I will see more later on." Katie seemed to relax. "Yes. That's it. I'll tell you as soon as things are clearer." She took a spoonful of oatmeal.

"Okay, then. Finish up and drink your cocoa," Carol said, slightly relieved. "We have to be at the bus stop in ten minutes." Katie dutifully finished her oatmeal. She was drinking the last of her cocoa when Tom came into the kitchen.

"Good morning, ladies."

"You're very cheery this morning," Carol said, rinsing the dishes in the sink.

"That I am, love of my life," he said, giving her a peck on the cheek. He gave one to Katie on the top of her head. "You too, beautiful." He poured some coffee for himself. "I was thinking about how happy Charlie was last night. I'm so glad he's here."

"Me too, Daddy," Katie said.

Carol dried her hands on a towel. "We all are," she said, heading for the door. "Put your dishes in the sink and let's get our coats, Katie."

"I'll do them," Tom offered.

Nine minutes later, Carol and Katie greeted Melissa and Barbara Lithcott at the bus stop. The two girls stood off to the side of their mothers. Melissa noticed the look of concern on Katie's face.

"What's wrong, Katie?" she asked.

"Oh, nothing," Katie answered. But her eyes remained downcast. Barbara heard her daughter and took note of Katie's expression, which was so different from her usual upbeat demeanor. She glanced over at Carol and raised her eyes inquisitively. Carol decided she didn't want to confide in Barbara about her concern. She shook her head and mouthed the word "hormones."

The bus turned the corner and arrived with its load of yelling, laughing, squealing children before anything more could be said. Carol and Barbara exchanged greetings with

Miss Chalmers and kissed the girls good-bye. The girls boarded and after final waves, Miss Chalmers closed the door and pulled away.

"So, uh, is everything all right, Carol?" Barbara asked as they began to walk to the corner.

"Why do you ask?" Carol said.

"I heard Melissa ask Katie that and, uh, well, after the bridge washout, well, Katie seemed so quiet so I, uh, well, maybe she felt something else was going to happen."

"No, Barbara," Carol said quickly. "Nothing like that. This morning she woke up on the wrong side of the bed. Hormones, I guess. The girls are growing up."

"I hear that," Barbara said, relieved.

"It's a long time ago. Remember when you were twelve?" Carol said lightly with a chuckle.

"Do I ever! Things were always sooo important and sooo unfair and sooo everything. I guess we're about to become our parents."

"I guess."

"Anyway, it wasn't that long ago, now, was it?"

Both women stopped, looked at each other, and had a good laugh.

CHAPTER 24

A LITTLE JOB FOR CHARLIE

Charlie stood in front of Kaplan's ringing his bell. Despite his jovial greetings to passersby, and their polite responses, he was not in the best of moods. Susan had come out earlier to break their lunch date. She explained she had a very bad headache. She wouldn't have come to work that day if it wasn't for the Christmas rush when the store was at its busiest.

"I'd be miserable company, Charlie," she told him, "and I don't want our date to be less than great." She saw that Charlie was disappointed, and so she immediately promised to have lunch with him the next day, "even if I have to go on a stretcher." Susan then noticed two more customers enter the store. "Gotta go. Sorry," she said, and hurried away.

Shortly after, Charlie's mood darkened even further when he saw Marty and Al walking straight toward him. Still comfortably thinking they had no idea who he was, he rang the bell.

"Ho-ho-ho, gentlemen," he called out. "And a Merry Christmas to you."

"Save the good-cheer stuff for the stiffs, Williams," Marty shot back with a sly grin.

Charlie felt as if he had been punched in the stomach. "How'd you know?"

"A little birdie told me," Marty sneered.

"Yeah," Al added with a chuckle. "A jail birdie."

Charlie looked around quickly to see if anyone was in earshot. He fought to control the anger rising in his chest. "So what do you want?"

"We want you. See, Charlie boy, we got this little job lined up that requires your talents," Marty told him as he moved closer.

"I have no talents you can use."

"That's not what Jimmy Falco says," Marty quickly said. "Ain't that right, Al?"

"Falco said you were just the man for the job."

"I don't know any Jimmy Falco," Charlie said dismissively.

"Maybe not," Marty said. "But you do know Winkie Cohen, don't ya?"

Winkie Cohen's name triggered the realization in Charlie's mind of just where Marty was going with this conversation. He gestured, waving his hand. "Go on. That was years ago. And besides—"

"Can it, Williams!" Marty cut him off, putting his hand up close to Charlie's face. "We got a safe to open and you're gonna be the can opener."

"Forget it," Charlie said. "I never used any of that stuff I learned from Winkie, and I'm not about to start now."

Marty turned to Al with a sneer. "Get that? He's not about to start now," he said to his partner, mimicking Charlie's voice.

"That's right, chump," Charlie said with some heat.

"And what if I was to say it's not for you to say, loser?"

Charlie grabbed Marty by his jacket. "Everything in my life is for me to say now, dirtbag. Now get out of here. I beat the hell out of you once and I can do it again—ten times better than I did before."

Al moved toward Charlie, but Marty held out his arm to stop him. Although he could feel the strength in Charlie's grasp, he knew he had a trump card. "Maybe you can, maybe you can't. But what would you do about that cute little niece of yours?"

Charlie's hand slipped off and away from Marty's jacket. His eyes narrowed. "What are you talking about? What little niece?"

"Your little niece," Marty repeated. "Your brother's little girl. The one who lives in that nice house not too far from here." Charlie could feel the air come out of him. His shoulders slumped. Marty noticed the change with satisfaction. "Yeah. That's what I'm talkin' about. So here's the deal, Williams," he went on, looking around and again moving closer to Charlie. "You do the job we want or we, let's say, take care of her. And the rest of your family while we're at it."

"You so much as touch a hair on her, or any of them, and I'll kill you," Charlie said, his voice dropping to a low, menacing tone.

"Yeah, yeah. That's big talk from a two-time loser. You'd have to find us," Marty said, smirking. "This is a *big* country and in the meantime, they'd all be dead."

Charlie, feeling trapped and frustrated, looked around, glad to see no one was near them. What he didn't notice was that Joan Kaplan, inside the jewelry store, was watching him and the other two men through the window.

"What's this deal?" Charlie asked, his voice telling Marty that he was resigned to getting involved.

"All in good time, Williams. All in good time," Marty answered in smooth tones. "We'll let you know. We know where to find you, too. Yeah, that's right. We know about your stayin' at Benjie's. And since we're goin' to be workin' together, this is your other partner, Al Steel."

Al nodded and extended his hand. "Nice to meet ya, Charlie," he said, trying to be friendly.

But Charlie just looked at him with a cold stare, then turned his back and began ringing his bell.

CHAPTER 25

DOTS ON THE WALL

As Marty and Al walked away from Charlie, Ed Kaplan joined his wife at their jewelry store window.

"You seem absorbed by something," he said.

"I am," she replied. "See those two men? It's the two who were here the other day. Over there." She pointed to Marty and Al. "Walking toward the cars."

"Oh yeah," Ed answered. "The guy who was sick. They never came back. I didn't think he would. What's going on?"

"They seemed to be having what looked like a confrontation or something with our Santa Claus."

"Confrontation? You mean like a fight?"

"Well, at one point, our Santa grabbed the smaller one by the jacket and it looked like he was going to hit him."

"Really?"

Joan nodded emphatically. "It looked like our Santa didn't want to have anything to do with them. To tell the truth, I can't blame him. I didn't like the looks of them the moment they walked in here."

Just then a group of three customers were buzzed into the store by Susan.

"Business," Ed told Joan. He walked away from the window. Joan Kaplan lingered a moment more as she watched the two men get into a black Chevy Blazer and drive away. She then looked at the Santa. He had stopped ringing his bell and was watching them drive away too.

Outside, Charlie watched Marty and Al leave the mall lot. As it turned onto the main exit road, he saw Marty's arm come out the passenger-side window and wave toward him.

Charlie was angry and frustrated. When he turned back to his job, his gaze settled on one of the stores in the row across from him: Kaplan's Jewelry!

"Jewelry store? I didn't hear them mention that the job was at a jewelry store. Did I miss it?" he muttered. "Jeez, it must be *this* one! Susan works there." His mind began racing. *They were casing the place when I saw them come out from behind it,* he thought.

Charlie picked up his chimney and went to Kaplan's door. He pushed on the outside bell. Ed Kaplan saw him. Charlie waved and indicated that he wanted to leave his chimney in the store where Ed had told him he could place it the day before. Ed buzzed him in and Charlie left the chimney in a corner in front, behind the first counter display. He then went back outside and walked to the alley where he had seen Marty and Al come out.

Moments later, he walked down the dirt path between the back of the stores and the woods until he figured out which store was Kaplan's. At first he saw nothing out of the ordinary. There was a small bathroom window there just like the small bathroom windows of the other stores. And, like them, the windows had visible alarm wires and bars.

Well, he thought, there was no way they could get in this way without sounding off the alarms, even if they did saw through the bars. He moved closer to the brick wall and looked around the window. It took a few moments, but he finally noticed a series of black dots on the bricks a few feet from the window. Dots, he realized, that if joined together would form a large rectangle. Curious, Charlie walked down past the rears of the other stores to see if there were any black dots on their bricks. There were none. Did Marty Richards make those dots? he wondered. If so, why? What did they represent? He had to find out.

Ed Kaplan was saying good-bye to a young man at the front door just as Charlie came back. As the man left, Ed held the door open for Charlie to reenter.

"Hi, Mr. Kaplan. Thanks for letting me park the chimney here. It has the money in it and I had to make a call and—"

"Next time use our phone," Ed said. "Susan told me you're Tom Williams's brother. We used to have coffee once in a while at Micky D's when he had the hardware store. And if you need to use the facilities, don't be shy."

Charlie hesitated a moment. "Did Susan also tell you I'm an ex-con and out on parole?"

Ed raised his eyebrows and shook his head slowly. "No, she didn't."

"Well, Mr. Kaplan, I am. If that presents a problem for you . . . I mean, my coming in here . . . uh . . . I can always go back down to McDonald's. And I could put the chimney in—"

"Whoa, whoa, hold on," Ed said. "I have no problem with your coming in here to park your chimney, use the bathroom, the phone, *or* have as much coffee as your kidneys can take. Your brother, Tom, is a good guy and if you're his brother, that's good enough for me. As they say, you did the crime; you paid your time, right?"

"Yes. Thank you, Mr. Kaplan."

"Let's drop that Mister stuff. It's Ed."

"Okay, Ed. As long as you're sure, now."

"I'm sure. Besides, how would it look if I were not to help

one of Santa's helpers? My stocking would end up empty, right?"

Charlie smiled. "Santa's elves might take offense too. Not to mention the reindeer."

"Oh no," Ed said in mock horror. "Not the reindeer." Both men laughed. There was a moment afterward when both men looked at each other silently. Charlie then knew that Ed trusted him.

"Ed? Is there a chance I could use the facilities now?"

Ed motioned with his hand for Charlie to follow him.

"I'll show you where it is," he said, leading Charlie to the rear of the store. Joan and Susan looked away from their customers for a moment. Joan watched with interest. Susan threw Charlie a quick, friendly smile.

Charlie followed Ed through the small gate in the rear counter to a large door just past Ed's work area. As they passed, Charlie noticed the large safe sitting behind Ed's chair.

"This leads into the storeroom," Ed said, pushing open the door and reaching for the light switch inside. Then pointing, he added, "There's the door to the bathroom."

"Thanks," Charlie said. "That's great." When he reached the bathroom door, he turned, expecting Ed to be standing there. But he was gone. The door leading back to the store was closing noiselessly.

Inside the bathroom, Charlie first used the toilet. Then, after washing his hands and wiping them with a paper towel from the dispenser over the sink, he walked over to the bathroom window. He saw the alarm wires covering and going up into the drop ceiling. They came out and also ran along the walls. But as his eyes followed the wires, he noticed they went up, across the top, and then down around the large, ornate medicine cabinet. He went back and traced the wires again. Then he knew. The medicine cabinet was not only the same size in area as the black dots on the bricks outside, but the same distance from the window!

* * *

When Charlie returned to the store, he saw that Ed and Joan were occupied with customers. Susan was just finishing with a teenaged girl. He waited until the young woman left.

"Hi, Susan," he said, smiling through his white beard.

"Hi, Santa," she said. "How about some coffee?"

"No, thanks." Charlie wondered if he should say something to Susan about the wires, but decided this was not the time or the place. "How's the headache?"

"A little better, thanks. It's going away. Slowly. But it *is* going away."

"Good," Charlie said. "And we're on for tomorrow?"

"Tomorrow's on."

"Good," he said again. He felt like a teenager with butterflies in his stomach, anticipating his first date. Susan picked up the tray of watches she had been working with and put it back into the display case. Though he knew he should leave, the faint scent of Susan's perfume drifted around Charlie, rooting him to the spot. He didn't want to leave her presence. "So, uh, how do you like working here?"

"Oh, a lot," Susan answered, locking the display case. "The Kaplans are terrific people."

"Yeah, they seem to be real nice."

"Believe me, they are."

To his surprise, Charlie now realized he was inhaling deeply.

"Good. Uh, you been here long?" he asked, talking for talk's sake to stay close to her.

"A little more than a year. And, thanks to this job, by next fall I'll have enough saved for nursing school."

The buzzer sounded. A young couple was standing at the door. Susan looked at Ed, who was walking toward the rear counter where the buzzer was.

"So you're going to be a nurse," Charlie said. Susan nodded, watching Ed as he reached under the counter for the buzzer. "I'll have to figure out some way to get sick so you'll have to, uh, administer to me."

"You wouldn't have to be sick for that, Charlie Williams," Susan said.

The low and sexy tone of Susan's voice, along with a flirtatious sidelong glance, set off a warning voice inside Charlie's head. *What are you doing?* the voice said. *Don't get involved.*

"You'll have to excuse me," Susan said. "I've got to take that customer. See you tomorrow." She walked quickly toward the young couple. "May I help you?" she asked. Her voice was now all business.

Charlie got his chimney and left. His emotions were disturbingly conflicted between his rekindled feelings for Susan and his plan to leave town as soon as possible.

CHAPTER 26

A PLAN AT P.J.'S

"Charlie? 'Zat you?" Benjie called out as Charlie opened the rooming house front door.

"In person," Charlie answered, going to Benjie's office door. He poked his head inside. "What's up?" Benjie was at his desk.

"Hi, Santa. Ya got a phone call 'bout an hour ago."

"My brother?"

Benjie shook his head. "No name. But it wasn't your brother. I woulda recognized the voice. And this voice I didn't like. Just said for you to be in P.J.'s Pub tonight at eight. You know where that is?"

"Yeah," Charlie said uneasily.

"You know who called?" Benjie asked.

"No idea," Charlie answered, spreading his hands apart as if to express ignorance.

"Hey, Charlie," Benjie said. "Didn't I tell ya not to try to kid a kidder? You mixed up in somethin' with Marty Richards?"

"No way," Charlie insisted.

" 'Cause if you are," Benjie continued, ignoring Charlie's denial, "I'll kick your ass right outta here. You understand?"

"Cool it, Benj. I hear you," Charlie said. "Thanks for the

message." Charlie went up to his room. Behind him, he heard the door to Benjie's office slam shut.

Shortly after eight o'clock, Charlie hopped off the bus and walked to P.J.'s Pub. Originally, it had been modeled after an English pub and had been one of the better taverns in town. Charlie had gone there when he was younger. It was where he had had his fight with Marty.

As Charlie walked through the door, he immediately noted that it had gone seriously downhill. The place looked seedy and dirty. All of the original "public house" charm was gone, replaced by tacky furnishings and fixtures. He went to the bar. A few older men sat at one end nursing their beers and watching a basketball game on the TV above the bar. At the other end, a lone middle-aged woman, dressed in a leather jacket and jeans, read a newspaper and sipped a bourbon neat.

The bartender, well over six feet with a big gut, a shaved head, and tattoos on his huge arms, walked down the bar to Charlie. The name VINNIE was tattooed above the barbed wire tattoo that most cons had done while in prison.

"What'll it be?" he asked.

"Bud," Charlie answered.

"Bottle or draft?"

"Draft."

Vinnie reached down, picked up a glass and placed it under a tap. As he filled the glass, he watched Charlie.

"When'd ya get out?" he asked.

"Out?" Charlie asked.

"I can always spot a guy come back to the world." He placed Charlie's beer down in front of him. "You got the look. Like you're wondering if you fit in anymore."

Charlie lifted his glass, made a toasting motion with it and took a gulp. "I guess then I'll have to start wearing dark glasses."

"Yeah." Vinnie chuckled. "Or somethin'. So when ja get out?"

"A few days ago." Charlie craned his head around, searching the tavern.

"Hey, Vinnie," called the woman from the end of the bar. "How 'bout another one here?" Vinnie looked at her and raised an index finger. "Hang on, Lucille," he called. "Be right there." He turned back to Charlie. "So, you lookin' for someone?"

"Guy named Marty Richards."

Vinnie pointed a thumb to the rear. "Booth in the back."

"Thanks," Charlie said. He downed his beer and walked in the direction Vinnie had indicated.

Charlie saw Marty seated at a table facing him. He assumed the hatless head with its back to him belonged to Al Steel.

"Well, here's our boy," Marty said as Charlie walked up to the table. "Sit down," he added as he slid over in the booth and slapped the bench next to him. But Charlie grabbed a chair from a nearby table and turned it around. He straddled it as he sat down at the end of the booth's table.

"How ya doin', Charlie?" Al said in a friendly voice. But Charlie didn't even nod to him.

"So what's the urgency to be here tonight?" Charlie asked, directly to Marty.

"We wanted to tell you not to plan any holiday trips," Marty said.

"You're talking Christmas for this job?" Charlie asked.

"Christmas Eve. Which is comin' on pretty fast. So I figured maybe we should get together to start makin' plans."

"Yeah," Al said. " 'Cause we got visions of sugarplums dancin' outta that sweet safe." His attempt at humor drew a sour glance from Marty.

"Who else is in on this?" Charlie asked.

"Me, Al, and you," Marty answered. "Oh yeah. And there's a fourth guy who, if you get any funny ideas, will take care of that cute little niece of yours and her folks."

Charlie tensed in his chair, as if to get up, and then settled back. He noted that Marty's reflex was to back off a bit.

"And like I told you, if you was to tell the cops this?" Marty continued. "We'd say we don't know what the hell you're talkin' about."

Charlie only smiled now and nodded. He knew Marty was afraid of being beaten up. Al, on the other hand, had not flinched, nor had he made a move to defend Marty. *Interesting,* Charlie thought.

"And even if the cops did believe ya," Marty continued, "how long would they put a detail on her? A week? A month? Two months? Lemme tell you, Charlie boy, she'd be marked. And if it took six months, a year, she'd still get it. And the parents too. Count on it."

Charlie's senses were reeling. Out of prison a few days and already he had put the life of a niece he hadn't known, and his brother and sister-in-law, in danger. The urge to hammer Marty, here and now, was strong. But he knew, as a two-time loser, he couldn't afford a felony rap. Marty and Al would deny everything and accuse Charlie of assault. A third felony and he'd be a lifer, and Marty knew it. He had no choice but to go along with them now. Maybe later he could figure out something.

Charlie took in a deep breath to control his voice.

"What kind of safe is it?" he asked.

"Freestandin'," Marty answered. " 'Bout this high, this wide," he said, making size motions with his hands and arms.

"I need the make or model. Otherwise I won't know what equipment I need."

Marty shot a look at Al. Charlie could see they hadn't thought this through. And they knew nothing about cracking safes. "Unless," Charlie went on, "it's Kaplan's Jewelry in the mall where I work." He had to contain himself from saying it with a smirk.

Marty and Al exchanged quick glances and their obvious

discomfort gave Charlie a momentary feeling of having the upper hand.

"Whaddaya talkin' about?" Marty bluffed.

"Yeah," Al joined in. "Who said anything about Kaplan's? Because that's where we found you?"

Again, Charlie felt a moment of pleasure at now being in charge of the conversation. "I saw you two guys coming around from behind it the other day. So I went back there today. Guess what I found? All these little black dots on the bricks. Which just so happen to be an outline of the medicine cabinet on the other side of the wall."

"Okay," Marty said. He knew it was too late to bluff anymore. Al slumped back in his seat and looked at Charlie with new respect. "So it's Kaplan's," Marty admitted.

Charlie nodded. "Right. I already scoped the safe in the office."

"Hey," Al said to Marty. "This guy's okay."

"How'd you do that?" Marty asked.

"Because I'm Santa Claus. Because I work outside the place. Because they let me use the can. And you can bet that the cops are gonna know that and want to talk to me after." Charlie leaned in closer to Marty. "So let's get some things straight. I'll have my butt covered. So now if you guys are thinking of makin' me the patsy, remember Benjie's a friend of mine. You hooked me with my niece and family. Okay. What's done is done. Now understand this. You rat me out like you did when I was a kid, you *both* go down big time. Benjie knows how to take care of business."

Al moved uncomfortably in his seat.

"Take it easy. No one's rattin' out no one," Marty said. "You do your end and we'll do ours."

"And what's my end for doing this?" Charlie asked.

"We go three ways. Even-Steven. Okay?"

"Okay. Now listen, this isn't going to be a cakewalk. That's one tough safe. I'll need first-class equipment. There's no way I can afford it. So unless you guys have enough cash . . ."

"We'll take care of that," Marty said. Charlie quickly reached into his pocket and took out a slip of paper. His sudden movement made Marty flinch again. Al took note.

"Good," Charlie said. "I figured making plans was why you guys wanted this meeting. So I brought a list of what I'll need." He shoved the paper over to Marty. "As you'll see, it includes a diamond-core drill, a video scope, and lots of other goodies."

Marty scanned the list. "We'll handle it."

Charlie looked from Marty to Al. "So, that's it?"

"We'll be in touch," Marty said. Charlie slid back his chair in one motion, stood, swung it around, and put it back at the table he took it from.

"Nice to see ya, Charlie," Al said, still trying to be friendly. Charlie gave Al a short wave of his hand.

"Yeah." He walked away.

Marty put Charlie's list in his jacket pocket. "Okay," he ordered. "Let's go." But Al merely stared down at his glass on the table, which he rotated in his hands.

"You didn't tell me there was a fourth guy," Al said softly.

Marty looked at him exasperatedly. "There *ain't* no fourth guy, dummy."

"Then you made it all up? About hurtin' the kid? And the man and woman? You was just bluffin'?"

"Of course I was bluffin'."

"That better be right, 'cause I don't want no part of hurtin' little kids. That wasn't part of the deal."

Marty let out a groan. "Hey, look, rocket scientist. As long as Charlie boy thinks we might hurt that kid, he's gonna stay in line. The last thing he'll want to do is take a chance that we might mess with his family."

Al looked back down at his drink and started to rotate his glass in his hands again, wondering. And Marty began again to think ruefully how he missed getting Billy Murray for this job instead of Al. "You feel better now?" he asked, finally.

Al shrugged in response.

"What now?"

"You ain't plannin' on screwin' him outta his share, now, are ya?"

"No."

" 'Cause I don't think he's bluffin' about takin' us out like you is about hurting that kid."

Marty shook his head in frustration. "Let's go," he said, sliding out of the booth.

But Al didn't move. Then, as if he had made a private decision, he lifted the glass of amber liquid in front of him, downed it, and followed Marty out of P.J.'s Pub.

CHAPTER 27

MY SWEET PATOOTIE

At one o'clock the next afternoon, Charlie was standing in front of Kaplan's thanking an older man for dropping money into his chimney when Susan tapped on the store window from inside to indicate she was ready for lunch. Charlie picked up his chimney and brought it into the store.

"Ready to go?" Susan asked.

"Never more so," Charlie answered. As they started to leave the store, Ed called out, *"Bon appétit."*

"Thank you," Susan called back as they left. When they were clear of the store and walking toward McDonald's, Susan said, "Somehow French phrases like *bon appétit* don't seem to go with eating at a McDonald's."

"No," Charlie agreed. "Seems something along the lines of 'Dig in' would cover it."

Susan laughed and was surprised to find she was feeling as giddy as a teenager on a first date. She realized that she hadn't felt this happy in a long time. She stole a sidelong glance at Charlie and her heart skipped two beats.

Ahead of them, a girl about ten was complaining to the woman holding her hand that she wanted a real Christmas tree and not "a fake one." The woman explained that with a tree they could use every year they wouldn't have to look for one and then keep it in water and dispose of it after the holiday.

"But that's all the fun, Mommy," the girl said.

Hearing this, Susan turned to Charlie. "Did you get a tree?" Then, with a laugh: "I mean fake or real?"

"Neither. I'd have to buy lights and ornaments and all the rest of that stuff. I have no place to store all that yet. I'm traveling light until I know . . . I mean, until I get a more permanent place to live. But I will miss not having one. Fake or real."

"Are you looking for a place?" Susan asked.

"Not yet. I have to see what kind of permanent employment I can find." Charlie felt guilty having not told Susan he was going to head for Florida as soon as the parole officer allowed it. But this was neither the time nor the place to start that conversation. "In some ways I'm still like a little kid when it comes to Christmas," he said, trying to change the subject.

"Me too. That's why I bought a little one for my apartment. It's like that one," she said, pointing to a little Christmas tree in the hardware store window. "Somehow I don't feel Christmas is Christmas without one."

"Yeah. I'm going over to my brother's house tonight to help them decorate their tree."

It was lunch hour, plus the mall was crowded with Christmas shoppers. McDonald's was busy.

"Why don't you get a table?" Susan suggested. "There's one over there by the window. I'll get us two Big Macs, fries, and Cokes. Okay?" When Charlie hesitated, she continued. "You'd have a better chance of holding it than I would. I mean, what if some guy comes over and insists on sitting down with me? And who would argue with Santa anyway?"

"Okay," Charlie relented. He went to hand her a ten-dollar bill.

"No, no," Susan protested, pushing his hand away. Her

hand felt warm on his. "This is on me. For breaking our date yesterday."

"Susan . . ." Charlie started. She raised her hand.

"I insist," she said with raised eyebrows. "Big Macs. Okay?"

"Okay."

Susan walked to the order line. Charlie saw a man heading for the table. He made a beeline for it and sat down. The man, a construction worker, frowned and then smiled.

"I thought Santa eats milk and cookies," the man said.

"Only at night," Charlie answered. The man nodded and walked to a nearby table that had just become available.

Charlie took off his hat and beard. As he waited for Susan to come with the food, he gazed out the window wondering where this renewed relationship with Susan was going to go. Several people who passed by outside waved to him, and mouthed, "Merry Christmas." Charlie wished them the same back.

A boy Charlie guessed to be about six or seven walked up to him. "Are you Santa Claus?"

Charlie smiled in his friendliest manner. "I'm just one of Santa's helpers."

"Like the elves?"

"Sort of."

"I saw an elf on TV last night," the boy continued. "He was small. You're not small." His tone of voice was accusatory.

"Some of Santa's helpers are small and some are not," Charlie said, trying to keep a smile on his face.

"I don't think you're an elf or one of Santa's helpers either," the boy said in a loud voice, pointing his finger. Charlie leaned close to the boy.

"You know," Charlie said in a very confidential manner, "I call Santa on my cell phone every night to tell him who's been good and who's been bad."

"You're lying," the boy said defiantly. Then, from behind Charlie's shoulder, a woman spoke.

"Elwood, are you bothering Santa?"

"He's not Santa," the boy said loudly. "He's just dressed like him."

"Elwood, that's rude," the woman said, stepping up to the table. "Say you're sorry."

"No!"

"I'm so sorry," she told Charlie. Then she grabbed the boy firmly by the hand. "We've got to go. Say good-bye to Santa."

"No!"

The boy's mother pulled him away, exhaling loudly with frustration. "What am I going to do with you?" As they moved away, the boy turned and stuck his tongue out at Charlie. Charlie made a funny face back at him just as Susan arrived with a tray brimming with their lunch.

"Spreading some Christmas cheer?" she asked with a smile as she put the tray down.

"Sort of," Charlie snorted, embarrassed. "Sweet kid. His old man's probably the Grinch." Susan laughed as she took the two neatly wrapped Big Macs, two salads, and two Cokes off the tray and put them on the table.

"I got us salads instead of fries. Okay?" she asked, sitting down opposite him.

"Healthy, huh? Sounds good to me," Charlie said, reaching for his hamburger. As he did, his elbow accidentally hit the edge of the tray Susan had put off to the side. The tray slid and hit Susan's soda, causing it to tip over. On reflex, both Charlie and Susan grabbed for the capped drink, and as they did, their hands locked.

"Jeez. Sorry," Charlie said.

Susan looked into his eyes and smiled as their hands unlocked. "No problem."

Charlie suddenly felt the same inner turbulence and confusion he had felt when he left Susan the day before. To mask his feelings, he quickly unwrapped his Big Mac and took a big bite. Susan sensed the awkward moment. She lifted the bun off her hamburger to squeeze some ketchup on it.

"You don't want any ketchup, Charlie?" she asked before taking a bite.

"Huh? Oh yeah. Sure."

She passed him a ketchup packet. Charlie took it and squeezed it onto his burger.

They both ate silently for a long minute or two. Then Susan let out a laugh.

"Your 'sweet patootie.' How could I have forgotten that?" She covered her mouth with a napkin as she began to laugh again.

"Well," Charlie said, grinning, "you were." He could feel his heart starting to pound again.

"I never did ask. Exactly what is a patootie?"

"I don't know." Charlie shrugged.

"Well, where did you learn it?"

"I can't remember. I know it's really old-fashioned. Probably from my aunt Belle, who raised us. It has a nice ring to it, don't you think?"

"Euphonious."

"What?"

"A word that sounds nice to hear."

"Like Susan," he said quickly before he realized the connection he had made. Susan blushed and looked down at the table. "I mean it, uh, it has sort of a romantic ring to it, huh? I mean . . ."

"Thank you. It does," she said. "So does 'Charlie.' In fact, I wouldn't be surprised if you didn't see 'Sweet Patootie' on Valentine cards one of these days." She grinned and blushed again, but this time didn't look down. She looked into his eyes for a long moment. The noise of the busy McDonald's faded and they were alone. She then reached across the table and touched his hand. "Charlie Williams, you're like that old song, 'Still Crazy After All These Years.' "

Charlie put his other hand over hers. "I wish there were times when I hadn't been so crazy."

"That's all behind you now."

"Yeah."

"You have your whole life ahead of you."

"You sound like my brother, Tom."

"Well, your brother is right."

"I suppose . . ."

Impulsively, Susan turned her hand that was sandwiched between his upward and entwined her fingers with his. She looked deeply into his eyes. "And if you let me, I'll help in any way that I can."

It was at this moment that Charlie realized that when the time came to move on, he wouldn't. Or couldn't. Or not, at least, without his sweet patootie.

CHAPTER 28

A SILENT VOW

Tom Williams pulled up in front of Benjie's at six thirty that evening and honked his horn. A three-quarter moon gave a silvery glow to the street and all the houses on it. The snow that had fallen a few days ago was still evident. Almost immediately, the front door opened and Charlie came out bounding down the stairs. There were vapor puffs of breath coming out of his mouth into the cold night air. In a few strides he reached Tom's Jeep and hopped in. He clapped his brother on the shoulder.

"Hey, Tom, how you doing?" he said cheerfully.

"Great," Tom answered, glad to see Charlie's exuberance. "Ready to put on the feed bag?" He put the Jeep in gear and moved off down the block.

"Been thinking about it all day." He rubbed his hands together in front of the heater vent. "That feels good."

"Benjie a little stingy with the heat?"

"Let's just say he's frugal."

"Yeah, I noticed how cool it was in there the other night. No wonder he wears that heavy sweater."

"I can't complain. The price is right."

"He's a friend, right?"

"Yeah. A real stand-up guy."

Two hours later, Tom and Charlie were sitting in the living room having a beer. Charlie took a sip, patted his stomach, and leaned back in the sofa's soft pillows.

"Carol is some cook."

"That she is. And my best friend. The luckiest day of my life was when I married her."

"That's what I tell all my girlfriends," Carol said with a laugh as she and Katie came into the room.

Tom gave a short laugh. "You weren't supposed to hear that." He looked at Charlie. "Now she'll get a swelled head."

Charlie could see the deep love between Tom and Carol. It was nice to see. It gave him an unfamiliar, but pleasing ache deep inside. *Maybe it could be like that with me and Susan,* he thought. His gaze drifted to Katie and the thought of the dangerous situation he was in with Marty Richards banished that sweet idea. His face clouded over.

Katie noticed it. Her stomach tightened.

"Is there something wrong, Uncle Charlie?" she asked.

Both Tom and Carol picked up the worried tone in their daughter's voice. They looked at Charlie.

The quiet room and sudden attention gave Charlie a suspicion that maybe Katie read his thoughts.

"No, Katie," he said with a forced smile. "How could anything be wrong being here with you, and your mom and dad?"

His answer satisfied Tom and Carol, but not Katie. *There is something wrong,* she thought. *But what? What* is *it?* She tried, but couldn't get an image in her mind. Her thoughts were quickly distracted by Carol, who clapped her hands.

"Well," she said, "it's time to dress the tree!" Tom set aside his beer and got up.

"Tree time," he announced. He went over to a pile of boxes

near the tree. "I have everything I need right here. Everything, that is," he added archly, "but some helpers."

"Well, helping is the least I could do to earn my meal," Charlie said, getting up off the sofa.

"Oh, wait!" Katie said suddenly. She ran out of the room and up the stairs, shouting back, "I'll be right down."

Tom, meanwhile, opened one of the boxes and pulled out a string of lights. Charlie and Carol went to the other boxes that contained ornaments and began opening them. Charlie lifted out a large star from the one he had opened.

"This is quite a topper," he said, holding it up to admire.

"My mother gave us that our first Christmas in this house," Carol said.

"It's a beauty," Charlie told her.

"That goes on after the lights," Tom said, mounting a small metal stepladder with a string of lights in his hand. They all turned as they heard Katie bouncing down the stairs. She came skidding into the room carrying three cutout angels and a cardboard menorah.

"Slow down there, rocket girl," Carol said, laughing.

"I just wanted to show these to Uncle Charlie," Katie gushed as she brought them to her uncle. "We made them in school." She held up the menorah. "This is for the Jewish Hanukkah. And next week the class will be making something for Kwanzaa."

"Our daughter is very ecumenical," Carol told Charlie.

"What's ecumenical?" Katie asked.

"It means respect and acceptance of other religions, and people, and their religious beliefs. Now," Carol said, "there's something I want to get too."

As she left the room, Katie brought her ornaments to Tom. "Where'll I put these, Daddy?"

"Wait till I get the lights all strung up, sweetie," he said, from atop the stepladder. "Otherwise, if we have to rearrange them, we might wind up knocking down some of the ornaments."

Katie placed the menorah and angels down on a chair. "Okay," she said.

"Uh, Charlie," Tom said, "did they celebrate Christmas, uh, where you were?"

"A bit, I guess. There was a little tree in the chapel when I first got there. Most of the guys got presents from home. And we had a decent Christmas dinner. Turkey. Like that."

Tom climbed down from the stepladder and began stringing the lights around the lower part of the tree.

"You said when you first got there. Why did they stop?" Tom asked.

"I don't really know if they did. I just stopped going after two years."

"Something happen?" Tom asked, and then quickly added, "I don't mean to pry."

"That's okay," Charlie said. Tom got down on his knees to finish putting the lights around the base of the tree.

"I guess," Charlie continued, "it's just that I found the peace I needed within myself. And I didn't . . . I don't feel I need to belong to any organized religion. I know it works for a lot of people, most people, but not for me. Everybody's different, right?"

"Right," Tom said, putting the plug on the end of the string of lights into the master socket. He stood and held out his hand to Charlie. "You can hand me that star now."

Charlie passed him the star. "Actually, they did have a tree the past few years after we got a new warden. He's a good guy."

"That's good to hear," Tom said. "The spirit of the season can be uplifting."

"Yeah, well, uplifting isn't a condition you find too often in the penitentiary."

"Sorry," Tom said. "I wasn't thinking."

"That's okay, bro. I'm totally uplifted now!" He put his hand on Tom's shoulder.

Tom got up. "Katie, you can start putting your things on the tree."

Taking the star from Charlie, Tom remounted the step-ladder and screwed the topmost light into the base of the star. Katie put the menorah in a prominent place and the cutout angels on either side of it. Then all three of them began hanging ornaments on the tree with Tom going back up the step-ladder to put some on the topmost branches.

Carol came back into the living room carrying an envelope. She gave it to Charlie. "This is for Saint Francis, Charlie. For your charity chimney."

"Thank you. It's a good cause. I don't remember there being so many people in need in this town."

"Things are expensive. Jobs are not paying so great. A lot of people are without medical insurance . . ." Carol began, and then stopped. "I'm sorry to get on the soapbox. It just doesn't seem right in this great country." She took a deep breath.

"So, Charlie, when does the job end?" Tom asked, changing the subject. He knew how passionate Carol was about some of the inequalities the poor suffered.

"Christmas Eve is my last day," Charlie answered.

"Do you get off at your regular time that day?" Carol asked.

"Not till the mall closes. Apparently there're a lot of last-minute shoppers. Lefty Lopez, the guy who runs this at the church, says they're the ones most generous 'cause they're the last ones to get into the Christmas spirit."

"What time does the mall close?" Tom asked.

"I don't know. I'll ask Lefty tomorrow. But I'm pretty sure it'll be well after five."

"But you can join us on Christmas Day for dinner, can't you, Uncle Charlie?" Katie asked.

Charlie smiled and bobbed his head emphatically. "You bet." He paused. "If I'm invited, that is."

"Of course you're invited. Right, Daddy? Mommy?"

"Of course," they both answered together.

"We're going to have turkey and stuffing and, and pumpkin pie and mince pie and," Katie went on enthusiastically, ". . . and now we're going to have *you* too!" With that, Katie ran to Charlie, jumped into his arms and hugged him with her eyes closed tightly. Almost immediately, a frown came across her face as she saw something disturbing in her mind's eye.

"Well, it sure sounds great," Charlie said over Katie's shoulder. He couldn't see the change in Katie's expression, but Carol did and a now familiar chill ran down her spine. It was a look she had seen before. Katie shook her head as if trying to brush away the vision. She opened her eyes and started to disengage from her uncle.

"I'll be thirteen on January twenty-first," she said as Charlie put her down. "And you'll come to my birthday party. Right, Uncle Charlie?"

A fleeting image of his last meeting with Marty and Al crossed Charlie's mind as well as what the ultimate result might be. And it caused him to stand a moment, frozen.

"Won't you?" Katie repeated.

"If I can, Katie. If I can," Charlie said, trying his best to smile. Then, seeing the slight look of disappointment on her face, he added playfully, "That is, if I'm invited."

Katie laughed. "Oh, Uncle Charlie. Of course you are."

The image of Katie's troubled expression remained with Carol.

"Let's put on the tinsel," she said, covering her concern.

Tom moved over to the light switch. "First, let's fire up this beauty."

"Before we put on the tinsel?" Carol asked.

"I think we'll be able to better see where it reflects the lights best if I put the lights on first."

"Okay," Carol said with a nod. "But let me put out all the other lights." She went to the wall switch next to the doorway. At the same time, Katie went to the two table lamps and turned them off. Seconds later, the room was in darkness except for some ambient light that came through the kitchen door.

"Ready?" Tom asked.

"Ready," everyone else chorused.

"You can make a wish if you want to," Tom said. "Charlie and I always did when we were kids. Remember, Charlie?" Charlie felt a lump in his throat.

"Oh yeah. I do. I surely do," he said, hoping they didn't notice the tightness in his voice.

"Everyone make a wish?" Tom asked. Carol, Charlie, and a very enthusiastic Katie said "Yes" together. Tom then handed the master switch to Charlie. "You do it, Charlie."

Charlie took the switch. His hand shook a little as he realized how much he had missed, and how happy he was to be home. He pressed the switch and the tree came to life with brilliant colors that blinked and ornaments that sparkled, reflecting the color throughout the darkened room.

"Wow!" Katie squealed.

"Beautiful!" Carol exclaimed.

"It's the best we've ever had," Tom said. Charlie was speechless. He fought tears. He remembered Christmases past and Christmases lost.

Tom put his arm around Carol and kissed her lightly on the cheek.

Katie took Charlie's hand. As he looked down into her smiling face, lit by the multicolored lights of the tree, he silently vowed to himself that no matter what he had to do, even if it meant going back to prison, he would never allow anyone to harm his beautiful young niece.

CHAPTER 29

KATIE'S GIFT

All morning and well into the afternoon of the next day, the locket around Katie's neck felt warm, and at times it seemed to glow. When she finally grasped it in her hand, she heard a soft, female voice. It was low and melodic, a little like her mother's. But it spoke in a language she had never heard before, and yet, she somehow understood the meaning of the words! It urged her to go to Radio Shack in the mall, not too far from the place where Uncle Charlie set up his Saint Francis chimney.

Deep inside her she knew it was the voice of her great-grandmother Miranda.

Late that afternoon, right after school, Katie and Melissa were at the mall, walking on the side opposite Kaplan's Jewelry Store. They were heading for Radio Shack. There were snow flurries in the air. While Katie was anxious and excited, Melissa was hunched over, cold and impatient to be on what seemed to be a purposeless trip.

"But *why* are we going to Radio Shack?" Melissa asked for the fifth time. "I'm cold and wet."

"And, for the fifth time, I don't know," Katie answered. "Just chill. We'll be there in a few minutes."

"You don't *know?*"

"No."

"I'm cold."

"It's winter, Melissa. Why didn't you wear something warmer?"

"I didn't know I was going on a hike," she answered sarcastically as they passed The Gap store.

"Why don't you go in here, look around, and warm up?" Katie suggested. "I'll come get you when I'm done."

"Oh, Katie," Melissa said in mock despair. "Why do I listen to you?" She looked at the store's window display. She loved fashion. "Look. They have the new bathing suits. Okay. Ten minutes. I'll give you ten minutes." With that, Melissa hurried away toward The Gap's door.

A few moments later, Katie was at Radio Shack. The store's wide window was in full Christmas décor with hundreds of electronic devices on display. But none of that caught Katie's attention. She was awestruck to see her great-grandma Miranda standing beyond the display, beckoning for her to come inside.

Mystified and yet joyful, Katie quickly entered the store just as a man walked toward Miranda. But he didn't seem to see her. In fact, the customer passed right through Miranda as if she did not exist. Miranda just smiled and shrugged. Katie heard that same sweet voice, the one that had beckoned her to go to Radio Shack. It said, "Don't be alarmed, my sweet child. It happens all the time." Miranda then stepped toward, or perhaps "floated" is a better description, a display of tiny digital recorders. She pointed to one of them. Katie followed, and when she was next to Miranda the older woman kissed her gently on the forehead.

"Hello, my darling," she said. "I'm so glad we have finally met." Again, Katie's great-grandmother spoke in the foreign tongue and yet Katie was able to understand every word. Still awestruck at the sight of her great-grandmother, Katie then felt a strange calm come into her body and mind.

She took a deep breath and relaxed. From that time on, she accepted Miranda's presence as though she had always been at Katie's side.

"Hello, Great-grandma. I knew somehow you would come."

"Yes. We are going to be great friends, Katie dear. Now that you understand the gift we share, we are as one."

"That's wonderful," Katie said, filled with love for the vision before her.

"We have some things to do, you and me," Miranda then told her great-granddaughter. "Your uncle Charlie is in a bad situation and I know you want to help him."

"Oh yes! Yes!" Katie said with youthful enthusiasm.

A young man, the salesclerk behind the recorder display, heard Katie. He came over and saw she was looking off into empty space and talking to herself.

"May I help you with something?" he asked politely.

"What? Oh. No. I mean, I don't know. I mean, uh, can you give me a minute?"

The clerk frowned. "Uh, yeah. Sure. Take your time. I'll be back." He then moved away to another customer.

Miranda smiled and put her hand on Katie's shoulder. "They can't see or hear me, dear heart. No one can. Only you. So it's best if you don't speak aloud, but just listen."

"Okay," Katie answered. Then she clamped her lips together, stifling a giggle as she realized she just did what Miranda had asked her not to do. Miranda smiled again and then pointed to one of the tiny recorders in the display.

"Purchase one of these, my child, and a chip to go with it. Then go to your uncle Charlie and give it to him as a Christmas present."

Katie was about to ask why, but she remembered what her great-grandmother had told her, and so remained quiet. As though reading her mind, Miranda continued. "It's something he will be able to use to stop being afraid for you. It can help him to get out of the bad situation that an evil man has put him into."

Katie understood. "I'm ready now," she called out to the clerk, who was free again.

"Ready to buy something now?"

"Yes," Katie answered, pointing to the tiniest of the tape recorders that Miranda had indicated. "I'd like this one and a chip to go with it."

"Fine," the young man said. He bent down behind the display case and brought out a boxed recorder. "Here you go. It comes with a chip."

"How much is it?"

"On sale. Special. Twenty-five dollars."

Katie took out her wallet and gave him a twenty and a ten. "Can you gift wrap it for me?" she asked.

"We don't wrap here. But I can give you the gift paper. No charge. And I have Scotch tape here."

"Okay. And do you have a little piece of paper or a card that I can write a note on and put in with it?"

"No problem, again. We have Christmas cards, or just Happy Holidays, if you want. No charge."

"Excellent. Let's make it Happy Holidays."

The clerk went off to get the paper and card. Katie turned proudly to Miranda, but she was gone.

Across the mall, Charlie stood near Kaplan's, ringing his bell, calling out, "Merry Christmas," and thanking people who dropped money into his chimney. Then, as if from nowhere, Marty Richards was in front of him.

"Well, look what the snow blew in," Charlie said with a sharp edge of sarcasm in his voice.

"Yeah," Marty agreed with a smirk. "The ghost of Christmas future."

"So what's up? I'm busy."

"Just checkin' while Al, my boozing partner, is gettin' a bottle in the liquor store. I want to be sure you're workin' tomorrow."

"Yeah. Late."

"How late?"

"When the last stores close."

"When's that?"

"Around ten, they said."

Marty moved his head up and down slowly. "And you get picked up by those guys in the van and dropped off at your place?"

"Yeah. So?"

"So you should get there about what, quarter after ten?" Charlie didn't answer. Marty raised his eyebrows. "Am I goin' too fast for you?"

"I'm following. Yeah, about ten fifteen," Charlie answered sullenly, repressing the urge to punch Marty in the face.

"So, ten, fifteen minutes inside should give you enough time to get out of your Santy Claus outfit and into civvies, right?"

"So it's tomorrow night? Christmas Eve?"

"I didn't say. Maybe it's just a dry run. We'll be there at ten thirty to pick you up. Don't disappoint me. You got that?"

The urge to break Marty's nose rose up in Charlie, but he once again restrained himself. "You get those things on my list?"

"We had a little problem with the diamond drill, but yeah, it's all taken care of." Marty then looked past Charlie and cocked his head. "Speak of the devil. Here comes that pretty little niece of yours. Remember, you want her to stay that way, so don't screw up." Marty turned and walked away in the direction opposite from Katie.

"Hi, Uncle Charlie," Katie called out. Glancing away for a moment, Charlie made sure Marty was gone. When he turned back, Katie and Melissa were next to him.

"Hey there, Katie. What's up?"

She hugged Charlie around his ample Santa waist. "I just did a little Christmas shopping. It's for you."

"You got something for me?"

"For Christmas, Uncle Charlie. But don't ask what it is."

"Well! Sure. That's really nice. Thank you, Katie."

She motioned toward Melissa. "This is my very best friend, Melissa."

"How do you do, Melissa?" Charlie said with a slight bow. "And a Merry Christmas to you."

"Thank you," Melissa said. "But I'm Jewish."

Charlie bowed again. "Well then, happy Hanukkah."

"Thank you," Melissa said.

"That's very ecumenical!" Katie said, proud to use the new word in her vocabulary.

"Katieee," Melissa whined, "it's snowing harder now and I'm getting cold again."

"Okay," Katie said. "You go on ahead and I'll catch up to you. I have some, uh, private business with my uncle Charlie."

Melissa scrunched up her face as if to say, "I know when I'm not welcome."

"Fine," was all she said as she hurried away.

"Don't go too fast," Katie said after her.

"So, what's so private?" Charlie asked in a mock conspiratorial tone.

Katie opened her coat and pulled out the locket chained around her neck. "Do you see this?"

"Uh-huh."

"It once belonged to my great-grandma Miranda."

Charlie leaned down for closer inspection. "It's really beautiful."

"Yes. And it's magical too."

"*Magical? Really?* How's that?"

"My mom said that when her grandma gave it to her, she said it was made from some of the gold The Three Wise Men gave to the Baby Jesus." Katie opened the locket. "And inside it contains some of the frankincense and myrrh they gave to Him too. Not too much. My mother called it 'the residue.' "

Charlie tried to keep the skepticism out of his voice as he asked, "Well, that's something. How is it magical?"

"Well," Katie began, searching for the right words, "I have this gift of sometimes seeing things, but since I've been wearing this, it's stronger. And sometimes I can feel what other people are thinking. Like when I just hugged you?" Katie stopped for a moment as a young man passed and dropped a dollar bill into the chimney.

"Thank you," Charlie said. "Merry Christmas."

"Same to you, Santa," the man responded. Charlie turned his attention back to Katie

"Go on."

"Well, it was the same feeling as when I hugged you last night. It felt like you were afraid."

Charlie kneeled down so he was eye level with Katie. "Afraid of what?"

She hesitated a moment "That something bad might happen to me."

Charlie stared at her, stunned and speechless.

"And I keep seeing a man," Katie rushed on. "I can't see his face, but I know he's a bad man. But don't worry, Uncle Charlie, Great-grandma Miranda said that there's a way we might stop him."

Charlie was puzzled. "What are you talking about, sweetie? I mean, how is it possible—"

"Here," Katie interrupted. She took a small package out of her coat pocket and gave it to Charlie. "This is the gift I got for you. Great-grandma Miranda's the one who told me to get it. She said it would be something you could use to stop being afraid for me. Now I have to run if I want to catch up with Melissa. If I don't she'll be really mad at me." Katie leaned over and kissed Charlie on his bearded cheek. "Goodbye, Uncle Charlie. I love you. And remember, don't be afraid anymore."

Before Charlie could say anything or stand up, Katie ran off into the snow flurries after Melissa.

Charlie examined the small package. His curiosity aroused,

he tore off the wrapper to find the tiny digital recorder with a handwritten note wrapped around it. The note read . . .

Dear Uncle Charlie,
This is what Great-grandma Miranda told me to get you. The chip is in the recorder. She told me you'll be able to use it, so I know you will. I love you, Katie.

Charlie rewrapped the tape recorder and put it into his pants pocket. *How could this help me?* he wondered. *How could it stop Marty? Or keep me from being caught up in this heist and become a three-time loser?* And what about protecting Katie? And Tom and Carol?

A middle-aged couple dropped a few bills into Charlie's chimney. But Charlie was so distracted by his thoughts that he didn't say anything until the man said sarcastically, "You're welcome," as he walked away.

"Oh," Charlie said, coming out of his thoughts. "Sorry," he called after them. "Thank you. And Merry Christmas!"

The man, now several feet away, waved in acknowledgment.

Charlie went back to the dilemma that had occupied him for the past few days since Marty and Al had trapped him into opening Kaplan's safe. He realized that whatever was to be done to stop all this, it was too complicated to do alone. He couldn't go to Tom with it. Then he realized that he did have some new friends in Lefty and Leon, and one very good old friend in Benjie. He wasn't alone. He began to ring his bell.

CHAPTER 30

PANSIES AND PEARLS

Charlie called out a cheery "Merry Christmas" and thanked two women who dropped bills and change into his chimney. As they walked away, he wondered about the gift Katie had given him and the strange tale she told about her great-grandmother's involvement. *I've got to get her something too,* he decided. He glanced over at Kaplan's. *Maybe Susan could help me,* he thought.

The shopping traffic had lessened as the snow began to stick. Charlie figured it would be a good time to go into Kaplan's, warm up with a cup of coffee, and have a quick word with Susan, if she was not busy.

"How is it outside, Santa?" Ed Kaplan asked after he buzzed Charlie in.

"Getting pretty cold."

"Like the North Pole, huh?"

"Yeah, but with this snow . . . not too good for navigating the sled. Or for the reindeer on roofs. Tiny hooves, you know."

Ed laughed. "How about some hot coffee?"

"You're a mind reader."

Ed smiled and went to get Charlie some coffee. Charlie

noticed that Susan was in the process of saying good-bye to a customer. She smiled at Charlie as he walked over to her.

"Hi."

"Hi. The snow sticking?"

"A little. Looks like it may just be flurries."

"Maybe we'll have a white Christmas."

Charlie's mind immediately considered the problems that a heavy snow on Christmas Eve might cause. It could complicate things with Marty and Al. "Let's hope not," he said.

"Why, Charlie Williams. Don't tell me you wouldn't like to see a white Christmas," she teased.

"No, it's not that," Charlie said, so worried about tomorrow night that he took her teasing seriously. "I'm just afraid it might cut down on the contributions. I mean, even just the flurries slowed things down and, well, the needy families—"

"Whoa there, Santa," Susan interrupted. "I was only joking. Are you okay?"

"Me? Yeah. I'm fine. It's just I'm sort of into this job and it's great to be able to help . . . you know."

Susan smiled at him and put her hand on his. "I know."

"Here's your coffee," Ed Kaplan said, arriving behind Charlie.

"Thanks, Ed. Santa will put something extra in your stocking for that."

"Just a little more business would be nice." The doorbell rang. "There you go. That was fast, Santa!" He saw Joan go for the buzzer. "I've got it," he called to her, and went to the front door to greet the customer.

Seeing the customers come in reminded Charlie of what he wanted to ask Susan. "Meanwhile," he said to Susan, "the reason I came in was to ask you about helping me with a present for my niece."

"What do you want to get?"

"That's just it. I don't know."

"How about a locket?" Susan suggested. "We have a sale on . . ."

Charlie shook his head and raised his hand to stop her. "She already has one she wears all the time." He smiled. "Says it's magical."

"Well, I can't beat that. How much would you like to spend?"

Charlie put on a rueful face. "I'd like more than I got, that's for sure. Maybe, uh, I don't know . . . twenty, thirty bucks."

Susan bent down and opened the back door of the display case.

"Are her ears pierced?" Charlie frowned.

"I really don't know." She lifted out a tray of earrings and placed it on top of the counter.

"How about something like these?" she asked.

Charlie looked at the earrings. He shrugged. "I don't know. What do kids like?"

"We're talking about Katie Williams, aren't we? How old is she? About twelve?"

Charlie gave a short laugh. "Yeah. Going on thirty, my brother says."

"Aren't they all today?" With that, Susan picked up a dainty pair of purple and yellow pansy earrings with tiny pearls in the center. She held them up for Charlie's inspection.

"They look nice," he said.

"I love them. I think they're perfect for a young lady."

"How much?"

"They're on sale. Twenty-five dollars. And if her ears aren't pierced, I'll do that for nothing. Or we can put clips on them."

Charlie examined the earrings again.

"So, what do you think? You want to see something else?"

"No, these are fine."

"Good. How do you want to pay for them? Cash? Credit?"

Charlie dug a hand into his pants pocket under his Santa outfit. "Cash. I don't, uh, I don't have credit cards, you see."

Susan realized that she totally forgot Charlie had been in prison for nine years. Her question about payment was just normal business, but to Charlie it might have seemed insulting.

"I'm sorry. I should have known . . . of course. It's just that I ask question by rote and—"

"Not to worry. I understand. No harm done. I have to get used to the world again." He pulled a few bills out of his pocket. "I'm lucky I still had a few bucks from before." He pulled off a twenty and a five and handed the bills to Susan.

"Uh, there's sales tax of about two dollars, but I think, I mean, Santa doesn't have to pay tax. Or any of his helpers."

"No, no, Susan," Charlie said, handing her two more dollars. "No more deals or shortcuts for me. Everything's got to be on the up-and-up now. If there's a tax, I'll pay it."

Susan was pleased to hear those words. She put the tray back into the display case and gathered up the earrings Charlie had chosen. "You're going to be just fine, Charlie Williams," she said. "Let me gift wrap these. I'll be right back."

Charlie glanced around the store. Ed and Joan were with customers. Susan was in the back, wrapping Katie's gift. He pondered his situation with Marty and Al. How was he going to deal with them? He had only twenty-four hours to find a solution.

CHAPTER 31

A REAL DATE

A few minutes later and Charlie no closer to a plan to resolve the problem, Susan returned to Charlie.

"Here we are," she said brightly, handing Charlie a small earring box wrapped in gold paper with a braided gold ribbon around it.

"That looks real great. Thanks," he said sincerely. "I know she's gonna love them."

"I'm sure," Susan said. Charlie slipped the box into his coat pocket and looked outside.

"Well, time to get back to the Santa business," he proclaimed. Susan furrowed her brow in thought, trying to decide something. Then she did.

"Listen, Charlie, there's a whole group of us who work around here. We meet at this bar in the mall, Clementine's, and, well, for the past few years have been having a sort of Eve of Christmas Eve party, the night before Christmas Eve. It's just drinks and fun and all. And we're doing it again tonight. After work. Here in the mall. Clementine's. You know the place?"

"I've seen it. On the other side, right?"

"Right. So . . . I was sort of. No, not sort of. I'd really like it if you'd come to it. With me."

A rush of excitement coursed through Charlie. He felt like a teenager being asked out by a girl he was crazy about. She was asking him! Then reality set in.

"Look, Susan, I'd love to but, uh, I mean after getting Katie the earrings and all I just don't . . . I mean, how much would it cost?"

"It's already been paid for!" Susan said.

"How's that?"

"Since we've been having the party there every year, and taking over most of the place, they told us last year that if we could guarantee we'd be back again this year, they'd give us the whole place for a flat rate. Like a private party. They said it would be easier that way for them, and cheaper for us. So we got together right after Thanksgiving and paid them. And I know at least two people who have canceled out, so it's paid for."

"Don't they get their money back?"

"No refunds. That was the rule. I mean, supposing you had ten people who suddenly couldn't make it? And we had to give them their money back. Then, everybody would have to chip in to make up for the loss and it'd wind up costing us more than if we hadn't booked it. So, would you like to come?"

Charlie nodded. "You're a great salesma . . . I mean salesperson. It's a date."

"Good. And listen, while we're on the subject of dates"— Susan's face flushed a little red—"and I hope you won't think me too forward . . ."

"You could never be too forward with me," Charlie told her, softly.

Susan relaxed. "Thank you. Well, what I wanted to ask is, are you doing anything for Christmas Eve?"

Charlie's insides tightened and his expression changed

involuntarily at thoughts of the safe just a few feet away and Marty and Al. Susan misinterpreted his expression, thinking his reaction was caused by her pressuring Charlie for another date.

"I'm sorry, Charlie," she said quickly. "I can see I was being too forward."

"No, no," Charlie protested. "It's not that at all." His mind raced to come up with something. "It's my brother and sister-in-law, and Katie . . . See, they invited me over tomorrow night and, uh, maybe going to church and all and . . ." His voice drifted off.

"Oh. Sure. I understand. Family comes first. Okay. I didn't mean to crowd you or anything."

"Oh no, no, Susan. I'm flattered you asked." Then, trying to pass off the awkwardness of the moment, Charlie continued. "I haven't been asked out on a date in I can't remember when. If ever! And to be asked out on two . . . well . . ."

"I understand. Getting back into the swing of things. I'll settle for the one tonight. Okay?"

"I look forward to it," a relieved Charlie said before adding, "What time do you meet?"

"Around seven," Susan said. "That way it doesn't go on too late into the night. Most of us work in the stores here, so tomorrow is an early day."

"Okay. I'll be back to my place by five thirty, the latest. And a bus runs from near there right to here."

"Why don't I come by and pick you up?" Susan suggested. "About six thirty?"

Charlie hesitated momentarily. Did he want her to see Benjie's house was in that part of town? Then he thought, *Okay, that's who I am and that's where I live and no more making believe I'm what I'm not.* "Sounds like a plan," he said. "But I have to warn you, I haven't had a date in nine years, so I may be a little, uh, socially rusty."

"I can't believe there's ever been anything rusty about you, Charlie Williams."

His heart skipped those beats once more and he felt alive and free.

CHAPTER 32

WHILE THE CHOIR SANG

By early evening, the snow had stopped. But a blustery, winter front from Canada had turned it bitterly cold. The wind swirled its icy fingers around those brave souls who were out for last-minute shopping. Charlie had packed up and was on his way to Benjie's in the van.

Across town, Katie sat alone in a rear pew of the First United Methodist Church where her family were active members. It was warm and peaceful there. Up front, Carol and Tom were participating in choir practice. Carol, who had a rich contralto voice, was a soloist. The choirmaster had done a special arrangement of "Silent Night." Carol's part was the two "Sleep in heavenly peace" lines.

As Carol's part came, her voice soared and reverberated in the empty church. The choirmaster stopped the rehearsal and was in the process of adjusting the choir's background humming when Katie felt a presence behind her. At first she thought it was the wind outside. She turned to see if the church door had blown open. It had not. Then she heard a familiar voice calling to her in that strange European language.

"Katie, dear child," it beckoned. "Over here." Katie looked left and right toward the rear of the church. On the left side, in the shadows, she saw her great-grandma Miranda step forward. The apparition gestured for Katie to come to her. "Come to me, darling." Katie checked to see that her parents were occupied, which they were. She quietly slid across the pew and made her way to the rear of the church where Miranda had slipped back into the shadows.

"I see that my granddaughter, your mother, has a beautiful voice," Miranda said as Katie stood next to her.

"Yes, she does, Great-grandma."

"My own mother had such a voice."

"Did she have the gift?"

Miranda smiled. Her beautiful face glowed in the darkness. "Oh yes. She explained it to me when I was just about your age."

At that moment, Katie felt a connection to her family that went back centuries. She touched the locket. "I see you have learned to hold it," Miranda said.

"It shows me so much, Great-grandma."

"Yes, my dear. It always will. And someday, you will pass it to your daughter, and she to hers."

The idea that she would have a daughter thrilled Katie and made her blush. But she knew she would and it also made her happy.

"And, please call me Miranda."

"Okay, Miranda."

"Good."

At that moment, the choir began to sing again, filling the nave with gentle and harmonious music.

"Silent night, holy night, all is calm, all is bright . . ."

Miranda listened for a moment. She then moved closer to Katie. "Now, my dear, I want you to listen carefully. Tomorrow night, Christmas Eve, you will have a great deal to do."

Katie was confused. She always went to church with her parents on Christmas Eve. Miranda read her thoughts. "First, we will have to find a way for you to stay home."

The two huddled for several more minutes, discussing what had to be done. When things were settled, Katie understood what she must do. She was not aware that the music had stopped and that the choir practice was over. Her father's voice focused her back to reality.

"Katie?" he called out. "Katie?" She stepped out of the shadows, into the aisle.

"I'm here, Dad," she answered, waving.

"Time to go," he said. "Get your coat. You don't want to be late to Melissa's."

"Okay," she answered. With that, she looked back into the nave one more time.

"Hold the locket tight and I will be with you," Miranda said. "You must not let anyone see it. Not till I tell you to show it to them."

"But when you do, won't the men take it from me?"

"All this will be clear to you when the time comes, my dear." On her final words, Miranda stepped farther back into the shadows, and as Katie looked on in wide-eyed amazement, her image slowly faded into the ether just as Tom and Carol arrived.

"How did we sound, young lady?" Tom asked.

Katie turned and said, "Oh, great, Daddy. And, Mommy, that carol you sang by yourself? That was so beautiful."

"Thank you, darling." Carol leaned over and kissed Katie on the forehead.

"Okay," Tom said. "Let's get you to the Lithcotts'. You don't want to be late."

Katie glanced into the corner one more time. Miranda was gone.

CHAPTER 33

SHALL WE DANCE?

At shortly after six thirty that evening, Susan pulled up in front of Benjie's. Charlie, who had been waiting just inside the front door, came out and went down the wide wooden stairs to her car. Climbing inside, he impulsively leaned over and gave Susan a quick kiss on her cheek. She blushed.

"Did that bother you?" he asked, wondering where he got the courage to do it.

"Oh no," she answered.

"Well, I wanted to do that in the store after you helped me with Katie's gift, but there were people around and Mr. Kaplan and—"

Susan interrupted him by leaning over and planting a kiss on his cheek. "It felt right," she told him. "Now let's have some fun."

Susan shifted the car into gear and as they drove off, her radio was tuned to a station playing harmonious Christmas carols.

In contrast, the music at Clementine's was loud and rocking. The restaurant was decorated for Christmas and crowded with people who worked in the mall, and their friends. Susan and Charlie were seated with three other couples, friends of Susan's. The atmosphere was festive, and a little raucous.

"Okay, okay, everybody. Calm down for a second." Micky, the manager of Old Navy, stood. "Okay. So we drank to Christmas past—"

"Those were the ones *before* you were engaged," Alex, Micky's best friend, interrupted with a dig. Everyone at the table laughed. Charlie, who felt like an outsider, had been warmly welcomed by the others at the table. Susan had introduced him as a prodigal son, returning to his hometown after living in New York. It was a story that she and Charlie had cooked up while driving to Clementine's. There was no reason to have to explain prison and all that.

"Right," Micky responded, looking down at his brand-new fiancée, Laurie, who sat next to him. She got up and gave him a hug and a long, loving kiss. Everyone applauded.

"Never mind. They're all just jealous, honey."

Everyone then cheered their agreement.

"True. True," Micky continued. "And we drank to Christmas present."

"You tell 'em, Scrooge," Hal, Micky's assistant manager, called out.

"He's Scrooge and you're Bob Cratchett!" Hal's girlfriend, Jackie, shouted. Everyone laughed and banged on the table. They began to chant, "Scrooge. Scrooge. Scrooge." Micky held up his hand to stop them.

"Because when I worked for your father, Jackie, he taught me well." Again there was raucous laughter. Then Alex, a six-five, handsome thirty-year-old who had played minor league baseball and now coached the high school team, stood up.

"Okay," he began. "Okay, everyone. If Micky's Scrooge, and Hal is Bob Cratchett, then I gotta be Tiny Tim! So, God bless us, every one." They all applauded. Alex sat down. His girlfriend, Agnes, gave him a big kiss on the cheek.

"Okay," Micky continued, "this toast is getting too long. Now it's time to raise our glasses to Christmas future!"

"And to weddings!" Laurie shouted.

"To weddings," they all shouted with glasses raised.

"And to good times," Alex added.

"Weddings and good times!" they all said.

"And good friends," Agnes added.

"And good friends," they all agreed. Then Susan stood up.

"And new friends!" she said. They all raised their glasses and looked at Charlie.

"To Charlie!" Everyone drained their glasses. Charlie was slightly embarrassed and at the same time filled with happiness he had not known for a very, very long time. Micky picked up the bottle of champagne that was in an ice bucket next to him and began to pour another drink in everyone's glass. The music changed to a ballad. He put down the bottle and took Laurie's hand to dance. The others also left the table to dance.

After a moment, Susan stood up and reached her hand to Charlie. "Dance with me?" she asked.

"It's been a long time."

"It's like riding a bike. As I recall, you were pretty good at both."

Charlie stood up and took her hand. They joined the others on the dance floor.

"I think Susan likes him," Hal said to Jackie.

"More than that," Jackie said. "I think she really, really likes him."

"Poor Charlie," Hal told her. With that, Jackie playfully slapped him on his bare, shaved head. The sound made their friends look at them. No one knew why Jackie had done that, but the gesture was familiar to them and they all laughed.

"What was that all about?" Charlie asked Susan as they danced.

"Jackie does that all the time, ever since Hal shaved his head."

"Oh," Charlie said. He felt her slide her hand from his shoulder to his neck. She felt warm against him. He enjoyed the closeness. Susan nestled her face against his shoulder and slipped both her arms around his neck. Charlie was dizzy with delight.

"Mmmmmmmm . . ." was all he could muster.

"What?" she asked.

"I can't begin to tell you . . ."

"Me too, Charlie."

"Can we just stay here for about nine years?" he said softly.

Susan caressed the back of his neck. "You can stay as long as you like."

Charlie's heart leaped and pounded. He pressed her closer.

CHAPTER 34

A HANUKKAH SECRET

Barbara Lithcott, Melissa's mother, brought the menorah into the kitchen. Katie counted the unlit candles. There were seven. One was higher than the rest. Melissa's two younger brothers, Bert, nine, and David, seven, moved up next to the table. They were excited.

"Why is that one higher than the rest?" Katie asked.

"It's called the master. We use it to light the other candles," Melissa told her best friend.

"Tonight is the sixth day of the holiday," Barbara told Katie as she put the menorah on the table. Lou Lithcott, Melissa's father, took a box of wooden matches out from a nearby drawer.

"Can I do it first?" David asked his father.

"Not tonight. We have a guest."

The boy was disappointed. "But Bert did it last night. It's my turn."

"Where are your manners, David?" Barbara asked her youngest. David sulked for a moment. He looked at Katie.

"Sorry," was all he said. Then he saw his brother making a face at him. He balled up his fist, but his father saw it and grabbed his shoulder.

"You're about to lose your present for tonight," he told David. The fist disappeared. "And you, young man," he said to Bert, "you should know better." Lou then turned to Melissa and Katie. "Okay, girls. Let's get started."

Melissa took the master candle from the menorah and handed it to Katie. Then Lou lit a match and handed it to Melissa. She lit the master.

"First we say the prayers," she told Katie. "Then we light the candles."

Lou Lithcott took out a prayer book and began to recite in Hebrew. Melissa roughly translated, whispering in Katie's ear. "Blessed are You, O Lord our God, King of the Universe, Who bids us to light the Hanukkah candles. Like that."

Lou Lithcott ended the prayer with "Amen."

"Now the one I like the most," Melissa said. Lou began again in Hebrew.

Melissa translated again. "Blessed are You, O Lord our God, King of the Universe, Who has kept us in life, sustained us, and brought us to this festive season."

Lou Lithcott said, "Amen" and put aside the prayer book.

"Okay, Katie. You can light the candles."

"Which way?" she asked nervously. She wanted to be sure to do it right.

"Left to right," Melissa told her, guiding her hand to the first candle. Katie carefully lit it, then the next, then the third. She looked over at David and handed him the master candle.

"Why don't you light the next?" she said to the boy. He smiled, then looked at his father for approval.

"That's very nice of you, Katie. Go ahead, David." David lit the fourth candle carefully, and then handed the master to his brother. Bert took it and expertly lit the fifth. He handed the master back to Katie. She gave it to Melissa, who lit the last candle and put the master candle back in the menorah above the others. The two boys then looked at their parents.

"Now come the presents," Melissa told Katie.

"You mean you get presents every night?"

"Eight nights—eight presents," Melissa said with a grin. "That's one of the best things about being Jewish!"

"I'll say," Katie remarked. "I think I'm going to talk to my parents about changing religions," she said as a joke.

"There's more to it than presents," Barbara said, overhearing the girls' conversation.

"But there *are* presents," Melissa said. With that, Barbara laughed and took out a large shopping bag from one of the lower kitchen cabinets.

"That's where she hid it tonight," Bert remarked to his younger brother. "I thought you looked in here."

"I did!" David insisted.

"You guys have to be smarter than that to fool your mother. She's an expert present hider." Everyone laughed. Then Barbara handed out the presents, including one for Katie.

"Happy Hanukkah, Katie," Barbara said. "It's a pleasure to have you here tonight."

"Thank you, Mrs. Lithcott," Katie said. "It was very nice." Then she and Melissa went up to Melissa's room.

A half hour later, after Katie had opened her gift, a CD of her favorite band, Wowii, she had this discussion with Melissa as the two girls sat on the bed in Melissa's room, facing each other.

"Melissa, can you stay over at my house tomorrow night?" Katie began.

"Christmas Eve?"

"Yes."

"Why?"

"When my parents go to the eleven o'clock service, I need to go somewhere."

"You're going somewhere at eleven o'clock at *night?* On Christmas *Eve?"*

"I have to be somewhere by eleven fifteen. My parents will be leaving around ten thirty, so I can leave after that and make it on time."

"Katie! Are you *crazy?* Where in the world are you going at that time of night?"

"I can't tell you."

"Oh, great. And you want me to be there and not know?"

Katie ignored Melissa's protest. "I'm going to pretend to be sick so I don't have to go to services with them. And if they think I'm sick, they'd never leave me alone. But they would if I had someone there with me."

"What *are* you trying to get me into?"

"Nothing, Melissa. Honest. I'll be home before my parents. So they'll never know."

Melissa shook her head vehemently. "Katie, I don't want to get involved in this. Sorry."

"You've *got* to help me. It could be a matter of life or death."

"What are you talking about? *Whose* life or death?"

"I can't tell you."

"I'm your best friend and you can't tell me anything? Then I'm sorry, Katie. If something were to happen to you, and my parents found out I was involved, I'd be grounded forever!"

Katie could feel desperation rising inside her. "No one will know. Pleeeeze, Melissa. It's really very important."

"I just don't like it, Katie," Melissa said, softening her objection.

"I'll give you my new Wii for a month."

"Your *new* one? Really?" Her objection was fast fading. Wii was her favorite pastime these days.

Katie nodded. "My new one."

"And if we get caught you're going to take all the blame?"

"Of course. I promise."

"Make it two months. And if something does go wrong, I say I knew nothing about it and you take all the blame."

"Absolutely."

"Okay."

"Good," Katie said, relieved. "Now let's go over how this is going to happen."

CHAPTER 35

CONFESSION

Susan parked her car down the street from Benjie's rooming house, and away from the streetlights. She turned off the engine. The Christmas lights from Benjie's and other houses on the block threw a soft array of colors, blinking bright red, green, blue, and white, onto the car and their faces. It helped mask that there were people inside. Charlie had suggested they park there because he had finally figured out that Marty and Al had been following people from the mall. That's how they found out where he lived. That's how they discovered Tom, Carol, and Katie.

"I had a great time," Susan told him. "And my friends think you are a really nice guy."

"They're nice too. It wasn't as hard for me to, you know, be with people as I thought it might. I guess I'm adjusting."

"I know you are. I'm proud of you. I know it can't be easy."

He leaned over and stroked her face gently. "Finding you . . . well, that's what's making it . . . I feel like I belong here again."

"You do, Charlie." She softly kissed the palm of his hand. For a long moment he stared into her eyes, deciding if it was a good idea to tell her what was happening with Marty, Al,

Katie, and Kaplan's . . . the whole story. Finally, he withdrew his hand and took a deep breath.

"Susan," he began. "I have something important to tell you." She was immediately attentive, captured by the seriousness of his tone. "I mean, if we're going to have any kind of relationship, and I surely hope what we have now goes to something more. . . ." Then he paused.

"Me too," she told him, thinking he was leading up to a romantic proposal. She wanted to encourage him.

"Well, there's something going on that you should know about."

His tone of voice had changed and she feared this was not what she had hoped. Kidding, Susan rolled her eyes trying to make light of Charlie's tone.

"Uh-oh," she said. "Sounds serious."

"It is," Charlie went on. "To begin with, I'm not going to my brother's house tomorrow night." He then told Susan all about Marty and Al, what his previous relationship had been with Marty, and what they wanted him to do under threat of harming Katie, Tom, and Carol.

When he had finished, Susan sat quietly for a long time, staring out at the blinking Christmas lights, as she pondered what Charlie had told her. Finally, she turned to him and reached for his hand. He let her take it in hers. She kissed it and held it to her breast.

"Dear Charlie," she began, as though she were writing a letter. But the way she said "Dear" made him feel warm and relieved. "Thank you so much for sharing this with me. It tells me that you trust me, and you should."

"I do," he said in a whisper.

"It also tells me that you're not going to do this robbery. So you must have a plan."

Charlie smiled and nodded affirmatively. "I'm not one hundred percent sure, but I do have an idea."

"Good," Susan continued. "Now please tell me what it is, and how I can help."

"One reason why I wanted to tell you all this now is if it doesn't work, you'd know the whole story."

She sensed he was still somehow unsure of her.

"Oh, Charlie, Charlie," she said. "Don't you know how I feel about you?"

"Well, yeah," he answered. Now it was his turn to stare blankly through the windshield. After a few moments he blinked his eyes and shook his head as if to clear his mind. "Yes, I do know how you feel. And I had to tell you all this because I feel the same. So I didn't want you to find out later on and wind up hating me for not having been honest with you up front. So this is like . . . I had to give you a chance to break—" At that point Susan silenced Charlie by reaching across the front seat and planting a hard, passionate kiss on his lips. He responded in kind and his heart soared.

Later, when their embrace ended, he shared his plan with her.

CHAPTER 36

SO WHAT'S THE PLAN?

The next morning, Charlie came downstairs in his Santa suit and found Benjie in the kitchen making coffee.

"Mornin' there, Santa," Benjie said. "Big night tonight, huh?"

"Good morning," Charlie answered, wondering how Benjie knew about the robbery. "What do you mean by big night?"

"Christmas Eve. Flyin' around in your sleigh with all them reindeer."

"Oh yeah. I gotta remember to take my goggles. That fresh coffee I smell?"

"Oh yeah. I grind the beans myself." Benjie filled a large cup of the aromatic brown liquid for Charlie and handed it to him. "Black, right?"

Charlie took the cup and sipped it. "Ah, that's good. You'll make someone a fine husband one day."

"In your dreams. So how'd it go last night?" Charlie had told Benjie about his date after he got home from work yesterday.

"Good. I . . . uh, yeah, it was good."

"Did ya make out?"

"She's not that kind."

"Listen, pal, they're all—"

"Not this one," Charlie interrupted.

"Oh," Benjie said, smiling and raising his eyebrows. "I see. Sounds serious. And happened so quick too."

"We go back a long ways," Charlie told him.

"True love, then, huh?"

"You might say. We'll see." Charlie took another sip of his coffee. "Listen, Benj, I got to talk to you about something."

Benjie heard the serious tone in Charlie's voice. He took his coffee to the table and gestured for Charlie to join him. "Shoot. I'm all ears."

Charlie sat down. He took in a deep breath. "You know that call you got for me the other night?" Benjie nodded. "Well, here's the deal." Charlie recapped his meeting with Marty and Al. He related the plan to rob Kaplan's Jewelry Store and how he was to crack the safe. When he got to the part about Marty and Al doing harm to his family, Benjie, obviously angry, curled his fingers in a fist.

"Creeps," is all he said. "I told ya not to mess with that guy."

Charlie nodded. "They would have found me anyway."

"I guess. So what are you gonna do?"

"I'm not sure. I spoke to Lefty and Leon when they picked me up after work yesterday. They said they'd do whatever they could to help."

"So you got a plan?"

Charlie held out his right hand palm up, then turned it palm down and then palm up again. "Maybe. Sort of. . . . Lefty and Leon suggested sending Richards and Steel to the hospital. But breaking bones won't help solve the problem of my family, my niece Katie, getting hurt."

Benjie poured more coffee for both of them. He was deep in thought for a moment.

Charlie watched the wheels turning in Benjie's mind. "You got any ideas?"

"Maybe. This thing goes down tonight, right?"

"After the mall shuts down. No one's gonna be around Christmas Eve."

"Gerry Reynolds will. He's the night watchman. And he owes me. Big time. So whatever we figure out, he can help. Now, tell me again about knockin' a hole in that wall in back and the medicine cabinet. . . ."

Benjie and Charlie talked for another half hour. A plan of sorts began to take shape. It had possibilities, but depended on timing and some luck. Charlie looked up at the clock.

"Jeez, it's eight already. The guys'll be here any minute. We've got to be at the mall by eight thirty."

"You wanna spend the rest of your life behind bars, or you wanna get to work on time today?" Benjie asked testily.

"Whadda you think?"

"Okay." Benjie stared off into space and then frowned, as though he was calculating something.

"On second thought," he suddenly said, "maybe we shouldn't try to stop it."

Charlie looked at him incredulously. "What?"

"I said," Benjie repeated, "maybe we shouldn't try to stop it." Charlie shook his head.

"I don't understand," he said.

"If we stop them, no crime's been committed, right?"

"Maybe," Charlie said. "They might still be nailed for breaking and entering."

"Think a minute," Benjie said coolly. "They let you out because of overcrowding, right?" Charlie nodded. "So if this guy, Richards, gets nailed for B and E and attempted robbery—"

"It's not robbery. No 'Stick 'em up.' It's burglary."

"Okay. Attempted burglary. His lawyer, even the dumbest lawyer, could plead it down to a misdemeanor. And then where are you? And your little niece? No, we gotta somehow nail the creeps with the goodies." Benjie closed his eyes to think.

"We're getting nowhere, Benj," Charlie said, frustrated. Benjie continued to figure out something. His lips moved silently. Then his eyes opened.

"You said they were gonna break in through the back wall of the store and go in through the bathroom?" Benjie asked.

"Yes," Charlie said curtly.

"So, if they get caught in the act . . ." Benjie's voice trailed off.

"If they get caught, I get caught too," Charlie said with some agitation.

"Not necessarily."

"And how would that work?"

"I'm not one hundred percent sure yet," Benjie answered. "But I'm working on it."

"And what about my family?"

"Aw," Benjie said with a wave of his hand, "that's the oldest bluff in the world."

"What if it isn't?"

"Charlie. Think about it. This guy, Richards, gets sent away? Who's he gonna get to go after a little girl?"

"I don't know. The bartender where he hangs out is an ex-con. I can't take that chance, Benj." At that moment, they heard the church van's horn honking outside. At the same time, Benjie's eyes lit up. He banged the table with his fist and then stood up.

"What?" Charlie asked.

"I don't have it all firmed up yet, but I will by tonight. Now go ask those two guys to come in for a few minutes. I wanna be sure they can handle what I have in mind."

CHAPTER 37

CHECK AND DOUBLE-CHECK

A few minutes after nine o'clock, on Christmas Eve, most of the mall closed down. The people working there hurried home or to gatherings to celebrate. It was Thursday, and that meant a three-day weekend for most. But many stores would be open Saturday to handle the returns of gifts not wanted, or gift certificates to be used—a fast-growing Christmas tradition. In addition, many stores ran huge "after Christmas sales."

An icy wind had been blowing all day. Now it grew stronger as Charlie waited for the van. A few minutes later, Lefty, with Leon on board, picked up Charlie and his chimney. They headed for Benjie's. As they passed the entrance to the main indoor mall, they saw Benjie's friend, Gerry Reynolds, the night watchman, making his rounds.

"Hold up a sec," Charlie told Lefty. He stopped the van and Charlie got out, waving to Reynolds. The burly watchman saw Charlie and came over to the van.

"I assume you're Charlie Williams," he said. His voice was deep and gruff. "Benjie said you was a Santa."

"Guilty," Charlie said with a nod.

"That word, guilty, ain't good to hear for guys like you and me," Reynolds remarked as he looked into the van. Lefty waved to him. Leon nodded. "Those the other guys?"

"Yes."

"Okay. So I'll be there when I'm supposed to be there," Reynolds said. He bent over a little as a gust of wind howled around them.

"Some night, huh?" Charlie said.

"Yeah. It'll make it harder for anyone to hear them knockin' down that wall." He extended his large hand to Charlie. "Well, then, good luck." They shook hands.

"Thanks," Charlie said, and got back into the van.

"Big guy," Leon commented as they drove away.

"Looks like he can do his part," Lefty added as he drove out of the mall and turned toward Benjie's rooming house. "They're pickin' you up at ten thirty, right?"

"Right," Charlie answered.

"That makes you back at the mall by eleven. If they ride around to see if you put a tail on them, maybe eleven fifteen."

"Right. But I doubt they'll do that."

"Whatever. So we'll pick up Benjie by ten forty-five or so. Be sure he knows when we'll be there."

"Jeez, Lefty, he knows," Charlie said. Lefty turned to Charlie.

"Listen up, Charlie," Lefty said sternly and slowly to make his point. "I'm old school. It never hurts to check and double-check everything. Just like I'm doin' right now. You hear?"

"You're right, Lefty," Charlie said quietly.

"I figure with settin' up and drillin' and all, that wall will be down by maybe midnight."

"It's only a brick facade," Charlie replied, "so once they drill holes in the spots they marked off, they'll be able to knock it right through."

"Sounds right. So we'll be there by then, in the woods."

"I'm wearin' my long johns, and my furry Santa hat," Leon commented.

"Yeah. A bright red and white Santa hat is perfect camouflage in the woods," Lefty said sarcastically.

"Hey, man," Leon responded immediately. "It's Christmas Eve. Anyone seein' Santa would think nothin' of it!" They all had a good laugh, then drove the rest of the way in silence as each pondered the dangers of what lay ahead this cold winter's night.

"Don't forget what I told you about checkin' with Benjie," Lefty said as Charlie got out of the van. Charlie, whose nerves were more than a little frayed, answered with slight annoyance, "I heard you, Lefty. I heard you."

"Don't get ticked off. I'm tryin' to help." Charlie said nothing. "You're a good guy, Charlie. But anything goes wrong tonight, it's your neck."

Charlie nodded his agreement. "I know. You're right. Sorry. And thanks." He then walked quickly to the steps and disappeared inside.

"Whaddaya think?" Leon asked as they drove away.

"Fifty-fifty. But it's Christmas Eve, so maybe Santa will give us all a nice present."

A little before ten-thirty, after Charlie and Benjie had a light supper of franks and beans, they waited in the foyer. Benjie handed Charlie a navy blue watch cap.

"Wear it right down over your eyebrows," he told Charlie. "Maybe someone comes by, they can't ID you."

"It'll be close to midnight, Benj."

"Hey. You play all the odds in somethin' like this. Cover all the bases."

"Okay. Sure." He looked at his watch. Almost time for Marty and Al to show up. Charlie felt worry rising inside him. "You think this'll work, Benj?"

"Hey, kid. What do they say? Death and taxes is all you can count on? But do I think we got a shot with this? If I was still takin' book, I'd give ya real good odds."

Charlie knew Benjie was sincere. He took a deep breath and blew it out slowly. Gradually, the weight of worry lifted.

Not completely, but enough so that when he heard the horn from Marty's Blazer honk outside, he was able to wink at Benjie.

"See you, Benj."

"Count on it, Charlie." He gave Benjie a thumbs-up and closed the front door behind him.

CHAPTER 38

A GIRL ON A MISSION

In the Williams home, Tom and Carol stood inside Katie's room with troubled expressions. It was ten thirty and they were almost late for Christmas Eve services. The choir had to be at the church before eleven. Katie was in bed. Melissa sat on the edge.

"You're not feeling any better?" Carol asked.

"A little," Katie answered weakly.

"How bad is it, sweetie?" Tom asked.

"Not that bad, Daddy. But I really don't feel up to going out. And it's getting late."

Tom looked at his watch. "Well, okay. If we don't leave now, our esteemed choirmaster will have a cow." He looked at Carol. "Remember, the service begins with your solo." But Carol was still concerned.

"Maybe we should stay home," she said.

"It's only an upset stomach," Tom said. He looked at Katie. "Am I right, sweetie?"

"Yes, Daddy." Katie nodded. She was getting anxious that her mother and father might stay home and upset her plans. "I'll be okay, Mommy. Melissa's here. She'll take care of me."

"I'll be the nurse if she needs anything," Melissa said, almost too brightly.

"You have your cell phone here?" Tom asked.

"It's here on the night table."

"Okay," Tom said. "We'll have ours on, so if anything goes wrong, or even *seems* to go wrong, call us immediately, you understand?"

"I will, Daddy. I don't want you to be late. Mommy sings so good."

"Okay. Ready to go, Mrs. Williams?"

Carol relented. She bent over Katie and kissed her on the forehead.

"Remember," she said, "you call us if you feel any worse. Even just a little bit, you understand?"

"Yes, Mommy."

After Tom and Carol left the room, Katie and Melissa stared after them, listening. When they heard the front door close, Katie pulled off the covers. When Tom's Jeep backed out of the driveway, Katie jumped out of bed.

"I still think you're crazy," Melissa told her.

Undeterred, Katie went to her closet and took out the clothing she had prepared. "It's something I have to do, Melissa."

"Well, before you go, where's the Wii you promised me? I have to do something while you're gone."

"As soon as I'm dressed. You are an addict."

"It's fun," Melissa answered with a shrug.

A few minutes later, both girls were at the front door. Katie opened it cautiously, peering out before stepping out onto the front porch. All of a sudden, she felt her locket getting warm under her coat. She pulled it out and saw it was glowing. She went down the front steps. She saw Miranda step out of the shadows across the street.

"Are you ready, Katie dear?" Miranda asked softly.

"Yes, Great-grandma, I'm ready."

"What did you say?" Melissa asked from the porch.

Katie smiled, knowing Melissa could not see or hear Miranda.

"Nothing," she said. "Just talking to myself. Now remember, if my parents call, say I felt better and fell sound asleep." Katie started to walk away.

"Katie?" Melissa called after her. "Be careful!"

"Not to worry. I have my very own guardian angel watching over me." Katie tucked the locket back inside her coat and walked to the awaiting Miranda. It would be a long, chilly walk to the mall.

CHAPTER 39

THE CAPER GOES DOWN

It was eleven thirty when Marty finished drilling through the marks he had made in the wall and chiseling away the outline of the medicine cabinet on the other side of it.

"Let's go for it, big guy," he said. Al picked up a twelve-pound sledgehammer. The head was encased in leather to muffle the sound when it hit the wall. But the wind was still howling so loudly that both Marty and Al doubted that anyone on the other side of the building would be able to hear anything. Al's first blow was directly into the center of the outline. The hammer sank into the wall and pieces of brick and mortar fell to the ground. Glass bottles and other items inside the bathroom cabinet could be heard crashing to the floor.

Several yards behind them, in the deeply wooded area, Benjie nudged Lefty and Leon. The corners of his mouth turned down and he nodded his approval of the job Marty and Al were doing so far.

At eleven forty-five, Al delivered the last blow. The gaping hole in the wall, roughly the size of where the bathroom medicine cabinet had been, was done.

At that very moment, Katie came walking around the corner behind the row of stores where Kaplan's was, and strode up to a very surprised Marty and Al, and an absolutely stunned Charlie. But Charlie was no more stunned than Benjie, Lefty, or Leon. Lefty lifted both hands to Benjie as if to ask, "What should we do?" Benjie held up a hand indicating, "wait" as they watched Katie walk up to Charlie, Marty, and Al.

"Hi, Uncle Charlie," she said as if it were the most natural thing in the world for a twelve-year-old girl to be greeting her uncle near midnight on Christmas Eve behind a row of stores in a mall.

"Katie! Wh . . . what are you . . . ?" Charlie stammered.

"What's the kid doin' here?" Marty demanded.

"How the hell should I know?" Charlie snapped back, still stunned at the sight of Katie and now frightened for her safety. "What *are* you doing here?"

Katie turned her head slightly and pointed to her side where, unseen by everyone else, Miranda stood.

"Great-grandma Miranda told me to come," she said matter-of-factly.

Oh my God, Charlie thought. *Has this young, beautiful niece of mine become delusional?*

"Katie . . ." he started, "what's with this—" But he was interrupted by Marty's angry voice.

"Get over here, ya nosy kid."

Charlie turned to confront Marty and saw he was holding a gun in his hand.

In the woods, Lefty and Leon once again looked at Benjie, who, once again, held up his hand.

"Hey, Marty," Al said. "I thought we agreed no guns."

"And whaddya do if this brat runs away to call the cops?" He raised the gun and pointed it at Charlie. "Get over here next to me, brat, or your uncle Charlie's gonna get a bullet through his head."

Katie was momentarily frightened. But then Miranda touched her on the shoulder.

"Do not be afraid, Katie. No harm shall befall you or your uncle."

"Okay, Great-grandma," Katie said. She went next to Marty.

"You touch one hair on her head," Charlie said, his voice low and menacing, "and I'll kill you. You hear me?"

"Yeah, sure. Just do as I say and no one gets hurt."

"It's okay, Uncle Charlie," Katie said. "Great-grandma said not to worry."

"Yeah, right, kid, you tell him. Great-grandma's gonna make everything okay," Marty said with a chuckle. "Okay, Al," he continued, turning to his partner. "We've wasted enough time out here. You go in first. I'll pass the stuff in to you, then the kid, then Charlie boy goes in and then me. Got it?" Al nodded and moved quickly toward the hole in the wall.

After several minutes, once Al, Katie, Charlie, and then Marty had disappeared inside the store, Benjie, Lefty, and Leon carefully moved out of the woods and up to the hole in the wall. Benjie listened for a moment, then flicked on his flashlight and peered inside.

"Good," he said emphatically. "The bathroom door's sprung shut. And I know the door leadin' back here from the front has one on it too. So be quiet and they won't hear us when we climb in."

"When do we go in?" Lefty asked.

"Let 'em get started on the safe," Benjie told him. "Be patient. We want this crime to be more than just a break-in."

Inside, Katie sat in a corner of Ed Kaplan's office. She looked up to Miranda, who was standing next to her, and started to say something. But Miranda lifted a finger to her lips indicating for Katie to remain silent.

Marty had placed a lamp from Ed Kaplan's workbench on the floor in front of the safe and draped a black cloth over it so there was enough light to see what they were doing, but not enough to be detected by anyone passing in front of the store.

"Okay, Williams," Marty said. "Do the deal." Charlie knelt down and emptied the canvas bag Al had given him in front of the safe. He put on latex gloves. He then took his handkerchief and wiped the box clean. Al let out a short laugh. "Bein' careful, huh, Williams? No prints."

Charlie did not react. He picked up the magnetic limpet drill and locked a diamond bit into place. He then put a stethoscope around his neck.

It took five minutes to drill two holes into the safe door. Charlie inserted a tiny video camera into one of them and a long, hooklike tool into the other. Then, manipulating the tool like a surgeon, he listened with the stethoscope against the safe door. Several seconds later, he heard the safe's tumblers drop into place. He grasped the safe's handle and opened the door.

"Done like the master himself," Marty proclaimed. He and Al rushed over to the safe and looked in. It was full of jewelry, watches, and cash.

Marty chuckled. "Yeah, old Winkie Cohen would be proud of you, Williams. Now move aside. Okay, Al? You got the bags?"

"Oh, Jeez," Al said sheepishly. "I left 'em in the Blazer."

Marty spun around and let out an angry sound in his throat. "I give you one simple thing to remember and you screw it up. One lousy thing! You know what? I think that damn Scotch has pickled your brain." Marty's chest was now heaving with anger. "Well, Dumbo! Don't just stand there. Go get 'em!"

In the dim light, Charlie saw Al's face flush with anger. For a moment he thought Al was going to tear Marty apart. But Al turned quickly and stormed out of the office and through the back door that led to the bathroom. Marty watched after him.

"And make it quick, ya jerk!" he shouted.

Charlie took this opportunity to reach into his pocket and turn on the disc recorder Katie had given him for Christmas. But Marty saw this.

"Hey! What're ya goin' in there for?"

Charlie had put away the handkerchief he used to wipe off his prints in the same pocket. He pulled it out.

"To wipe my nose," he said. "DNA and all that . . ." He wiped his nose as he reminded himself to be careful what he said since everything was now being recorded. "So, is this heist like the jewelry store you knocked off in Hillsdale, Marty?" he asked. "The one you framed me for?"

"Nah, that was easier," Marty replied. "A small safe. We just had to break in, grab it, and take off. We were outta there before the cops or anyone showed up."

Charlie noticed that Marty didn't admit that he had framed him.

"So why'd you frame me? I was just a kid."

"You forget what had happened a few months before that, kid?"

"You mean the fight?"

"You broke my nose and knocked out a tooth." Marty bared his teeth to show a gold tooth.

"Nice tooth. But you started it."

Marty smiled broadly. "Yeah. And I sure finished it, huh? Framin' you as the driver on that job and sendin' you to juvie hall for three and a half was worth every shot you gave me."

"How many other guys have you framed, Richards?"

"Just you, Charlie boy. And be glad we're not gonna frame you for this one too."

"What about my niece?"

"You mean puttin' a hurt on her and her family if you didn't cooperate?"

"That's exactly what I mean."

"Too bad." Marty snapped his fingers. "That's life, sucker."

Satisfied with what he recorded, Charlie stuffed his handkerchief back into his pocket.

Benjie, Lefty, and Leon waited outside the hole in the wall. They heard Al enter the bathroom and start to crawl out the hole. They flattened themselves against the bricks. When Al was halfway out, he saw them, but it was too late to go back in. He was about to shout to Marty, but Lefty grabbed him, put his hand over Al's mouth, and pulled him out. Flailing, Al threw a punch. Lefty ducked and responded with a thundering left hook that knocked Al out cold.

"That's why they call him 'Lefty,' " Leon said to Benjie.

"He's not left-handed?" Benjie asked. Leon shook his head. "It's 'cause he can knock out anyone with that left. Anyone."

"Let's wrap this guy up," Lefty said. "Who's got the tape?"

"Right here," Leon answered.

Marty paced back and forth in Ed Kaplan's office. Charlie and Katie exchanged glances. Katie smiled. Charlie was amazed at how calm his niece was. Miranda watched them both and smiled to herself.

"Where the hell is that moron?" Marty said aloud. Frustrated, he went to the back door and pushed it open. "Hey! Al! Where the hell are you?"

In the bathroom, Benjie, Lefty, and Leon froze in silence. A still-groggy Al stood with them, his mouth taped shut and his arms taped behind him. Benjie motioned for him not to make a sound.

Marty, getting no response, turned and went back to Charlie. "All right, Williams," he said, pointing his gun at the sledgehammer, "while we're waitin' for the idiot to come back, pick up the sledgehammer." Charlie picked it up. Marty then pointed his gun at the display cases in the front of the store. "Start smashin' open them cases. Put the trays on top. Start with the ones that got the most gold."

Charlie stepped out of the office and went to the front of the store.

"Get up, Katie," Miranda told Katie, "and take out your locket." Katie followed her instructions. Her movement caused Marty to look at her. He spotted the locket.

"Oh my," he said. "Speakin' of gold, what do we got here? C'mere, kid." Katie went over to Marty. "Let's have a look at that."

"No, it's mine!" Katie said. "My great-grandma says it is only for me."

"Leave her alone, Richards!" Charlie called out.

"I ain't gonna hurt her. I just wanna see what Great-grandma gave her." Marty grabbed the locket and tried to snatch it from Katie's neck. But as soon as he did, it glowed red hot and sent a tremendous shock through his body. He cried out in pain and fell to the floor. The gun fell out of his hand, slid across the floor, and stopped at the back door. Marty scrambled to his feet to go after it, but before he could, Charlie had him by the arm. He spun Marty around and hit him with a right cross that was filled with all his pent-up anger. The blow sent Marty crashing into the back door, where he collapsed to the floor.

The back door flew open and Benjie, followed by Lefty and Leon holding Al, stepped into the store. They saw Marty lying on the floor unconscious.

"Looks like we missed all the fun, champ," Benjie said, grinning at Charlie.

When Marty came to and realized that Leon was in the process of securing his wrists with duct tape, he tried to struggle. Leon grabbed him by the neck and lowered his face until it was inches from Marty's.

"You want me to drop that sledgehammer on your stupid head?" he asked. Marty slumped, frustrated, as Leon finished taping his hands.

"We knew everything would turn out all right, Uncle Charlie," Katie said.

Charlie looked at her quizzically. "We?"

"Great-grandma Miranda and me." She touched the locket around her neck. "And this gift from the Magi."

Charlie took a deep breath and smiled his acceptance. "Whatever you say, sweetheart. We couldn't have done this without you."

"Done what?" Marty asked with a smirk. "You're involved in this whole thing too, Mr. two-time loser."

"Sez you," Charlie said, smiling.

"That's right," Marty answered. "Sez me. You were with me when we broke down the wall. You opened the safe."

"There's only one thing wrong with that, Richards."

"Like what?"

"Like, I was never here. And neither were any of these gentlemen. Or my niece. Right, Katie?"

Benjie, Lefty, and Leon spread their hands and shrugged, indicating they had no idea what Marty was talking about.

"We were at Saint Francis putting away the Santa stuff," Lefty said, putting his arm around Leon.

"I was watchin' Midnight Mass from Saint Patrick's in New York," Benjie said. "In high-def," he added, grinning.

"And I was home with a stomachache," Katie announced proudly.

"In about an hour," Charlie continued, "this guy, Gerry Reynolds, the night watchman? He's gonna come by in back on his rounds and see the hole in the wall. He's gonna call the cops. So this felony gets added on to your other one and, then," Charlie said as he took out the disc recorder, "I give the cops this. A recording I made before where you admit to framing me for the jewelry store heist in Hillsdale. And that was with a gun, so it's armed." Then Charlie played the recording for Marty. "How did that sound, Mr. three-time loser?" Saying those words made Charlie feel elated.

"Is that what you think?" Marty sneered.

"Sounds like three strikes and you're gone for good!"

"Well I got news for you, genius. It ain't gonna fly."

"How's that?"

"Because when you play that little thing for the cops, it'll prove you was here with me!"

"But, Marty. Marty, baby," Charlie said, smiling broadly. "I didn't record it here," he lied.

"You say. Where the hell did you record it?"

"In P.J.'s Pub! The night you, me, and Al had our little sit-down. Vinnie, the bartender, will remember I was there. He showed me his barbed wire tat."

"But, wise guy, Al was there too. He knows what we said." Everyone looked at Al, who was taking all this in. Benjie gently pulled the tape off his mouth.

"Hey, Al?" Charlie asked. "You want to be an accessory to armed robbery? Plus conspiring to kidnap a little girl? Or you wanna walk out of here and disappear?"

"Don't listen to him, Al!" Marty commanded. There was a tone of worry in his voice.

"I don't want no part of this guy anymore," Al said, seeing his way to get back at all the abuse Marty had heaped on him. "I'm no 'Dumbo'!"

"Shut up!" Marty yelled.

But Al was on a roll. "And I didn't know he was packin' a gun. I told him I didn't want no part of hurtin' any kid or her family."

"Idiot!" Marty lunged to kick Al, but Benjie stuck out his foot and tripped him. He fell facedown on the floor.

"Me an idiot?" Al gave out a contemptuous laugh. "Me? Hey! Who's gonna go away for life and who's walkin' outta here?"

Marty got to his feet. He swung his gaze back to Charlie and sneered. "So, this moron wasn't here. You wasn't here. The kid wasn't here. These guys wasn't here. So I broke into this place all by myself, broke open the safe, and then tied myself all up with this tape. Is that what you're sayin'? What a joke!"

"No joke, creep. Sort of yes and no." Charlie spoke to Marty as if he were a child. "Yes, Marty, you were all alone. Yes, Marty, you broke into here all by yourself. And yes, Marty, you cracked the safe. But no, Marty, you didn't tie yourself up with that tape. What happened is before Gerry the watchman called the cops, he caught you red-handed. Gerry's a real big guy—"

"Professional wrestler," Benjie interjected.

"There you go," Charlie continued. "Do I have to draw you a picture? You, Marty Richards, who couldn't take me, an eighteen-year-old kid, versus a three-hundred-pound professional wrestler. Case closed!"

"Good old Gerry," Benjie added. "The Meat Grinder, they used to call him."

"Yeah," Lefty said with a chuckle. "He was my favorite. I loved his propeller body slam."

Marty's eyes now darted about like a trapped animal's. "I'll get you for this, Williams. I'll get all of you! You hear me? All of you!"

Lefty caught Leon's eye and made a motion with his head.

Leon ripped off a piece of duct tape and, as Marty ranted on, clapped the tape over his mouth. Lefty then scooped Marty up, as if he were a sack of flour, and carried him into Ed Kaplan's work area. He dropped him next to the open safe.

"Might as well grab a nap, genius," he said. "It's gonna be a long, cold night." He began taping Marty's ankles.

"Let's get this show on the road," Benjie said. "It's nearly twelve thirty. Midnight services will be over soon and there'll be people in the streets." He took Al by the arm and led him out the back door. Lefty and Leon followed. Charlie took Katie by the hand.

"Just a sec, Uncle Charlie." She turned to Miranda, who was standing at the end of Ed Kaplan's workbench. "Thank you soooo much for everything," she said.

"A great pleasure, my child. You were wonderful. And so brave. A very Merry Christmas, sweetheart. I will always be with you."

With that, Katie felt a soft and loving kiss on her forehead as Miranda's image disappeared.

"We can go now, Uncle Charlie," Katie said brightly.

"Great-grandma Miranda, right?" he asked.

"Of course," Katie answered. They moved away from Ed Kaplan's work area and left, closing the back door behind them.

When they were all through the hole in the wall, Gerry Reynolds appeared. Benjie greeted him. The watchman was a head taller than and half again as wide as Benjie.

"Give it about ten, fifteen minutes," Benjie told Gerry. "That'll give us all enough time to be far away from here."

"No problem. Like I told ya, Benj, I know this punk Richards. I was not happy to have to work on Christmas Eve, but this makes it all okay. I know I owe ya."

"You owe me nothin'. Merry Christmas." Then they all

heard the door of a car open and shut. Everyone froze. A moment later, Susan appeared behind the stores.

"What's this about?" a stunned Charlie said as Susan came running toward them. Benjie, Lefty, and Leon exchanged quizzical looks. Gerry frowned with worry. He knew Susan worked at Kaplan's. He was about to intercept her.

"Charlie! Charlie!" Susan called out. "Are you all right?"

"I'm fine," Charlie replied, going to her. "What are you doing here?"

"Well, when you told me what they were forcing you to do I just . . . I had to be sure that, well . . ." Her voice trailed off.

"Charlie," Benjie said with a grin, "the lady cares about you. We all do. But before anyone else shows up, I suggest we all blow this joint. This caper is toast."

"Right," Charlie said, grinning. "And thanks, guys. I mean, what can I say?"

"It worked out fine," Benjie answered. "Say good-bye."

"It was a pleasure, bro," Leon said.

"A great pleasure," Lefty added. He turned to Al. "That your Blazer out front?"

"Yeah."

"Then get into it and disappear. If we ever see you around here again . . ."

"I'm history, man," Al said with a wave as he headed for the Blazer. "And thanks," he called back over his shoulder.

"Merry Christmas, everybody," Benjie said. "And especially to you, young lady," he added, touching Katie gently on her head and smiling.

Lefty and Leon added their Merry Christmases and went back through the woods with Benjie.

"I parked just around in front," Susan said. As Charlie, Susan, and Katie walked away from behind the stores, Charlie turned back once to see Gerry Reynolds struggling to get through the hole in the wall. He wondered if the big guy could make it. When his legs and shoes disappeared into the bathroom, Charlie smiled to himself. The caper was really over.

A minute later, as they were about to get into Susan's car, Katie put out her hand to Susan. "Hi!" she said with a big smile. "I'm Katie Williams."

CHAPTER 40

MERRY CHRISTMAS

It was twelve forty-six when Susan drove into the Williamses' driveway. Tom's Jeep wasn't in the driveway.

"We're okay," Katie said, relieved. "They're not home yet."

"That's good. Back upstairs and into bed," Charlie told her. "And good night."

"What do you mean, 'Good night'?" Katie asked. "Aren't you coming in?"

"What will your mom and dad think when they come home and see us?"

"Uh, hold on a sec," Katie said. "Let me think. . . ."

"I don't want this night to be . . . I mean, there's no need for them to know . . . It's our secret, right?"

"Forever, Uncle Charlie." Her eyes lit up. "Got it!" Katie exclaimed. "Here's the story. Susan and you went out after you both finished work and you called to wish us a Merry Christmas. When you found out I wasn't feeling good and they were in church, you decided to come over and cheer me up. I mean, it is Christmas Eve, and you didn't want me to be alone."

"You've got a great imagination, young lady," Susan said.

"Imagination *plus!*" Charlie said.

"Well, I think that story will fly, Charlie," Susan said. "And I'd like to meet your family."

"Okay. Okay," he said reluctantly. "We go in. When are they coming home?"

"Around now, I guess," Katie answered.

"Well then, let's move!" Charlie exclaimed. They got out of Susan's car and made it to the front door just as a wide-eyed Melissa opened it.

"There you are!" she said, obviously relieved. "Are you all right?" Then she looked at Charlie and Susan and wondered what they were doing there. Before she could ask, Katie went past her, followed quickly by Susan and Charlie.

"I'm fine. We're all fine. Everything's perfect. Just close the door. Quickly."

Melissa obeyed, but was still confused. "So what's going on, Katie? Where were you?"

Katie ignored the question while she took off her coat. "I was having an adventure, Melissa. You met my uncle Charlie. And this is his friend, Susan. Susan, this is my very best friend, Melissa." Just as Susan and Melissa finished exchanging greetings, they heard the sound of Tom's Jeep coming into the driveway. Katie hugged Melissa and spoke to her rapidly.

"They're here. Here's the story, Melissa. Susan and Charlie called and you told them I was sick so they came over to see how I was and keep me company. Got it?"

"I suppose," Melissa said. Katie hugged her.

"You're the best friend!" They all turned as they heard Carol and Tom walking up the porch stairs.

"I don't know whose car that is," Tom was saying.

"Quick! Everybody into the living room," Katie said.

They no sooner got there than they heard the key in the front door and it opened.

"Katie? Melissa?" Tom called out.

"In here, Daddy," Katie said. Tom and Carol walked into the living room. When they saw Katie dressed and Susan and Charlie standing there, they were both surprised.

"Charlie? What are you doing here? And, Katie. You're up. And dressed."

"I feel much better, Daddy. I got up and dressed when Uncle Charlie and his friend Susan dropped in. Uncle Charlie called to wish us Merry Christmas and when he found out I wasn't feeling so good, he decided to come by and cheer me up."

Susan, who was sitting in an easy chair, rose and extended her hand. "Hi, Mr. and Mrs. Williams. I'm Susan Cole. Charlie's friend."

Tom and Carol, who had been silent and a little suspicious of the whole setup, shook Susan's hand.

"Nice to meet you," Carol offered.

"You look familiar," Tom said.

"I worked part-time in Kaplan's when you had your hardware store. I'm there full-time now."

"That's where we met again," Charlie said. "Well, actually out in front. You wouldn't remember, but we went to school together."

"I see. That's, uh, that's nice," Tom said.

"Anyway, we were just leaving—" Charlie announced.

"No, wait," Tom said. "Listen, sit down, sit down."

"It's late, Tom. We don't want to disturb you. I just wanted to see that Katie was all right."

"You're not disturbing us," Carol insisted. "Please. I'll make some coffee."

Charlie held up his hand, and shook his head. "No, really. Susan and I, uh, we have a party to go to and, well"—he took Susan's hand—"I'll see you guys for dinner tomorrow." Carol was disappointed, but then she noticed how Charlie was holding Susan's hand and rubbing it with his thumb. *He likes this young woman,* she thought, *and she likes him.* It made her feel happy for Charlie.

"Let me ask you," Charlie suddenly said. "Would it be okay if I bring Susan with me tomorrow?"

"Absolutely," Carol answered immediately. "Dinner's at four, so come early."

"Thank you," Susan said. "Sounds great." Charlie took Susan's arm. They started to leave, but Charlie stopped.

"Hey," he said, "Merry Christmas."

"Merry Christmas," everyone responded.

"And, since it's Christmas Day now and you already gave me my gift, Katie," he said as he reached into his coat pocket and pulled out the little gift package that Susan had wrapped so nicely in the store, "let me give this to you now." He handed her the package.

"What is it? Uncle Charlie?" Katie said as she took it.

"You'll have to open it to see, won't you?" Before Katie undid the wrapping, she read the card taped to the top of the box aloud.

"Merry Christmas to my one and only beautiful and special niece. Love, your uncle Charlie." Katie beamed and repeated, "Your uncle Charlie. Sounds wonderful, doesn't it? Thank you, Uncle Charlie!"

"You are most welcome." And then Katie opened the box and took out the earrings.

"Oh, they're sooo beautiful. Look, Mommy. Pearls." Then she hesitated. "Uh-oh. They're for pierced ears. I don't have pierced ears, Uncle Charlie."

"I can do that for you at the store," Susan said. "It'd be my Christmas gift to you. That is, if your parents say it's all right."

"Oh, Mommy. Daddy. Can I? Can she? Please? Melissa has hers pierced, right, Melissa?" Melissa, who had been quiet all this time, afraid Katie's parents might ask her how the night went, just nodded and grinned.

"Yes, darling," Carol said. "Whoever heard of a girl with a Gypsy great-grandmother who didn't have pierced ears?"

"What Gypsy great-grandmother?" Charlie asked.

"Why, Miranda, of course," Katie answered. She instinctively lifted her hand to touch her locket. And, as she did, her lips formed a smile exactly like that of young Miranda in that faded photograph from far away and long ago.

If you enjoyed A CHRISTMAS GIFT,
don't miss these two other holiday novels,
written by David Saperstein and George Samerjan.
Turn the page for a special taste of

A CHRISTMAS VISITOR and
A CHRISTMAS PASSAGE,

both available from Kensington.

CHAPTER 1

IN MEMORIAM

Each year brought a different perspective. As with changing seasons, the passage of time revealed different hues of color, from bright to muted to bright again, reflecting the loss he carried deep inside. The emptiness seemed not to diminish, nor ease, though thirteen years had passed.

The cold, threatening November day had kept people indoors. As the crisp autumn night rapidly descended, the Town Square was deserted. George Boyajian stood motionless on the narrow, gray stone sidewalk that led to the town's War Memorial. His six foot, sixty-year-old frame was erect; shoulders square—the physique of a man twenty years younger. George's full head of brown hair gave no hint of age, though some gray flecks had begun to appear at his temples. Under his weathered leather jacket, and fleece-lined gloves, were powerful, sinewy arms and hands—the result of a life's work in the building trades. He was a master carpenter.

George Boyajian had, for the past thirteen years, observed a private ritual on the night before the somber public assembly took place at the memorial. He moved forward down the walkway toward the five polished native granite columns, which formed a circle of honor. Each column was fronted with a brass plaque. His heart pounded. A chill ran down his spine as he heard the rattle of the rope tapping against the lit hollow flagpole, and the crack of the American flag snapping briskly in the breeze above. It caused him to gaze up at the stars and stripes, illuminated against a brilliantly starry sky.

The sound and image transcended time, stringing his memories of this place together like dark pearls in an endless necklace. He did not feel the chill wind. The acuity of his vision was almost surreal. He could see every broken blade of grass along the path, every stone, and every patch of earth—all fitting together in a sentient mosaic.

George stopped again. It was 1966 and he was standing at attention in his fatigues in Vietnam at a jungle base camp as the chaplain read the names of that week's fallen. In that faraway, long-ago place, he might well have been one of the names announced . . . names recorded on lists of wars—wars begun millennia ago with rosters of the dead in the millions. And still there was no end to them in sight.

His memory and reflection was but a momentary diversion. He walked on, wanting to be strong for John's sake. It was the reason why George Boyajian would come to this place the night before the annual ceremony—to inoculate himself against any public display of hurt and loss, his private emotions locked away while he performed his public duty.

"Oh dear God," George whispered inside himself. "My dear God . . ." Gathering courage, and remembering his pledge to honor John, he reverently walked into the circle of the five stone columns.

The names of deceased servicemen from New Chatham were displayed on the columns' brass plaques. The Great War, the one they said was to end all wars, contained eight names; World War Two listed twenty soldiers, sailors, and marines who had fallen; five men had been killed in the Korean Conflict—a "police action" they called it; the Vietnam War plaque listed twelve men who had made the supreme sacrifice in South Vietnam, Laos, and Cambodia. George shook his head in somber

lisbelief at the number of souls his small town had offered
o America. He paused briefly before the Vietnam plaque. It
isted the names of his schoolmates and friends who had died
n Vietnam. He knew them all. It still amazed George, after
nearly four decades, that his name was not engraved there. He
vas here, living and breathing. Yet part of him had been left
behind, forever entwined in the souls of those who fell beside him.

The last plaque, memorializing the first Iraq War, contained
only one name, his son, John Boyajian. He removed a small
plastic baggie from his pocket. In it was a cloth he had partly
dipped in Brasso. He gently rubbed the brass letters of John's
name with the caustic fluid and then wiped it dry with the
rest of the cloth.

"There you are, son. All spit and polish." George knelt.
First with his eyes, then his heart, and finally his hand, he
reached out across a lifetime. With a tender touch, more an
embrace, his finger found the name, John's name, shining in
moonlight that gave the brass a blue patina. He stared at the
raised characters, and then through them, seeking to catch a
glimpse of John on the other side. He closed his eyes and remembered a place nearby. The New Chatham train station . . .

John, a strapping twenty-five-year-old, stood before him, tall
and slender, exuding the easy, wiry, physical presence of youth
and the deep inner confidence of a man who knew who he
was and where he was going. John had completed his train-
ing and was a proud member of the elite 5th Special Forces
Group. He wore his Class-A uniform. Black spit-polished boots
were bloused in the distinctive custom of the Airborne. His
Green Beret proudly displayed the Special Forces insignia.

Clutching John's right arm tightly was Elizabeth Meyers,
Lizzie, his girlfriend since junior high. Her sandy blond hair,
tossed by a gentle breeze, fell across John's shoulder as she
rested her head there. John squeezed Elizabeth's hand and

kissed her softly on her forehead. It was a hard moment for them, but there were things George needed to say.

"So remember . . . stay in the middle. Never volunteer for nothing . . . and don't let 'em get to know your name too easy," he told his son.

"Yes, Dad," John said, laughing. "That's the same thing you told me when I enlisted, and it's the second time you told me that this morning."

George smiled and nodded. "A senior moment, huh?"

"Hey . . . you made it back from Vietnam okay. I'll make it too. Six months in the Gulf, and I'll be home. Piece of cake." John looked down the platform toward the parking lot. "I wish they would have come."

George felt impotent, unable to change events. He glanced around nervously. A scattering of men in business suits stood waiting for the train. Another day at the office for them.

"They love you, son. You know that."

"Yeah."

"Your mother's scared to death. You're her baby, you know. First born. It's how women . . . how mothers get." George glanced at Lizzie. She smiled shyly. "Just look at you, son. You're a man, now." George smiled. "A warrior."

John laughed, and slapped his father on the shoulder.

"Yeah. I know. Just like you were. Lean, mean, and almost bulletproof."

A woman with a young boy at her side approached them. The child tugged at his mother's sleeve and pointed.

"Look Mommy. A soldier!" The boy threw a child's salute at John, who smiled and returned the salute. The mother pulled her son away.

George saw John glance away again toward the parking lot, hoping that his mother and sister might magically appear. But they didn't.

"Nothin's going to happen to me, Dad. I'll . . ." The sudden wail of a train whistle turned their attention away. Up the racks a bright headlight signaled the approaching train. The wooden platform trembled slightly beneath their feet. John pulled Elizabeth close to him. The moment George dreaded was here. The three of them stood frozen as the train pulled in, and with a final creak and bang, it stopped to gather the travelers. Sensing the moment, Elizabeth disengaged and George stepped forward to embrace his son. Around them, the other passengers hurriedly boarded the train. For them it was just a little trip into the city. They would return later that evening. For John it was the start of a journey into an unknown fraught with danger.

"I love you, Dad," John whispered as his father held him close, closer than he ever had in his life. George tried to speak, but no words formed. His throat was dry. John pulled away gently and smiled. George nodded and placed his hand on his son's cheek, then stepped back to allow the few moments left to be between John and Elizabeth. Tears welled up in Elizabeth's eyes and spilled out. Her body trembled. Wisps of her hair matted on her wet cheeks. John gently stroked the hair away and kissed her. He tasted her tears on the softness of her lips and inhaled the scent of her love. Embracing Elizabeth tightly, he kissed her neck and whispered, "I'll be back. Let's surprise everyone at Christmas and get married."

Elizabeth looked into his eyes. "You really mean that?" She felt lifted and thrilled.

"Yes." His voice was hoarse. He swallowed hard.

"Oh, John, I love you. I don't want you to go. I'm afraid and . . ."

"I'll be fine . . . And home for Christmas." He kissed her quickly, hard on the mouth, then picked up his duffel bag and hefted it onto his shoulder. Smartly, he turned away and walked toward the train. Once aboard he looked back and waved one last time. Moments later, as the train disappeared down the track, George and Elizabeth were alone on the platform.

"God love you, son," George whispered as he placed his

arm around Elizabeth. She got weak in the knees and sagged
a bit. George held her close while she wept. She did not see
or feel his tears as they melted into her golden hair.

The vision faded. George Boyajian was at the monument, his
finger still pressed against the name he loved, but his expression was now serene.

Behind George, three grungy, drunken teenagers sauntered
into the park toward him. They wore black engineer boots
with dog chains strung around them, loose fitting blue jeans,
and overly large, heavy plaid shirts. Two sported baseball caps
cocked sideways. Their moonlit shadows moved along the
deserted walkway, spilling onto George's as they stopped close
by him. The leader of the motley group smeared his finger on
the Vietnam War plaque.

"Hey man, where's Rambo? Like Rambo's gotta be here,
man." He chuckled at the wittiness of his remark. The others
laughed with him.

A sudden hot rush of anger made George shake his head
rapidly to clear away this rude intrusion into his privacy. He
strained to ignore the young barbarians; to recapture the seren-
ity of the emotional moment they had interrupted. A second
teenager did an insulting mimic of "Taps."

"For God's sake," George said with precise pronunciation
of each word, "This is a cathedral! Have respect!"

The leader looked at George with a cynical smile. He
glanced at his cohorts for support. "You got a problem, old
dude?" He chuckled. "Yo, man—We just looking for Rambo.
With all these here dead mothers . . . Hey, gotta be Rambo
too. Ain't that right, old dude?"

Rising to his feet, George eyed the leader and then the
others. He figured he could take down one big mouth before
the others got him. If that was the price of protecting John's
sanctity, he was ready to pay it.

"If you can't show respect, please leave."

"Yo, man . . . You're the one who needs to show respect," another boy said, opening his shirt and revealing the butt of a 9mm Glock automatic pistol.

"School the old dude, Frankie," said the leader.

"Yeah. Show him who we are, man," the third kid chimed in. They moved threateningly closer to George.

"Hey there old man," the leader said with a wide grin, "It's showtime!" They closed in slowly, like a pack of hyenas on the savannah, cornering what they thought to be an easy victim. George quickly glanced over his shoulder at John's name, as if to gather strength or perhaps to say good-bye. He saw the shadows of himself and his tormentors on the brass and granite. As he turned back to the confrontation, the indistinct shadows of two more men appeared from behind. A clear, deep voice cut through the tension.

"Is there a problem here?"

"Something we might help with?" the second man asked. George kept his eyes on the gang leader, now assuming that whatever the punks tried to do the strangers behind him would help. The expression on the gang leader's face changed as he looked beyond George. The young man's eyes grew wide and afraid, unable to comprehend. His bravado was gone as a great danger was suddenly staring him in the face. A cold blast of wind blew his arrogantly placed baseball cap off his head. It pushed him backward. He shuddered. His skin, a moment before flushed red with heated blood and arrogance yearning for action, had now turned a deathly gray.

"No. Uh . . . No man. No problem." George watched in confusion. The leader was responding to something the stranger had said, but George had heard no words.

"Yes, sir," a different gang member said, hearing another voice that escaped George's detection. Respectfully, the frightened kid bowed his head.

"No problem, sir," the leader said again, his voice now thin and fearful. "We uh . . . we didn't mean . . . What?" A flash of pain twisted his face in anguish, yet George didn't see anyone touch him. "No, man. We . . . we're sorry." The leader backed away. "Like really sorry, man . . ." He then turned and ran. The others quickly followed.

George turned to thank the strangers. But they were gone. He looked all around the memorial park, then up and down the Town Square. But not a soul was in sight.

"I'll be damned," he muttered as he returned to John's plaque. "If that doesn't beat all." He knelt again. "Listen Johnny . . . I'm gonna talk to your mother and sister. Get them to come. To understand . . ." He felt a chill though no breeze had blown. "Oh God! Yes. I know you can see me, son." He touched John's name again, this time with the palm of his right hand. "You're here, aren't you . . . just on the other side. You know they didn't come to say good-bye at the station. But here . . . maybe . . . Maybe I can get them to understand. It's time. Maybe tomorrow."

CHAPTER 2

VETERANS DAY

George stood in the warm kitchen with his back to his wife and daughter. The aroma of pancakes on the griddle blended with brewing coffee and the tang of freshly squeezed oranges. His gaze was fixed on the rolling fields between the old farm-house and the distant foothills. He was rehearsing his lines as though he were an actor in an impossible play, about to step on stage to face an unwelcoming audience. Yet he had no choice but to perform. After the events of last night at the monument George felt he was driven by a force he could not resist. He was a strong-willed man but now something compelled him to act.

He sipped from his gray ceramic coffee mug, then turned his gaze away from the outdoors, over his shoulder, to his daughter, his "baby," Jennifer. But Jenny was grown up. She was now in her late twenties—grown, married, divorced, and a single parent. A woman. Where had the years gone? She had George's brown hair, but not his blue eyes. Hers were duplicates of her mother's—brown, warm, bottomless pools that drew you into her soul. Jenny sat slumped at the oak butcher-block kitchen table that George had built five years ago when they'd remodeled. Nicks, scars, and stubborn stains on the table bore witness to the kitchen being the center of life in their home—a locus of all good, bad, joyful, and tragic events that had befallen the Boyajian family. It all seemed to have centered around this sturdy, serviceable table in the kitchen.

Jenny cradled her coffee mug between her delicate hands as if it were an offering to some deity and she the supplicant seeking an answer to her prayer. She wore a loose fitting pale blue sweater and jeans. Her pretty features bore the same troubled and distracted look George had observed for months. But it had become more pronounced over the course of the last few days. George's wife, Carol, a stunning woman in her early sixties, sat next to Jenny.

George had fallen in love with Carol the first time he had seen her, and though heated passion had abated over the years, there was no diminishing of his deep and total love for her.

Carol sat pensively with her left hand on Jenny's. She sensed George's mood. Thirty-five years of marriage will do that. Her eyes narrowed. Her head tilted slightly to the right.

George read the suspicion on her face; she knew him too well, and all of his moods and methods.

"Listen, guys," he began, "I uh . . . Last night I had this experience. I can't explain it exactly, but it was, well, something." Jenny now looked at him too. Daughter and mother—a pair of skeptical bookends. "What I want . . . I mean what I'd like is for you two to come to town with me today . . . to—"

"Don't start, George," Carol curtly interrupted. "We settled all that long ago. Jenny's home to be with us. We're not going to the ceremony. And that's that!"

"But if you'll just . . ." he said stubbornly.

"For God's sake, George!" Carol grasped Jenny's hand.

"Don't you think we have enough to deal with without your raking up more pain?"

George moved to the table and took their clasped hands in his. "Jenny? Honey? Please. It's been so many years. Too many. It's time we . . ."

"No," Carol said as she pulled her hand away. "It was like yesterday. It will always be yesterday for us." She extricated Jenny's hand from his and stood up.

"Please . . ." he begged.

Carol shook her head slightly and looked away. She was making an effort to control her emotions. She took a deep breath and looked at her husband.

"You're the one who let him go. He's a man, you said. He wants to serve his country, you said. You're the one who took him, in his uniform, to the American Legion Hall. You—the proud father! I don't need to see his name on that cold plaque. I buried my son next to your parents. His name is on the family stone. That's more than enough for me."

"No dear . . . It's not about that."

"What else is there but names?" she said sarcastically. "Lots of names. Others we knew and grew up with. Will seeing them bring them back to us? What is the point in going there again, and again, and again?"

George knew that when Carol dug her heels in like this, nothing could move her. His only hope to get them to town was Jennifer.

"Please, Jenny. Please trust me on this."

"Maybe I should go," Jennifer said bitterly. "After all, it may be my last chance before I'm in the ground next to Johnny."

"No! No . . ." George quickly said. "That's not what I meant, sweetheart."

"We have a living child here who needs us," Carol announced, wanting no more of this talk. "Jenny has to concentrate on only one thing—getting better."

"Well, damn it, I'm going. I haven't missed a year since . . ." George plucked his brown tweed sports coat from its peg on the nearby pine coatrack, thrusting his arms through the sleeves. He paused before the mirror above the coatrack and adjusted his collar. He stared at the reflection of the Combat Infantryman's Badge in his lapel. He looked at Jennifer one more time, asking with his eyes for her to go with him. She turned her head away. Carol's gaze stayed locked on him, showing neither anger nor compassion.

George left, shutting the kitchen door gently behind him. He took a deep breath and exhaled. The pleasant scents of the farmhouse kitchen melted into a mist in the cold morning air. He inhaled the scent of nearby pines. He walked toward his pickup, passing the door to his workshop in the barn. Down the path past the barn, the barren brown fields spread and stopped at the low, tree covered, rolling hills. He approached his old but reliable Chevy pickup. Heavy white clouds moved slowly across a brilliant blue sky with a swiftness that evoked something familiar and ingrained in his memory. These days his mental wanderings seemed to come with more and more clarity when emotionally intense events occurred in his life. George watched the clouds and drifted with them, back in time.

A raw recruit in Vietnam—he and two fellow squad members took on nicknames and wrote them, with a black magic marker, on their helmets. George became "Tracker," one buddy became "Death Dealer," and the third, "Silent Death." As green as their fresh, dark fatigues, they modeled themselves after the older guys—the nineteen- and twenty-year-old enlisted combat veterans and their twenty-three-year-old captains. Tracker would come home. Alive. The other two, both with the word "death" in their nicknames, would not.

George climbed into the truck and started the engine. He drove up the gentle slope to the country road that led to State Road 16, and town. The two lane blacktop took him past his neighbors' farms—working family farms, a rare and fast disappearing enterprise. Stone walls, dating back to the American Revolution, lined both sides of the narrow road. He drove past the wide, single story, brown aluminum barn where the monthly farm animal auctions were held. The rusted and faded HELP WANTED sign swayed slowly in the wind. It seemed like the sign had beckoned forever, but George had never met anyone who had been hired there. Farther down the road the John Deere dealership displayed the newest tractors, threshers, reapers, and trailers, all bright green with the distinctive yellow John Deere logo on their sides. Beyond the dealership, down a hill into a pocket valley, a spring-fed pond where George used to catch stocked rainbow trout now hosted a flight of Canadian geese who had stopped to rest on their annual trip south. They paddled across the pond, darting their graceful necks below the surface to snap up what little nourishment remained before winter set in.

George passed an abandoned farmhouse set back behind long dormant fields now occupied with shoulder-high weeds. Its once white clapboards were stained with rusty, long, pale brown threads that seemed to be tears shed by the abandoned structure. All of the windows were broken, no doubt shot out by local kids with BB guns. George wondered about the fate of families who had once lived there. He imagined birthdays and Thanksgiving dinners. Were names of any of their kin engraved on the town's memorial? And what memories, sad or gay, might be contained, echoing within the walls of those now barren rooms? Did ghosts haunt the old house, peeking out when no one was looking? Did apparitions gather once again to celebrate special occasions? Or was the house merely an abandoned shell? In time, boards would rot around rusted nails and the structure would collapse. Eventually there would be no physical sign that a family, that a history, had ever happened on that piece of earth.

These days George did not farm anymore. The local construction business, which had been a sometimes thing, had suddenly boomed since that fateful day of September 11, 2001. Growing numbers of people with money were moving upstate from New York City, seeking a rural haven should the unthinkable happen again. The population had increased dramatically with scores of building permits still being filed every week at the county seat. George and the other tradesmen in the region were busy full-time, remodeling and rebuilding old estates and doing finishing work on new ones. George's specialty was the reproduction of eighteenth-century American carpentry, using many tools from that era. The word spread quickly that George was a reliable, consummate craftsman. His talent was in great demand. Everyone wanted to make new things look old.

Nearing the town of New Chatham, he passed the Hess Oil distribution depot with its massive white storage tank. Then the Chevy dealership came into sight with its display of new pickups and SUVs out front. A quarter mile down the road, on his right, he passed the county fairgrounds where once a year the toothless folks from the hill country and the khaki clad weekenders from the big city, sporting fashionable logos on their colorful polo shirts, mingled in an odd ballet of country-meets-city. Beer drinkers were banished to a tent surrounded by police. Three-hundred-pound hungry fried-dough eaters, dressed in bib overalls and work boots, stood in long lines for tasty hot treats.

Beyond the fairgrounds, George could now see the brick smokestack of the ancient, long abandoned shoe factory. At the start of the twentieth century, New Chatham had been a center of milling, leather tanning, and a bustling shoemaking industry. It had hosted a mixed population of nearly twenty thousand Italian, German, Polish, and Scandinavian immigrants eager for jobs and a better life. But by mid-century, the mills, tannery, and factory had moved south and west. New Chatham settled back into its core industry: dairy.

Now that, too, was passing into history. The real estate boom brought many of the locals work, but it would only last as long as there was land to build on or places to refurbish. It had a finite future. Some people, like George Boyajian, had rediscovered many of the old-time crafts and trades. Others had become landscapers, contracting as the lawn mowers, gardeners, and groundskeepers of new estates fashioned from former farms. George knew that some of the locals resented the inconsiderate ways of the city people—taking two parking spaces, cutting ahead in lines, talking loud and fast, and openly disdaining what they called "provincial customs."

"Call them what you will," he'd tell his friends, "there's more money and work floatin' around here than we've ever had before. So don't look a gift horse in the mouth or he might just bite you." And, to George, there was another benefit. Wilderness was returning to the region as the new, larger landholders posted and patrolled their properties. To the chagrin of some of the locals, mostly seasoned poachers, the newcomers forbade illegal hunting and fishing. But the result was a resurgence of wild turkeys, bear, and a rumored mountain lion or two. George liked that. He liked to hike in the woods behind his farm fields after a light rain, or early snow, and look for game tracks. He'd taken John in those woods as a child, and had taught him how to hunt and shoot. But now that seemed a hundred years ago.

George drove into town from the north. He passed the small playground with jungle gyms and slides, the new swimming pool, the old boot factory now converted into loft apartments, and finally rows of clapboard houses that lined the road leading to the old iron bridge that spanned the diminutive Chatham River. Two thick, dark stone columns, built in the late nineteenth century, stood at the entrance to the bridge—mute sentinels to the passage of time. He drove over the bridge. The roadway was pitted in a state of disrepair. He glanced downstream and marveled at the progress being made on the new bridge, a steel-and-granite structure, soon to be completed. Then this bridge would be removed, its iron sold as scrap, or so the town fathers promised.

He slowly drove down Main Street. Cars were parked bumper to bumper, filling all the available spots. Small shops faced each other on both sides of the street. An upscale gourmet market now stood where the old Grand Union had closed. Next to it was a mini-mall with a well-stocked liquor store, a Coach outlet, an Old Navy store, and a Baskin-Robbins. On the other side of the street was the New Chatham Public House, one of the few remnants of times past. Next door was a Chinese/Sushi restaurant, and on the other side a new, upscale furniture store. Other than the pub, there were only two of the original stores left on Main Street—Carmine's Barbershop, its red and white striped pole standing out front and spinning, announcing there was still a refuge for men seeking merely a haircut and not a hairstyling experience; and Williamson's Hardware, with a green and white canvas awning that shaded its rippled plate glass display window.

Ahead, George could see some familiar faces—townspeople gathering around the war memorial where he had been last night. Every year the same people gathered for the ceremony, though the ranks of the World War Two and Korea veterans were noticeably thinning. George parked in the lot of the railroad station. As he always did, George peered down the platform where he and Elizabeth had said good-bye to John. Sometimes in his daydreams George imagined that he could see John once more, but this time he stopped his son from getting on that train. But then, no matter how hard he tried to manipulate the outcome, the dreams would end with John on the train, disappearing into the distant horizon.

George walked to the small War Memorial park. His blue and silver Combat Infantryman's Badge, pinned on the lapel of his sports coat, glinted in the bright sunlight. The five granite pillars and their brass plaques seemed less dramatic in the cold light of day. The New Chatham police had blocked off Main Street.

Nearly one hundred townspeople were at the monument. Some of the older citizens, men and women, wore ribbons and military decorations on their chests. Younger onlookers stood in silence, awed or curious about the ceremony. Many held small American flags. The town's American Legion color guard stood at attention. The flag bearer was a middle-aged man with an ample paunch overhanging his wide, white dress belt. His pale face was flushed red while a breeze made a wisp of his thinning hair dance on his forehead, the rest held down by his overseas cap. His flagstaff swayed, pulled by gusts. On either side of him stood men with WWII vintage M1 rifles held at right-shoulder arms. They, too, wore the same wide, white dress belts over their aging military uniforms. They nodded toward George as he approached.

The American flag, on its pole, flapped in the wind, its ropes causing the same rattling sound George had heard last night. From his position George could see the Thanksgiving displays in the stores. Soon they would be replaced by Christmas decorations, wreaths, lights, and bunting. George walked slowly and deliberately to a spot within a few yards of the memorial. He exchanged nods with a few more friendly faces and listened to the low hum of conversation as all waited for the ceremony to begin.

Mayor Andy Lockwood, dressed in a navy blue suit, white shirt, and a blue and red tie—an imposing rotund man, with broad shoulders and a thick neck—shuffled papers in his hands and appeared to count the number of voters assembling, no doubt identifying the loyal Republicans who always voted for him. He surely also noted the Democrats and Independents who rarely gave him their support. George imagined him making a mental reminder to talk to each one of them anyway before they departed from the ceremony. He'd also seek out the influx of outsiders who might become voters, never overlooking an opportunity to expand his loyal base.

Mary Simpson, a short, weathered, red-haired woman in her early seventies, outfitted in bright green slacks, a red jacket, and a white wool scarf walked up behind George.

"Morning, George," Mary said softly, startling him out of his reverie.

"Oh! It's you, Mary. Not nice creeping up on a fellow that way." He smiled. "Good morning . . . How are you?"

"Just fine," she chuckled, "for an old creaky battle-ax, that is. How's Carol?"

"Fine, thanks."

Mary glanced around furtively. "And Jenny?" she asked, her voice lowered.

"She's okay."

"But how is she doing, George?" Mary asked softly.

"She's doing just fine, Mare. She's staying with us for a while. We took her up to Albany . . . to the medical center. They've got a good program up there. Did a needle biopsy. We're waiting for the results."

"Carol mentioned it. They do such wonders today, now don't they?"

"Yes . . . I guess they do." George's jaw clenched.

Mary took his hand. "You know, I remember when you had Jennifer. All those years after Johnny. Why, Carol had given up all hope of conceiving again, and those doctors told her to forget it. Ha! And then, out of the blue, there was Jenny! 'Our beautiful little miracle,' you called her." Mary leaned closer. Her voice was hushed. Private. "This illness, if it is . . . you know . . . Well, there's just so much they can do now. So much more hope. And new things every day."

"You're right. And thanks." He genuinely meant it.

"If there's anything I can do . . . Anything . . . You just ask. You hear me, George Boyajian?"

"I do, Mary. I surely do."

She reached up and kissed him on the cheek. "This town might be getting big, but the folks who count love you and your family. We'll never get so big that we don't take care of our own. You hear?"

"I know." George glanced toward John's name on the nearby plaque. "You know, Mare, I was talking to Johnny last night."

Mary nodded and smiled. "What did he say?"

"He said," George whispered in a conspiratorial tone, "that he thinks we ought to have Christmas this year."

"Oh George! That's wonderful. Whatever I can do, let me know. I bake today. Maybe I'll bring you over something sweet for the holidays." She then handed him a single red rose. "Seems this has become a ritual. Now you take care."

George watched her walk away. Mary Simpson, like so many friends in New Chatham, was an extension of his family. He sniffed the fragrant flower. The sun glinted off the brass tablets, as though the names inscribed there were shouting for attention. The bronze letters seemed like so many tiny doors that were open to allow the light from the other side to shine through. He felt a hand on his shoulder.

"George," said Tom Jennings, extending his hand and shaking George's vigorously. Tom was nearly six feet six inches tall and slender as an old illustration of Ichabod Crane. His face was just as angular. Jennings's gray postal service uniform was starched and pleated in a military fashion. "Carol and Jenny not here?"

"They just can't do it, Tom. I tried, Lord knows, but it's still too much for them. Maybe next year . . ."

"Sure. See you later." As Tom walked away Larry Williamson, confined to a wheelchair, rolled into view. Larry wore a jungle fatigue hat and a fatigue jacket with staff sergeant's stripes on the sleeves and his Combat Infantryman's Badge. He had served in Vietnam with George where his encounter with a Soviet-made antipersonnel mine had left him a paraplegic.

"Larry," George said, stepping toward the hardware store proprietor. He patted his old friend on the shoulder.

"Alone?" Larry asked.

As George nodded, Larry looked over at the plaque bearing John Boyajian's name. "You know I . . ." Larry was interrupted by the New Chatham High School Band as they struck up "God Bless America."

Silently, George stood at attention, his arms to his sides, his legs together. The music, and the sharp crisp red and white stripes and silver stars on a field of deep blue that fluttered above them once again brought to the fore the realization of how their lives had forever been changed by their war, and for George, John's war as well. Two soldiers, one standing, one irreparably crippled, experienced a common, silent, personal memory. The band finished and Mayor Lockwood stepped out in front of the silent granite pillars.

"Residents of New Chatham and visitors, we welcome you to this observance of Veterans Day—a day of homage and respect for all who have served . . ." He droned on in politician talk until he turned toward the five plaques behind him. "The names of our families, friends, and neighbors here enshrined—generations of our town's young men and women defending America, bearing witness to the terrible price freedom demands. We honor the men and women whose names are forever inscribed on these plaques, and their families who have endured such a great loss, and those who today serve and wait."

The Mayor stepped forward and placed a wreath at the base of the World War One pillar. Lonnie Sanderson, a World War Two veteran, with help from a friend supporting him, bowed, and placed a flowered wreath under the plaque bearing the names of the World War Two dead. Marjorie Blackman, the widow of Terry Blackman, who was killed in 1952 at the Yalu River, when the Chinese Communist Army entered that war, followed with a wreath under the name of her husband, and his lost comrades. Then, Larry Williamson wheeled forward and placed a bouquet of flowers under the Vietnam plaque. Finally, George Boyajian stepped forward with the single rose that Mary Simpson had given him for the Gulf War plaque. He touched the only name—John Boyajian. George said a silent prayer, saluted, and stepped back among his comrades—a tight circle of honor and an unspoken bond among the combat veterans present.

"Let us all observe a moment of silence," the Mayor coninued, "to honor all of our veterans among us and especially those whose names are here . . . engraved in brass on stone, and forever in our hearts." The tinny sounds of the lanyard tapping against the hollow aluminum pole, and the large American flag, snapping in the breeze above, traveled through the town center. For a long moment, the townspeople present bowed and prayed silently as one. Then Judy Carmichael, a pretty sixteen-year-old with a zest for life and world-conquering dreams, the lead trumpet player in the high school band, stepped forward. She lifted her shiny, silver trumpet to her lips and played a mournful and heartfelt "Taps." George and Larry shivered at that simple melody they had heard so many times before.

"Ladies and gentlemen, that concludes this year's remembrance of our veterans," Mayor Lockwood announced. "Thank you for attending." He moved off to have words with the voters as the crowd broke up by twos and threes. People strolled back to their cars, or to the nearby stores that were open for Veterans Day sales.

"Hey, George!" the Mayor called out. George and Larry were leaving the park, but turned to him. "Wait up." They waited as Lockwood joined them. "George, I want to do right by you, and by John."

"What is it, Andy?" George asked.

"We uh . . . the thing of it is . . . well, we might need more room."

George could see Lockwood was uncomfortable.

"Room?" George asked.

"We've got kids—soldiers—from town, and the county, in the 554th MP Reserve Unit. They're called up—heading for Iraq. And there's the two Henson boys with the 10th Mountain Division plus Lonnie Fredericks's son with the Rangers. They're in Afghanistan . . ."

"So you might have to add another plaque."

"Christ, I hope not, but the town council wants to be prepared. I mean we're not expecting anything but . . ."

"Yeah . . . but," George said, looking back at John's plaque.

Andy Lockwood put his arm on George's shoulder. "At first we thought, if it came to it, we'd put one plaque for Afghanistan and one for Iraq. But then we decided on one plaque. I mean they're sending our kids all over the world now . . . this terrorism business. Preemptive."

"It's all blending into one," George muttered.

"The world's cops," Larry added. "Our kids . . . For what?"

Andy Lockwood was a staunch Republican, but as Tip O'Neil, the once Speaker of the House of Representatives, used to say, "All politics are local . . ." Lockwood avoided confrontation with his hometown people whenever possible.

"We thought we'd add plaques, if we have to, in the space under John's . . . if that's all right with you."

"You don't have to ask me, Andy," George said. "I don't own the space on that monument."

"No," Lockwood quickly replied, "but John does, which is why we want your blessing."

"Do what you need to do, Andy. God help us all if we start adding more names to that monument."

"I pray we don't. How's Carol and Jenny?"

"Fine. Just fine." The Mayor hustled off to press some flesh. George glanced over at John's plaque one more time. It looked lonely. "I guess if it has to be, John could use some company." Larry nodded and wheeled his chair toward Main Street. "Just a sec, Lar," George told his friend. He trotted over to Mayor Lockwood, chatted with him for a minute, and then returned.

"What was that all about?" Larry stared into George's eyes, one brother in arms to another.

"I told him . . . well sort of volunteered that if . . . or when . . ." He looked away from Larry for a moment, past Main Street, far, as if he could see the forbidding mountains of Afghanistan and the endless desert sands surrounding the Tigris and Euphrates Rivers. "If the news comes to another family in town he should call me. Maybe I can . . . you know . . ."

"Maybe we both can, pal."

An hour later George drove down the gravel driveway to the one story ranch house that was the local veterans' organization headquarters. Small pebbles bounced up against the undercarriage of the truck like hail. Off to the right was a field occupied by rows of picnic tables and brick barbecue pits. To his left, the ground sloped down to a pond stocked with fat rainbow trout where the vets' group held its annual fishing derby for the kids. An oversized stuffed figure of Santa Claus was propped up against the headquarters' flag pole. Next to it was a hand-painted sign that read "Annual Xmas Toy Drive." A long dining room where they held ceremonial dinners and events occupied the front half of the building, while the back half was fitted out with a bar that ran the length of the back wall. Behind it was a large picture window that overlooked the pond.

"How the hell are you!" shouted Robbie Crippens, red faced and portly, as he mopped the bar with a rag. "Get you a cold one?"

"Too early for me, Robbie. How about a Pepsi?"

"You got it." Robbie reached behind into a cooler and extracted a frosty can, popped it open and handed it to George along with a tall, ice-filled glass. "Red, white, and blue can. The right drink for today."

"Thanks." George poured the dark liquid and lifted it to no one in particular. "To absent friends."

"Hear, hear." Half a dozen veterans at the far end of the bar responded. George knew them all. Another group of older men were wrapping toys in gaily colored paper. He smiled at the contrast—the veterans taking time and what little spare money they had to help the less fortunate, and the professional veterans; the would-be and wannabe heroes whose lives were changed forever by war. It didn't matter, George thought. They all paid the price of admission.

"Hey George," Seth Williams said as he approached. Seth was average height and sported a paunch. He limped. He and George had been bounced around together in Vietnam, and the punishment on Seth's body now claimed his senior years—arthritic knees and cervical and lumbar discs compressed to where any activity was painful. Seth joined him. They shook hands.

"Ain't seen you in a while, George."

"I've been real busy."

Seth eased onto a stool. "Hey Robbie, let me have a coffee, will you?" Robbie nodded.

"That time of year, again, George."

"Yeah. They come faster now, don't they?"

"And they don't get easier . . . I mean your Johnny."

"No. Never will." Seth accepted a coffee mug from Robbie. "Thanks, Robbie." He took a long sip while staring through the glass window at the pond beyond.

"Sometimes it seems just like yesterday, huh? Or like maybe it's all going to happen again tomorrow. I guess we had some times, George."

"I'll drink to that." They clinked drinks. "And to the strange ones like those psy-ops spooks?" George said.

"Yeah, I remember them. Two Harvard Ph.D.s with the military intelligence insignia. No rank."

"And that interpreter of theirs," George added. "The spooky lookin' dude with one eye that sort of snaggled off into space."

"That was a real plan to end the war, huh?"

"Damn near ended us," George mused, triggering a vivid memory of fighting alongside Seth.

*   *   *

The downwash from the Huey's rotor pummeled their chests, causing their jungle fatigues to flap wildly as if in a storm. Vibrations caused the bird to shudder in syncopation with pounding hearts. His legs, dangling over the edge of the Huey were washed in sunlight, his upper torso hidden in shadow. The wind flattened the dry ginger ale brown rice stalks below.

Shoveling himself off the Huey, George fell to the ground with his knees bent in a modified parachute landing fall. A twisted ankle in this clearing would make him a slow moving target. He wouldn't hear the report of an AK-47, but anticipated the sledgehammer blow to his shoulder, or the splinter of the bones of his skull above the bridge of his nose.

From the corner of his eye he saw Seth sprinting toward the dark wall of jungle a hundred yards away. George inhaled deep gulps of one-hundred-and-twenty-degree air; his lungs burning as if he were running the Wannamaker Mile. The straps of his eighty-pound pack cut into his shoulders as he counted the strides between him and the tree line glancing rapidly from right to left and back to his front to see if anyone fell. With two yards to go he leapt, passing from the brilliant yellow sunlight of the abandoned, dried up rice paddy to the cooler jungle darkness.

Slumping in a heap, George curled up behind a tree, his rifle thrust forward. Hot, salty sweat burned his eyes, soaked his clothes, and attracted flying and crawling insects—an incredible variety. The company of South Vietnamese irregulars he and Seth were with organized itself and took off toward the mountains to the east. A few men in front of George, Captain Daiuy Van led the way.

George was comfortable with Daiuy Van. He'd been fighting this war for twenty years; back to fighting the Viet Minh. It was amusing that the U.S. Army made George advisor to Daiuy Van. There wasn't anything about infantry small unit tactics that George could teach Daiuy. What George and Seth did bring, however, was the power of their radio that could summon rotary winged carriers of rockets and miniguns. They could cause the sky to rattle as one-hundred-and-five-millimeter projos rent the air and tore into the jungle. They could cause speeding silver shapes to appear in the sky, and ugly yellow clouds burning black to fill the jungle with gagging fumes and burning corpses. They could summon slow moving olive drab birds piloted by the bravest men in the war, with large red crosses painted across white backgrounds.

It was dusk as George and Seth sat with Daiuy Van.

"Ba xi de," Daiuy Van said, nodding to George and then to the dark hills surrounding the small valley. "Many Vee Cee tonight."

George accepted the old warrior's canteen and took a sip of the pungent fish juice and kerosene-tasting liquid. In the gathering darkness the first Harvard Ph.D., late of the U.S. Army Military Intelligence School, Fort Devens, Massachusetts, tapped George on the shoulder. He spun, plucking his .45 from its holster, thumbed back the hammer and thrust the weapon squarely into the abdomen of the terrified psychological warrior. The man turned a ghostly white. George lowered the pistol.

"Don't come up behind us. Got it?"

"Got it, sergeant," said the spook, regaining his breath. "How deep should my foxhole be?"

"Well," said Seth, "that is a matter of discretion. Personally, I like to get mine down to the water table."

"Okay. What I needed to know." The young doctor trotted off to inform his compatriot.

"Down to the water table?" George, Daiuy Van, and Seth had a good laugh.

While Daiuy Van's company, the Mot Mot Ba, the "One One Three," formed a three-hundred-and-sixty-degree perimeter, the sound of an entrenching tool chopping into the jungle soil hovered over the gathering. The spooks were digging.

Later they set up a loudspeaker and had their interpreter

rapid fire a string of Vietnamese words echoing up the walls of the valley. George listened carefully; making out a few words he could understand. "Surrender. Hectare. Rice." Good luck, thought George, hunkering down.

It didn't take long for all hell to break loose as a shower of rocket propelled grenades answered the psy-ops announcement. A cry of pain called out nearby, but none of the rockets reached them. George and Seth crawled over and felt the earth give way to a void before them—the cavernous yap of the foxhole. Low groans of pain came from the bottom. Plucking the red filtered flashlight from his web gear, George turned it on.

Before him, six feet below the surface of the ground lay the second Ph.D. spook. Across the foxhole was what was left of the man's hammock where he had strung it several feet below the surface. In the dim red light, George could see the unnatural angle of the man's leg and knew with a certainty that it was broken.

"Probably get a medal for that stunt," Seth said. No attack came that night, though George, Seth, and Daiuy Van remained alert until sunrise. George figured that the stupidity of the effort was what probably had saved their lives—any unit dumb enough to expect a loudspeaker to get the NVA to surrender probably wasn't worth the ammunition to destroy. They never did see the psy-ops guys again, and were left alone in their little corner of the war.

"To Ph.D.s," said Seth, raising his coffee cup. "Sure knew how to screw up a war."

"Yeah," said George, "and to the horses they rode in on." The television over the bar was showing an Iraqi road. Plumes of black smoke came from a Humvee.

"Turn that thing off," Seth said angrily. "That's the 101st for God's sake. Our old unit—out there like sitting ducks. Damned politicians ought to be there instead."

George patted Seth on his shoulder. "I got to get going, pal."

"Happy Thanksgiving, George."

"Yeah . . . you too."

From *A Christmas Passage*

CHAPTER 1

MARTA

Normally quiet Fulton County/Brown Field, servicing corporate and private aircraft and a few commuter airlines, was crowded with holiday travelers this Christmas Eve morning. The modern drudgery of air travel—overbooked flights, time-consuming security checks, delays, cancellations, and general rudeness—was held to a minimum at this small facility. But this morning, with snow falling and a heavy influx of hurried, tired, infrequent travelers, civility was discarded as unceremoniously as last year's gift wrapping. The terminal was hot, damp, loud, and odiferous. At the entrance to the one row of kiosks and stores, a banner proclaimed—LAST STOP FOR YOUR CHRISTMAS SHOPPING. Marta Hood wore a pastel yellow sweatshirt and form-fitting Levis over her plump thirty-five-year-old body. Her boots, a pair of well-worn Uggs, were still wet from the accumulating snow outside. The heat in the terminal caused her to carry her ski parka as she ushered her children—Ronny, age eight, and Nancy, age eleven, toward the gate area. Marta stopped in front of the TV monitor that served as a departure board for the airfield. She was nervous. She hated flying. With one eye on her children and one eye on the unsympathetic monitor, she searched for her flight number and gate. The title of an old movie echoed in her mind, *Quo Vadis?* "Where are you going?" She vanquished the thought and zeroed in to find the listing she needed: Blue Ridge Flight #6224 to Asheville—Gate 6.

What the hell are we doing? she wondered, as she had so often during the past weeks.

Carlisle Lane had its Christmas traditions, some that began months before the holiday season. Knute Lincoln, a retired engineer from an aerospace company, and a man with entirely too much energy to be retired, decorated his house, a red and white clapboard saltbox reproduction, with Christmas decorations after Columbus Day. Disapproving looks and anonymous notes from his neighbors had forced Knute's pre-pre-Christmas activity back to Halloween. But that was not acceptable, either. Finally, for the sake of neighborly peace, he acquiesced and pushed his luminous exhibition back to the more traditional time—the day after Thanksgiving. But the unforeseen consequence had been that Knute expanded his glittering exhibit to a much more elaborate display. His house became a beacon, an explosion of light and color that lit up the entire street all night long. He made the installation and maintenance of his extreme holiday show a full-time job. Word of the "radiant display on Carlisle" spread, and so, from November twenty-seventh until well into January, hundreds of cars slowly made their way to Carlisle Lane for what many described as a cheerful and uplifting observance.

The journey took them past Claudia's gray Cape Cod, sorely in need of paint, but with a fresh Christmas wreath hung on her door by her son-in-law; then past the colonial of Pieter, an expatriate from Holland who in a feat defying gravity had hung Christmas lights from atop a tall ladder with a leaf rake, projecting wires and lights thirty feet above his shingled roof like a giant, incandescent teepee. Next was Steve and Stephanie's house, also a colonial, where a big menorah, strategically placed in the large picture window, tastefully signaled it was also the season of Hanukkah. Finally they arrived at Knute Lincoln's Victorian and his storied display. There they stopped for a long moment as though they had arrived at an important shrine. Aware of the traffic behind, people lingered only a minute at most.

Next door to Knute Lincoln's electrified showplace stood Marta Hood's house, a contemporary knockoff of a classic Dutch colonial. But this year there were no candles in the windows, door wreaths, or the old-fashioned sleigh pulled by four life-size reindeer with a jolly smiling and waving Santa in tow. This year passersby on the lane, out for a stroll in the chill December air, saw no warm green, red, and yellow lights gaily festooned on the Hood Christmas tree in the large front bay window. The house was unadorned. The dismal mood of it, especially compared to the rest of the lane, was striking. Inside the house, Marta's children had their holiday, and lives, dampened with anxiety. Childish anticipation of gifts beneath the tree had given way to fear of the unknown that lay ahead. Their parents were divorcing. Bitterly. The children felt helpless and afraid.

Ronny, a precocious third-grader with a knack for annoying his teachers by reading ahead in the curriculum, had been oblivious to the problems at home. Then one night, in a bedroom cluttered with war toys, tanks, aircraft, and thousands of plastic soldiers, while reading under his blankets by the light of a flashlight, Ronny heard loud and angry voices coming from the dining room.

"Mortgage . . . credit cards . . . empty bed . . . affair . . . frigid . . . let yourself go . . . overweight . . ." None of these words made sense to him as they floated up from below and through his bedroom door, but the hostile tone of the voices frightened him. He bravely crept to the top of the stairs and listened. His mother then made a sound he had not heard from her before. She was crying. There was no doubt. The instinct to help her rose in his young body with a rush of adrenaline.

But fear of his father's size and short temper kept Ronny from descending the stairs. As his father's voice grew angrier, his mother's sobbing grew quieter. Then there was silence. Suddenly Marta raised her voice with a vehemence that Ronny had never heard before.

"Get out!" Marta screamed. "Get out of my life!"

Ronny clenched his fists as an abiding hatred for his father grew in his heart. He gathered his courage and stood to go downstairs. The touch of his sister's hand on his shoulder stopped him.

"No," she said softly. "Stay here. There is nothing we can do."

"What's going on?" he asked, as tears welled up in his dark brown eyes.

"We're getting a divorce," Nancy said.

"You're insane," their father said in the room below. "If I leave, I'm not coming back," he threatened. Marta then unleashed a diatribe that both children would never forget. It would be the stuff of nightmares for years to come.

"All those years!" Marta shouted. "All those years you criticized me about everything . . . the checkbook, the house, how I drove your precious car . . . even the laundry and dry cleaners. I couldn't get your French-cuffed shirts done the right way. I didn't dress to please you. I wasn't a good lover. I was inadequate. You remember that? Inadequate, you called me, like I was subhuman or retarded. You almost convinced me I was worthless. Almost. Not coming back, you say? Thank God, I say. Go to your girlfriend and abuse *her*. Get out of our lives! Get out! Get out! Get out!" Marta screamed those words over and over until Nancy and Ronny heard the door slam. Then they heard their mother sobbing. They hurried downstairs and found her on her knees in the foyer. The children embraced her and joined their tears with hers. It was three days before Christmas.

* * *

The next morning Marta hurled the gaily wrapped Christmas gifts, one after another, out of the front door. Silver wrapping and bright ribbons glittered brightly in the sunlight. The packages fluttered like wounded ducks shot from the sky. They were aimed at her husband, who had returned. He dodged the last package, but in doing so slipped and fell backward onto the wet lawn. He lay there, looking up at Marta as she stood with her hands on her hips, forbidding him entry and access to Ronny and Nancy, who stood behind her.

Knute Lincoln and his wife, Laurie, had come out to see what was going on. A few other neighbors had also gathered.

"Damn it, Marta! Have you lost your mind?" Robert, six feet, five inches tall, with well-coiffed blond hair, stood up and brushed some mud from his tweed overcoat. Breathless from dodging the gifts, he glanced at the gathering neighbors and decided not to press for entry. The words "Hell hath no fury as a woman scorned" rolled around in his thoughts. And he knew his neighbors, with whom he had purposely little contact, would bear witness against him if he got physical.

"That's it!" shouted Marta. "Go away!" She wore a pale blue silk blouse with the collar turned up, and pleated navy blue slacks. Wisps of hair fell over her eyes, and she brushed them back with her right hand, like a prize fighter clearing sweat from his eyes before launching the next set of punches. "You have any problems, you can tell it to the judge. I called Harold Buckman this morning and told him to file for divorce. Adultery!" she yelled loudly for all to hear. "Adultery with your so-called assistant."

"I just want to give the kids their presents," Robert said plaintively. He took a timid step forward. His body language, the step forward, and an incipient smile on his thin lips angered Marta. But she felt empowered.

"You think that dumb smile, raised eyebrows, and syrupy charm works? Ha! Presents? You gave them their present last night. They heard everything. No!" she said emphatically. "Get lost!" Marta felt a surge of strength course through her body.

She knew he was no longer in control of her life, and though the prospect of being a single mom was daunting, she found the thrill of her ability to confront him addictive.

"Are you saying you won't let me see the kids?"

"You got that right." Marta stepped outside, closing the door behind her. She walked forcefully to where Robert stood, stopping inches from him. She was in his face; eyes wide, teeth clenched. "Your relationship with the children will be decided in court. Harold will contact you the day after Christmas with the details. We'll be in Asheville for the holidays. Don't try to contact us there. You know you really don't want to deal with my father." She turned her back on him. Then, over her shoulder, she shouted back, "January fourth. Noon in Harold's office. Get ready to pay for your adultery, big time!"

Marta let a few tears fall as she walked back to the house, but she wouldn't let Robert see them. Slamming the front door behind her, she leaned against it with her arms across her chest. The wide foyer was dimly lit. A long, narrow table with an antique mirror stood against the wall. Memorabilia of a marriage, residue of incomplete events, was still in place. Framed photographs of birthdays, vacations, once cherished souvenirs like a gray pottery jug with the words *Current Realities* imprinted on it. . . . Marta glanced at the mini-gallery of her married life and sat down on the second carpeted step of the staircase that led upstairs to the bedrooms. She cradled her face in her hands.

Ronny, with tousled hair and his plaid shirt buttoned one hole off, sat next to her. Nancy sat on the other side. Marta wiped the tears from her eyes, and reached out to them.

"Are we ever going to see Daddy again?" Nancy asked.

"Yes," Marta said, embracing both of her children. "Of course you will. But there will be rules about it."

"Does he love us?" Ronny asked.

"Yes, dear. He's your father. He'll always be your father." She took a deep breath and stood up. "Okay, guys. Now we've got to pack. Grandma and Grandpa are excited that we're coming. We'll have a wonderful Christmas there."

"But, Mommy?" Ronny asked. "If Christmas is going to be wonderful, why were you crying?" Marta forced herself to smile. She hugged Ronny tightly.

"Someday, young man, you'll understand that people cry sometimes when they're happy."

"And you're happy now, Mommy?" Nancy asked. Marta embraced her children with even more ardor.

"Yes. Very."

"But you threw our presents at Daddy," Ronny said.

"This is Christmas, and there will be presents," Marta told them. "This year we're having a real Christmas."

CHAPTER 2

ANDY

Marta, her kids in tow, pressed through the crowded terminal toward the gate area. Outside, she observed that jumbo flakes of snow were blanketing the tarmac. De-icing equipment had rolled out adjacent to aircraft getting ready to depart. As they walked past the crowded airport bar, Marta glanced inside. Smokers sat in their special section, veiled in a cloud of nicotine-filled air, enjoying their cigarettes. Fools, she mused, paying for overly expensive drinks in return for refuge from the dictates of the smokeless world. Sucking death into their lungs. Strangers brought together by a fatal, addictive habit, pausing momentarily on their journey home for Christmas. Marta shook her head to clear a wisp of melancholy. Christmas and divorce. *No*, she thought, *I will not let him ruin one more day of my life*. Ronny tugged at her sleeve, anxious to get on the plane.

Nancy watched a pretty young woman at the bar take a long, deep drag on her cigarette while the man in the expensive suit talked rapidly to her. But the young woman seemed disinterested in what he was saying. Her gaze wandered away and caught Nancy watching. The woman smiled and winked. As Nancy smiled back, Marta gathered her children up and moved away with a bounce in her step. Okay, single-mom-to-be, a new year! A new life! She guided the children briskly toward the gate.

Inside the crowded bar, in the no-smoking section, Anselmo Casiano nursed his second Rolling Rock. He had not had one of those in nearly thirty-eight years. Andy, as he preferred to be called, smiled to the notice of no one around him as he reminisced—a beer run to Xuan Loc. *Now why did I go there?* he wondered. Andy was lately aware of how often, since Maria died, he reflected on the past. They were married a few months after he returned from his second tour in Vietnam. Thirty-five years. So many plans for retirement. Gone. Ovarian cancer took her in six months. And now he was on his way to see his old army buddy George Spillers in Asheville, North Carolina. George was dying too. Leukemia. Agent Orange, George suspected. But the docs at the V.A. wouldn't admit that was the cause.

Andy's thoughts drifted back to the Rolling Rock. The images flooded in, blotting out the snowy landscape outside. A tropical sun baked the flatlands beneath the hills of III Corps. Their jeep's floor was layered with stuffed, pale gray sandbags. A fifty-caliber machine gun was locked and loaded, on its mount, welded to the floor behind the driver's seat. Wild-ass Captain José Morales, a West Pointer on his third tour, drove. Andy and George held on in the back as they sped at sixty miles an hour down the dirt road. A rooster tail of dust rose behind them. *God*, Andy recalled, *Charlie could have seen us coming from miles away*. It had been a beautiful day. Three young, stupid, and self-proclaimed immortals on a beer run to Xuan Loc because the word had come over the radio that Rolling Rock was going for a buck-fifty a case. All the way there Andy's heart had pounded wildly, yet now, in the anonymity of the airport bar, he recalled loving every minute of the adventure. The madness of indestructible warriors.

Andy sipped his beer and smiled, shaking his head. No one around him noticed. His thoughts again drifted to that day and their arrival at Xuan Loc. There was that stupid, young MP corporal facing Captain Morales down.

"Roll down your sleeves and get into proper uniform, sir," he announced moments after they had parked. His sleeves? Andy smiled, vividly recalling Morales was wearing black pajamas with infantry crossed rifles on one collar, and his captain's railroad tracks on the other. A black patent-leather gun belt was slung around his waist. There was a notch in it for each firefight he'd been through. Ho Chi Minh sandals adorned his bare feet. The "sleeves" were the least of his military-dress violations. The captain's jungle hat bearing rust stains from grenade pins around the band would have given a more experienced MP a clue as to the person he was dealing with.

All Morales said as he turned to those still in the jeep was, "Did you hear that, guys?" Spillers clutched his M16 while Andy leaned on the fifty. The captain's hand was on the butt of the .45 dangling loosely in his belt. The two MPs standing behind the young corporal suddenly paled, realizing they were in danger of replaying something akin to the *OK Corral* scenario. The men in the jeep were on a serious mission. There was beer at stake: dirt-cheap cases of Rolling Rock. Thankfully, good old steady George Spillers kept a cool head. He dismounted and stepped between the jeep and the MPs.

"We just drove twenty nasty clicks for some beer. We're not here for a dress parade, Corporal." Spillers was a staff sergeant, speaking to a corporal. "My captain and buck sergeant are thirsty, is all." He nodded toward the captain and Andy. Whether it was Spillers's reasonable tone, or what the MPs saw in Andy and the captain's eyes, or the fact that in their line of work, these guys were already dead, the MPs relented. A compromise was struck: thirty minutes to load up and get out of Dodge.

* * *

Lazily, Andy's nail peeled the damp label off the Rolling Rock bottle. He would remember the beer-run story in more detail and reminisce tonight with George Spillers in Asheville. He never did tell Maria about it. He never talked much to her, or anyone else, about those otherworldly, bloody days. That past would be recalled fondly with George. But it would always be overshadowed with the pain and emptiness of losing Maria.

Andy checked his watch, then took one last swipe into the plastic, finger-stained bowl of goldfish crackers, munched them down and knocked down his beer. It was time to head for the gate. He glanced at the snow piling up outside and wondered how long the flight delay might be. No matter. He had time. Nothing but time. He paid his tab, slipped off the stool, grabbed his carry-on bag, and exited the bar.

Out on the concourse, Andy nodded at a pretty, young female soldier, dressed in desert fatigues and tan boots, as she approached and passed close to him. The sight of her, and his daydream at the bar, gave Andy an image of himself nearly four decades ago passing through the Nome, Alaska, airport on his way to Saigon. But here he noticed that civilians smiled and nodded warmly to the soldier. In his day, Andy saw mostly contempt when walking through airports. He paused, contemplating catching up to her to say . . . Say what? He could not find words to connect the young soldier's present and his past. He sighed and continued on toward the gate.

CHAPTER 3

ILENA

Specialist Ilena Burton thought about the eye contact she had made with the older man on the concourse. She was used to stares and found some comfort in the nods and smiles she often received. But he had a different look about him as though he somehow understood the fear and pain of loss that dwelt beneath her copper-toned skin—a mixture of Iraqi desert sun and her Cherokee heritage.

Inside the airport gift shop, she studied a mirrored shelf of tiny glass animals, turquoise and white dogs, ceramic cats, and little clear crystal trees with red glass leaves that reflected the shop's bright fluorescent lighting. Her long black hair was neatly tied in a bun beneath her fatigue cap. She turned away from the display, deciding that nothing there was appropriate for her Aunt Bess and Uncle Benjamin waiting for her arrival in Asheville. An illustrated political multiracial poster of a soldier, sailor, marine, and jet pilot, males and females, standing side by side in dress uniforms, caught her attention. The headline on the poster read "Support Our Heroes." Ilena looked around self-consciously, hoping no one connected her with this stateside depiction of military life.

We're not that pretty, and it ain't that clean, she mused to herself. That thought brought back the yearning she felt—a yearning to be back with her comrades in Iraq that grew with each mile she had put between there and here. Her best friend, Beth. She could see her, Kevlar vest strapped tight, behind the wheel of an ordnance-packed diesel, flop sweat dried instantly by the near unbearable heat, running "balls to the wall," as the major liked to say, up the Alley of Death, the infamous road to Baghdad airport. Why does it take testosterone-based terms to define heroism? Heroism and guts know no gender. Beth and she had seen their National Guard buddies swept away by IEDs, while in convoy, like the hot desert wind blows sweat from a worried brow. Silently, Ilena spoke to Beth. "Foot on the gas, baby, and don't slow down. Not for no one or nothing." Mad dash from one spot on the map to the next with no thought but engine RPM, fuel, tires still on, and I'm alive. For a fleeting moment Ilena thought of turning back to her unit and comrades. She felt she had somehow deserted them. But then she remembered the major, and Beth, and six or seven of her buddies insisting she take her accrued leave, as they had. So be it.

Ilena turned back to the glass shelf. Her hand shook slightly as she lifted a glass owl from among the diminutive glass animals. Somehow it seemed appropriate to the moment, with its eyes wide open, alert, wise. An offering to the gods of war? The owl is also a hunter, like the hawk and the eagle. Perhaps this glass airport owl was the one amulet that would keep Beth safe. This might be Ilena's moment of destiny to have been here and performed an act of supplication to save her friend. She would bring Beth the owl. It would keep them both alive until their tour, twice extended, would finally end.

She waited as the struggling cashier deciphered the meaning of the data on the monitor of her computerized cash register. Ilena took her carefully wrapped package and change. As she left for the gate she watched the cashier tend to a tall, imposing black man. She noted his purchase was a book, *Notes of a Native Son*, by James Baldwin, and today's *Atlanta Journal*.

Baldwin. Jerrold Baldwin had been the first soldier killed in her unit, the 444th Transportation Company. His Humvee had no armor underneath. The 444th had not been issued any Kevlar or even flack vests. An IED had disintegrated his vehicle. Unlike the author of the book the black man was going to read, Jerrold Baldwin was white, twenty-two, married to his childhood sweetheart, and the father of two babies. He had worked days at the Heritage Furniture Factory and managed a McDonald's on weekend nights. Ilena recalled he was always griping—bitter for having joined the Guard for the extra money to support his young family. He kept saying, "I can't believe I'm in the middle of a war. I'm in the National Guard. We're supposed to guard the home front." Ilena knew his wife, Clarisse, and planned to visit her on Christmas Day.

"Rest in peace, Jerrold, my compatriot," Ilena whispered to herself with a pressing sense of guilt at being alive. "At least you're not in the middle of it anymore. I'll tell Clarisse how you were the bravest, and how you loved her and the children deeply." She sighed and walked slowly toward the gate area.

CHAPTER 4

REGGIE

He watched the crowd on the concourse as they struggled with their Christmas packages, luggage, laptops, and knapsacks. He checked his watch, an Omega Seamaster that Yvonne had given him for his fiftieth birthday. Happier times. There was a good half hour before he had to get to his gate, so he settled down on a bench outside the one restaurant in the terminal, a Jack in the Box. He'd gone through the *Detroit Free Press* on the six A.M. flight to Atlanta.

Reggie Howard opened the *Atlanta Journal*, a newspaper he had never read before, to the sports section. He was a big man—six-three, and two hundred fifty pounds. His large hands that had served him well as a wide receiver at Northern High, but not well enough to earn a football scholarship, grasped the paper and held it wide open. There was nothing about his Lions, something else he would have to get used to. Asheville had no professional sports teams. Georgia had the Falcons and the Braves. Carolina had the Panthers, but was it North or South Carolina? He wasn't sure.

Reggie closed the sports section and briefly perused the headlines. Politics and politicians. Lies and corruption. Reggie was disgusted with all of it. It didn't matter which group

controlled the White House or Congress. Red States; Blue
States; Liberal; Conservative; Evangelical; Catholic; Pro-Life;
Pro-Choice; Islamo-Fascist; War on Terror; NAFTA; Undoc-
umented Workers; Market Up; Market Down; Fed Raises Rates,
Lowers Rates . . . words from headlines drifted through his
mind. The country was going to hell in a handbasket, as his
long departed father had predicted. One headline at the bottom
of the front page of this newspaper caught his eye: WHITE
CHRISTMAS—HEAVY SNOW EXPECTED TODAY. Reggie glanced
out the nearby window that faced the main entrance to the
terminal. The snow was piling up rapidly. Taxis, arriving with
holiday passengers, looked like yellow cupcakes topped with
three inches of white icing on top. "Just great," Reggie muttered. "Spending a night on the floors of this place. One more
indignity to suffer."

It always amazed Reggie that he had blinked awake on or
about four A.M. every morning for the past three weeks. There
was comfort in his bed, in his house, and most of all in his
wife asleep next to him. Dear Yvonne. A lover and friend.
The thoughts that awakened him were always clear and de-
liberate, flowing in his subconscious like an underground
river, coursing through his sleep, carrying the same anger
and confusion in its eddies and backwaters.

He was a strong man who had spent his adult life, more
than thirty years, working on three different GM assembly
lines. Reggie Howard came back from Vietnam grateful to be
alive and eager to live a quiet, peaceful life. Those were still
the days when prejudice and nepotism in the Auto Worker's
Local put up an invisible wall to keep a black man from the
best jobs on the line. He had climbed up and over that wall,
just as he had several rice paddies under fire. He had suc-
ceeded, for a time, in what was still the white man's world.
Though his temples grayed and his step became a bit slower,
he was more than capable of holding his own with the
younger men.

Reggie and Yvonne were the first African-American couple

to move into their neat, suburban Detroit neighborhood. It had been difficult, but he had Yvonne, and their nightly union of souls to talk each other through the trials of the day and prepare for the next, one day at a time. Their bond was the synthesis of Reggie's urban Detroit upbringing and Yvonne's experiences growing up in the sleepy craft-paper mill town of Prentiss, Mississippi, where her parents had settled. Their marriage was a true partnership. Their love was deep, abiding, and after thirty-six years, still passionate and fiery.

Yvonne was a tall, wiry, slender woman. She resembled the light-skinned women on her mother's side of the family who had originated in the hill country of Kentucky. Most had lived to well into their late eighties, some into their mid-nineties.

Reggie's thoughts drifted back to those early mornings when he lay awake beneath perspiration-dampened sheets. He had worried about the thumping of his heart and the nightly sweats. The doctor had prescribed Valium when he felt this way, but he was loath to take it for fear of addiction. He remembered several of his buddies in Vietnam who had become opium and heroin addicts over there and brought their habits home to the streets of Detroit. He had witnessed their decline into druggie hell and unable to help, wept for them.

Reggie and Yvonne always saw themselves as an independent family living within certain limits of white society, frustrated at times by affronts to their dignity. But Yvonne was there for him, and he was there for her. There were no secrets between them. Their love was a shield against a hostile world. Yvonne, he knew, was his sustenance. Many nights, when the only light in their bedroom came from the streetlamp at the corner of Holland and Stevens Streets, Yvonne stroked Reggie's hands, scarred from years of working on the line, and listened. Her counsel was Socratic. She did not preach, but rather guided his path with thoughtful understanding.

But now their love was being tested as never before. After

decades of playing by the rules set by management and the union, and the culture of productive work—after prospering as a result—all had abruptly changed. And so the racing heart-beat and sweats. Confusion and anger. He remembered a conversation a few days before he left for Asheville.

He had felt Yvonne awake, as he lay sleepless.

"Up again, baby?" she asked, moving her warm body next to his.

"It's wrong," said Reggie softly. "Just flat-out wrong."

"It's temporary." Yvonne rubbed her eyes. "You've got to let it go."

"Says you."

"Says reality. You're not Don Quixote, and I'm not Sancho Panza."

"How do you know?" Reggie asked softly, half smiling at her analogy.

" 'Cause I've seen the GM windmill, and it's too big to fight. We have time left on this earth to live, Love. We can do that."

"I don't know anything but building cars. It's all I've ever done."

"You've done a lot more than that. You've been strong for us; raised two fine children with me; fought for your country; bled for it; stood tall and took your rightful place in this world. . . . And, my love, there was a time when you didn't know how to build cars." They both laughed.

"That was a long, long, time ago, baby," he said as he rolled over and pulled her on top of him. He embraced her. Yvonne stroked the back of Reggie's neck. He looked up as if he could see the stars and full moon of a tropical night sky through the roof. This bed was paradise.

"Like yesterday," Yvonne whispered in his ear. "We'll always be young."

"How'd you end up with a laid-off, broken-down wreck like me?" Reggie asked. "I remember some of those guys you dated before me. Remember that guy studying law at Howard?"

"Clarence?"

"Yeah, Clarence. He was gonna be the first black this, the first black that—"

She put her hand over his mouth. "Shhhh, you fool. Enough. You're my man. Always my man. The first Reggie. That's who I wanted and that's who I got." Reggie felt Yvonne's fingers tighten on his neck. "Don't you ever low-rate yourself. Look at our life, our family. Can't you see? Does anyone have better kids than Donald and Samantha?"

"We're selling our home," Reggie said softly, stubbornly refusing to let his sense of failure go. "And not because we want to. It wasn't our choice."

"It was a house when we bought it, and we made it a home. We fought to make it a home, as I recall. So now we're moving on, and once you get settled down in Asheville, we'll find a perfect house and make it a home again."

"I let you down."

"You haven't let me down. You've got to stop this. You didn't get fired. You didn't quit. You got laid off along with thirty thousand others. White, black, brown. You didn't let me down. Don't let yourself down."

"I don't know about going to work for Donald."

"That's your pride talking. You know what happens when your pride talks?"

"Yeah. Nothing good. I'm nearly sixty."

"Fifty-six. Don't rush it. It'll be all right."

"You say. You know I haven't been on a plane since I got back from Vietnam."

"So you're not a world traveler." Yvonne sat up and looked at Reggie. "Vietnam? You haven't said that word in a long, long time." Reggie looked back up through the ceiling to a jungle moon of thirty-five years ago.

"I ran into Ray Clifton at the tire place."

"Ray Clifton? Good Lord. There's a name from the past."

"Yeah. His paycheck went to his bar tab every week. I figured he'd be long gone. He tells me he came darn close. Scared him. So, after all these years he goes to the V.A. They tell him he's got post delayed stress." Reggie took a deep breath. "Two wives, dozens of girlfriends, a couple dozen trainloads of bourbon . . . So he goes to the shrink. Man, I wish I'd been there. He told me it was the first time since he's back that he opened up."

"You guys never spoke about it?"

"We didn't have to. We knew . . ."

"So how is he?"

"Sober. Cleaned up good. Resurrection."

"I'm glad," Yvonne said sincerely. "We ought to have him over before we leave."

"Yeah, we should. I'd like that. We were . . . you know . . ." Reggie felt the soothing touch of Yvonne's fingers as she stroked his wrist. He soon fell into a sweet, deep sleep. It was safe, like the first night back at a firebase after a jungle patrol, surrounded by trusted others, like Ray Clifton, manning the wire.

CHAPTER 5

JOHN

As Reggie Howard set the *Atlanta Journal* aside and opened *Native Son*, a Lexus, its roof covered with snow and the windshield partly obscuring the driver's view with ice, drove into the Hertz return area and skidded to a stop. As John Sullivan got out of the car, he slipped on the slick pavement, and cursing, grabbed the open door to steady himself. He carefully made his way to the rear and popped the trunk. While the Hertz attendant, wrapped in a parka, checked the mileage and gas, John hauled his luggage and attaché case out onto the snowy ground. He waited impatiently as the attendant double-checked his entries.

"Using the same credit card, Mr. Sullivan?"

"Yes," he answered curtly. "It's in my profile, isn't it?" The handheld computer slowly spit out the bill.

"We have to ask, sir." John grabbed the bill from the attendant's hands, popped up the handle on his large suitcase, and without acknowledging the attendant, wheeled it off toward the waiting Hertz bus.

"And Merry Christmas to you, too. . . ." The attendant's sarcastic words trailed off, unheard, as the snowy wind whipped around John's bare head. He stopped and pulled up the collar of his inadequately light topcoat to cover the back of his neck. As he trudged toward the bus, John's thoughts were of being home after six weeks away.

Earlier that morning, John Sullivan, a tall, blond, thirty-five-year-old master of the universe, had been in fashionable Buckhead, shouting into the Crowne Plaza Atlanta's telephone, uncertain if the person at the other end spoke enough English to understand him.

"Damn it, I ordered two eggs over easy! These are fried to a crisp. This is supposed to be a first-class hotel." He paused, listening to silence. "Do you understand? *Comprende? Verstanden?*"

"Yes, sir, I do. And I speak English."

"Good. Then let's get it right and make it fast. I've got a plane to catch." John slammed down the receiver and glanced out the window of his executive suite. What had earlier been a few flakes drifting by his window was now a steady and heavy snowfall. His chest rose and fell with rapid breathing from the surge of anger-induced adrenaline in his bloodstream. Poor service like this was simply unacceptable to John. He had grown up in cloistered privilege, educated in privilege, and was accustomed to being treated as a privileged person of importance.

Richard Sullivan had elevated his only child to heir at his moment of birth. John's mother, the former Meredith Simpson, was a product of overly inbred descendants of early colonists and old Charleston aristocracy. Her coming out was at the lavish cotillion thrown in the Plaza Hotel in New York City. She was a member of the Daughters of the American Revolution and the Daughters of the Confederacy. But only a few short years after her coming of age, the Simpson fortunes were decimated by her father's gambling in the stock market—specifically junk-bond speculation.

Her marriage to Richard Sullivan, a self-made entrepreneur from Louisville who controlled interests in Black Angus cattle, rice, and oil wells throughout the South, saved the Simpsons from certain bankruptcy.

John Sullivan was a bright child, who quickly assimilated life's survival lessons from his father, and, when time permitted, social graces from his mother. Richard Sullivan was an imperator. In a prior age he might have been a Roman provincial governor or Saxon baron. He intuitively understood power in all its trappings and guises. To Richard Sullivan, wealth and power were inseparable—a primary lesson he continually stressed to his son.

"Benchmark, John. Benchmark," Richard would repeat. From the day John entered his first exclusive private school until he graduated with honors with an MBA from Harvard, John was taught to measure himself against the best around him, no matter the situation. Who wrote the best? Who was the best at math? Soccer? With whom did the girls want to dance? John reported to his father, and they adjusted strategies and plans for winning. There was no shame in encountering someone better at something; but there were penalties for not surpassing the achievements of others. Richard and John were a cabal of two, plotting and manipulating John's future. In the process, Meredith's role was marginalized. Secretly, she wondered if Richard were driving John too hard to mimic his life rather than allowing him to have one of his own.

John learned the lessons of power well. After he graduated cum laude from Harvard he went on to earn his MBA there, too. He plunged into the family business with focus and intelligence, anxious to please his father, and, secretly, to surpass him.

The next step in his carefully planned life was to find a wife—a suitable mate to provide a social front and bear heirs. Richard tapped Meredith to fill the role of matchmaker. A Junior League charity event at the Sullivan estate in Asheville in late June was the setting. Canopied outdoors by a pale, blue sky, the west lawn held several circular tables covered with white cloths, set with crystal and sterling-silver flatware, and festooned with fresh lilies. A string quartet played softly as the chosen mingled, champagne flutes in hand. Bored, with business stratagems coursing through his mind, John was startled by the sound of a strange voice behind him.

"Hello, John." Turning, John noticed the woman's deep blue eyes first, accentuated by dark lashes and eyebrows. Those eyes locked with his, unwilling to lose the moment. His gaze lowered to her subtly glossed pink lips that framed a sparkling smile. Her brunette hair fell casually across tanned shoulders. Two narrow white straps held her low-cut, backless dress that ended where her long, trim legs began. John's eyes found the gold bracelet on her left ankle and felt a provocative chill run down his spine.

"I'm Anne," she said. "Anne Blakely." She extended a graceful hand. Seven months later, they married.

Two years to the day after that, Richard Sullivan died of a massive myocardial infarction in his hotel room in Hong Kong. At the wake John learned that his father had not had a checkup in ten years and had apparently suffered a "silent" heart attack during that time. He'd been too busy to look after his health, John thought, or simply believed he would live forever.

John finished packing while he waited for his reorder of breakfast. Thoughts of his father's obsession with the business and monetary success had been troubling him lately. Was he going down the same road? There was an ache inside and something disturbing that he saw in the faces of Anne and the twins, Kate and Carly, when he left on these ever more frequent business trips. The business was growing far beyond anything that even Richard Sullivan had projected. And its demands were pushing John farther and farther away from the family he loved. Even his mother, who had seemed to blossom after Richard's death, had warned him to take time to live and love.

There was a tentative tap on the door.

"Room service."

John stepped to the door in quick, long strides and opened it. A dark-haired, heavyset Hispanic woman with a broad smile nodded. She wore a starched white uniform.

"Good morning. May I come in, sir?"

"Yes. Set it on the coffee table, please," he instructed. She lifted the stainless-steel circular cover.

"Eggs over easy. I hope they're to your liking this time."

"They look fine," he answered curtly. The woman bowed slightly and presented the slender black, plastic wallet containing the bill. He opened it and signed it, but added nothing to the service charge that was included. He handed the wallet back to the woman.

"Thank you, sir. Will there be anything else?"

"No. No, thank you." John looked at his Rolex Oyster. The woman picked up the eggs cooked the wrong way, walked to the door, opened it, and then paused.

"Traveling home for Christmas?"

"What?" John asked, taken aback by the question.

"Going home for Christmas?" she repeated.

"Yes. Yes, I am."

"Well," she said with a smile, "I hope Santa brings you what you wish. Merry Christmas, sir."

"Yes," John answered softly as she closed the door. Suddenly he felt very lonely. "Whatever that is."

CHAPTER 6

AMELIA

The snow increased as the Hertz bus passed an area where a small commuter plane was parked. *I hate those things*, John thought, knowing that he would soon be aboard one and that it would have no first-class section. He shrugged at the thought, took a deep breath, and summoned the courage to prepare himself to be just another coach passenger like those he observed now deplaning into the snowy morning.

Amelia McIntosh stepped out of the aircraft onto the platform at the top of the stairs. She immediately looked skyward. Snow gathered quickly on her cheery face. She enjoyed the refreshing sensation of crisp air and an open space, especially after the heat and humidity of Florida and the cramped multi-stop trip from Fort Lauderdale.

"Some of us have a life to lead," the young man directly on the stairway behind her muttered rudely.

"Well, yes. Of course," the perky seventy-four-year-old retired teacher replied. "I hope it's a happy one." She smiled coyly. The young man couldn't help but smile back and nod.

Amelia had that effect on people. When she got to the bottom of the stairs she felt a strong hand grip under her arm.

"It's slippery out here," the young man said. "May I help you?"

"You are a gentleman," Amelia told him, "and that is a lovely gesture." She relaxed her body and allowed him to guide her to the warmth of the terminal.

"I've got to catch a flight to Birmingham," he told her. "You take care."

"I will. I surely will. Merry Christmas."

"Yes, ma'am. Merry Christmas." He nodded his head slightly and left. Amelia looked around to find the gate for her flight to Asheville. She felt a warm flush and unbuttoned her coat.

"Cold-warm, cold-warm," Amelia muttered as she recalled her life the past few weeks.

The sweltering heat and high humidity common to South Florida had abated. It was December. The hurricane season was over. A more temperate time of year had arrived. But even so the year-round residents kept their air conditioners at sixty-eight degrees.

In the wake of an abrupt, but common afternoon thunderstorm, steam rose from the hot asphalt street outside the two-story condo building at 5665 Black Olive Drive in a senior development called Plantation Cedars. It seemed to Amelia that the short, violent downpour was a rite of ablution, cleansing the fouled atmosphere lingering between her and her sister-in-law, Jenny.

No comfort here, Amelia thought. Standing in the frigid confines of the condo that she and her late husband Joseph had purchased for his sister, Amelia shivered. She knew what was coming. Still, ever the optimist, she searched for new words, a new approach that might somehow change the all too familiar course of the conversation.

Nearly a half-century of being Jenny's sister-in-law had taught Amelia that no matter what she said or did, it was never right, never enough, never acceptable. For decades, Amelia had allowed Jenny the latitude of believing Amelia was not "good enough" for her brother. The most civil of conversations in Joseph's presence would abruptly change to accusation when he left the room.

"You're holding Joseph back. He can be so much more than a teacher," Jenny would start.

"He's not just a teacher," Amelia would answer. "He's a professor. A Ph.D. Highly respected in his chosen field."

"At a Negro college. He could be at Harvard or Yale."

"An African-American college. Highly accredited and respected. It's where we chose to teach." Eventually, the accusations grew more vicious and personal.

"He should have married a black woman," was the final blow. When Jenny said it, Amelia stormed past the other woman to the guest room. Jenny followed like a dog on scent. She was fifteen years younger than Amelia. Her straightened hair was showing gray at the roots. Her hazel eyes were sharp and focused. Today, like most days, she wore tight-fitting clothing that displayed a full, firm figure. Her body had always been Jenny's pride and meal ticket. She had taken very good care of it and used it, with what she called her "feminine wiles," to have men around, mostly white, to do her bidding. Of course, that wasn't always the case. In her younger days, she was unable to sustain any relationships because of her self-centered nature. There were three marriages and three nasty divorces. There were no children. No really close friends. Her older brother, Amelia's husband, Joseph, was her rock and her lifeline. She considered Amelia an impediment to that relationship. Now Joseph was gone and Jenny was unable, or unwilling, to accept Amelia's reaching out with an offer of friendship and family.

The guest room was painted pastel pink with aquamarine

trim. Like the rest of the condominium, it was jammed with furniture, spoils from Jenny's three unsuccessful but highly profitable marriages: a four-poster bed bought by husband number one, a Tiffany lamp provided as a peace offering by husband number two, an ornate antique music box from husband number three. These trophies were visible proof of victory for Jenny. She stood at the door and relentlessly continued her attack.

"You always put your career first. . . . You never bore him the children he wanted. . . . Joseph was always unhappy. . . ." Amelia did not respond. She had, long ago, painfully learned when it was time to walk away. Confrontation was useless. And now, especially after Joseph's passing, she was tired. This last attempt at reconciliation had been a failure. Sadly, it was time to say good-bye, perhaps forever. Amelia smoothed the front of her skirt, and faced Jenny. "I'm sorry, Jenny. I'm leaving now for the airport."

"This is so like you, Amelia," Jenny said caustically. "As long as I've known you it's always been about you." The accusation was calculated to incite. The rhythm and intonation of her words were like sparks sizzling along a lit fuse, running to detonate their explosive relationship. But Amelia would not be baited.

"This, uh, coming here to try to . . . to offer you . . . I'm your only family, Jenny, and you mine. But it was a mistake. My mistake."

Jenny stepped forward.

"You make it sound so noble," Jenny said, taking a long swallow from her martini. She swished the dark green olive on its toothpick around in the oversized martini glass, then brandished it as though it were an empowering amulet. Aware that Amelia once had a bout with alcoholism, Jenny relished the act of partaking in an afternoon drink in front of her.

"I thought after Joseph passed we could try." Amelia grasped the handle of her suitcase. "I'm sorry." Unconsciously, Amelia's tone of voice had changed from reconciliation to resignation. That only served as a trigger for Jenny, a crouching beast waiting to pounce.

"Try what?" Jenny snapped. "I don't need you!"

"No, you don't," Amelia answered calmly. "Not now. Maybe someday. . . ."

Jenny laughed. "Someday? You're old. Your damned life is almost over. I'll dance on your grave."

"How cheerful of you, Jenny. It's comforting to know that at least you'll be at my funeral." Amelia, fatigued, her patience gone, looked directly into Jenny's eyes. "Merry Christmas, Jenny. Have a good life." She pulled out the handle of her suitcase and began rolling it toward freedom. Then, for an instant, Amelia thought she saw hesitation in Jenny's eyes. But like the shadow of a fast-moving cloud racing across blue water, it was gone. Amelia allowed herself a moment of satisfaction, realizing that an old and tiresome thorn in her side was finally removed.

Mercifully, the horn of the taxi sounded out front. Amelia walked past Jenny, down the thickly carpeted hallway, opened the front door, and then gently but firmly closed it behind her.

More by Bestselling Author

Lori Foster

Available Wherever Books Are Sold!

Check out our website at **www.kensingtonbooks.com**

More by Bestselling Author

Janet Dailey

Bring the Ring	0-8217-8016-6	$4.99US/$6.99CAN
Calder Promise	0-8217-7541-3	$7.99US/$10.99CAN
Calder Storm	0-8217-7543-X	$7.99US/$10.99CAN
A Capital Holiday	0-8217-7224-4	$6.99US/$8.99CAN
Crazy in Love	1-4201-0303-2	$4.99US/$5.99CAN
Eve's Christmas	0-8217-8017-4	$6.99US/$9.99CAN
Green Calder Grass	0-8217-7222-8	$7.99US/$10.99CAN
Happy Holidays	0-8217-7749-1	$6.99US/$9.99CAN
Let's Be Jolly	0-8217-7919-2	$6.99US/$9.99CAN
Lone Calder Star	0-8217-7542-1	$7.99US/$10.99CAN
Man of Mine	1-4201-0009-2	$4.99US/$6.99CAN
Mistletoe and Molly	1-4201-0041-6	$6.99US/$9.99CAN
Ranch Dressing	0-8217-8014-X	$4.99US/$6.99CAN
Scrooge Wore Spurs	0-8217-7225-2	$6.99US/$9.99CAN
Searching for Santa	1-4201-0306-7	$6.99US/$9.99CAN
Shifting Calder Wind	0-8217-7223-6	$7.99US/$10.99CAN
Something More	0-8217-7544-8	$7.99US/$9.99CAN
Stealing Kisses	1-4201-0304-0	$4.99US/$5.99CAN
Try to Resist Me	0-8217-8015-8	$4.99US/$6.99CAN
Wearing White	1-4201-0011-4	$4.99US/$6.99CAN
With This Kiss	1-4201-0010-6	$4.99US/$6.99CAN
Yes, I Do	1-4201-0305-9	$4.99US/$5.99CAN

Available Wherever Books Are Sold!

Check out our website at **www.kensingtonbooks.com**

Discover the Magic of Romance with
Jo Goodman